Under the Lights

Dahlia Adler

Spencer Hill Contemporary / Spencer Hill Press

Contact: Spencer Hill Press,

27 West 20th Street, Suite 1102, New York, NY 10011
Please visit our website at www.spencerhillpress.com

First Edition: June 2015
Dahlia Adler

Under the Lights: a novel / by Dahlia Adler – 1st ed.
p. cm.

Summary: Frenemies Josh and Vanessa are forced to co-star on TV, making for a tricky triangle when she falls for her publicist's (female) intern.

The author acknowledges the copyrighted or trademarked status and trademark owners of the following wordmarks mentioned in this fiction: Advil, American Express, American Idol, Bacardi, Band-Aid, Bang & Olufsen, The Beatles, Ben Sherman, Beverly Hills 90210, Beyoncé, Bikram Yoga, BlackBerry, Blu-ray, Botox, (Los Angeles) Clippers, The Coffee Bean & Tea Leaf, Coke, Cosmo, Diet Coke, Entertainment Weekly, Escalade, FaceTime, The Foo Fighters, Fred Segal, Fresca, Grand Theft Auto, Gray's Papaya, In-N-Out, Instagram, iPod, Jack Daniels, Jacob the Jeweler, Jeep, Keurig, Korea Times, Louboutins, Louis Vuitton, NIN, Nirvana, Oreo, One Tree Hill, Patrón, Ping-Pong, Pinkberry, Post-it, Pumas, Radiohead, Rage Against the Machine, Range Rover, Screen Actors Guild Awards, Skinnygirl, Skype, Sherlock, Snow Queen, Stella Artois, System of a Down, Taylor Swift, Thermos, Transformers, Twitter, Yoda, Yves Saint Laurent, Vanity Fair, Victoria's Secret

Cover design by Maggie Hall
Interior layout by Jenny Perinovic
Cover image by Jen Grantham

ISBN 978-1-63392-017-0 (paperback)
ISBN 978-1-63392-018-7 (e-book)

Printed in the United States of America

To Yoni and to Maggie,
for holding my hands through the best and the worst,
both behind the scenes and under the lights

Chapter One

Josh

*E*ither my best friend or my assistant is about to punch me in the face. As usual, the fact that they're dating really isn't doing me any favors.

"You barely even looked at any of them," Ally Duncan complains through gritted teeth. She's been working for me for over a year, but her patience hasn't grown any in that time. I'd assume she just needs to get laid, but given she's been with Liam Holloway for almost as long as she's been with me, I'm all too nauseatingly aware that's not an issue.

"Josh, can you stop being a dick and just pick a script so she can get out of here?" Liam sounds pissed, like he's the one responsible for finding me a new project. Which, maybe he should be. If he'd convince his damn girlfriend to stick around LA instead of running off to college, I wouldn't have her shoving scripts in my face, desperate to make sure I've got one last job before she abandons me.

"How about you stay, and I let you pick one for me?" I suggest to Ally, handing back the pile of scripts. "There. Problem solved."

She snorts. "Sure, I'll just tell Columbia I'm turning them down so I can spend another year getting your dry cleaning and picking out jewelry for every girl you nail."

"Wouldn't be the first time," I remind her.

"Yeah, because my deferring last year was so obviously about my desire to be your slave." Her phone beeps with a text, and I catch a quick roll of her eyes as she checks it. "It's Van. Again. I gotta go." She presses a kiss to Liam's mouth before getting up from the pool chaise they're sharing and muttering loudly enough for me to hear, "Get him to pick one already, will you?" She drops the pile in his lap.

He squeezes her hand briefly, and we both watch her ass as she walks out to her car.

Liam turns to me as soon as she disappears. "Dude, you *have* to stop that."

"What?" I ask innocently, taking a sip of beer from the bottle on the table next to me.

"She's going to New York, period. Refusing to pick a script isn't gonna keep her here."

I raise my eyebrows and take another sip. "For someone who's supposedly in love with her, you're pretty damn chill about letting her go."

"I'm not *letting* her do anything," he says tightly. "This is her dream. She makes her own choices, and I respect them and want her to be happy."

"So you're just...totally cool with the fact that your girlfriend is moving three thousand miles away. For four years." Liam is so full of shit.

"She'll be home for breaks and summers." He's obviously given himself this pep talk a few times. "Anyway, what am I supposed to do? Tell her not to go?"

I shrug. "Why not? I tell her that every day."

"Because you're a selfish asshole."

"Maybe, but at least I won't be spending four years jacking off to Skype."

Liam scowls at me, and I'm guessing my grinning only makes it worse.

"Man, you're too easy," I tell him, taking one last swig before putting the bottle down. "Gimme those scripts."

He hands over the stack, and I lie back and check out the first one. The title screams sci-fi, and I toss it aside without reading it.

"I thought you were gonna take these seriously."

"I am. And I seriously do not want to put on some lame-ass futuristic outfit and prance around like a Han Solo wannabe." I check the next one. *Hmm, Meagan Scanlon.* It's tempting to consider, given she's definitely one of Hollywood's more bangable writers, but the title's a dead giveaway that this is yet another one of those Jane Austen chick-flick things. *Pass.*

"What's wrong with that one?"

"I have no interest in playing Bridget Jones with a dick." My phone rings, and I put the scripts aside and check who's calling. Wyatt. "Hey, cuz."

"Hey, your assistant still leaving?"

"Yeah, why?"

"I've got a friend who needs a job."

I snort. Of course he does. My cousin attracts losers like a game of beer pong at a frat party, and has a new favor to ask of me every hour. That's what happens when your growth spurt never comes and you realize you peaked at eleven. "Is your friend hot?"

"Depends. How gay are you feeling today?"

"You stupid dick. I told you—no male assistants. Call me back when you find a hot *female* friend who needs a job washing my car in a thong." I hang up and toss my phone on the pile of scripts.

"I thought the whole point of hiring Ally was that you wanted an assistant you weren't gonna try to nail," says Liam.

"Yeah, well, I'm trying not to be too picky."

"But no male assistants?"

"I don't want anyone around who's gonna steal my shit. That means clothing *or* chicks."

"Did you seriously just refer to girls as your 'shit'?" Liam rolls his eyes. "Christ, no wonder you're single."

"Actually, I'm single because it's fun as hell, chicks are boring after a day, and I like to sleep in the middle of my bed." I toss the last script—one of those ensemble pieces of shit that drop your cred faster than a crotch shot—and grab my phone back to mess around on the Internet. I fucking love adoring tweets. "Remember when you used to enjoy being single?"

"About a billionth as much as I enjoy not being single."

I roll my eyes. "You're so whipped."

"If you think I've got any shame about that, you're talking to the wrong guy."

"Don't I know it." The truth is, for all the shit I give him about Ally, it's cool to see Liam this happy. He's been through so much, I can't be pissed about this, no matter how badly I miss my top wingman. And at least Ally doesn't suck at life. "I forget sometimes that you're one of those happy pod people now."

"You will be someday, too," he assures me with a smug grin. "And when that happens, I'll laugh my ass off."

"Not a chance. Lifetime bachelor, man." I bring the beer back to my lips, but it's so warm it's like drinking piss. I put it back down. "You wanna grab some boards and go down to the beach?"

"Pick a script, Chester. Seriously. You haven't done anything but Aspen ads in months, and Ally's worried about you. Just *try* one so she can stop feeling like she's leaving a baby on a convent doorstep by abandoning you for Columbia, will you?"

"Oh, fuck off." I reach back into the pile and grab one, then hand it to Liam without even looking. "There, now you can tell your girlfriend you did your job, which is really *her* job. And since I actually have you without her for five seconds, can we talk party?"

He groans, and I know what's coming. He's convinced Ally will hate having a goodbye party, but I don't give a crap, even though he's probably right. If I'm losing my assistant, I'm losing her in style.

"Don't even think about trying to talk me out of it," I warn him. "This party is happening, and it's gonna be epic."

"Talk to Vanessa about it," he says with a sigh. "You know I suck at this."

"Ah, yes, how *is* your former fake-girlfriend?"

Liam glares at me. "Never mind. You're beyond help."

"Oh, buy a sense of humor, Holloway. You need to get out more. What are you doing tonight?"

"Reading scripts until Ally comes over for dinner. Probably watching a movie."

"You two watch more movies than anyone I know," I say with disgust, "which, considering we're both actors, is ridiculous. Please tell me you don't actually *watch* them."

He shrugs, but he's incapable of stopping a smile from spreading across his face.

"Good man. Though I don't know how you guys manage to do the sleepover thing so often while she's living at home. Doesn't she have mythical unicorn parents who actually give a crap?"

"Yeah—that's why we tell them she stays in your guest house when you keep her in Malibu too late. Thanks for the great excuse, by the way."

"Oh, come on. They don't actually believe that shit."

"It's amazing what parents will *want* to believe when it comes to their daughters."

"They must despise you."

He laughs. "If they do, they hide it really well. And in return, I make no references to the fact that I can find every single freckle on their daughter's body with my eyes closed. Everybody wins." He glances at his watch, then pushes himself up to standing. "And on that note, I gotta go. But call Van, okay?"

"Yeah, yeah." We bro-slap five, and he heads out, leaving me to my quiet backyard, a pile of crap-on-paper, and no clue how I'm gonna function without the girl who keeps my life together.

I don't really need a new assistant. After all, before I hired Ally, I was doing just fine with only an agent (who's since been replaced), a manager (who quit after I hooked up with his daughter...okay, daughters), a driver, and a maid. But as I walk around my bedroom in the Malibu beach house I've turned into my full-time residence, I feel like she's inserted herself into my life as a necessity.

Nannette's birthday—send sunflowers! her purple pen screams from the August 4th square of the calendar she replaces on my wall every month. *Always wear Ben Sherman to Esquivel—hostess is dating a designer's brother* is on a Post-it wall in the closet. *Call your grandmother on Fridays at three* is next to the Bang & Olufsen on my nightstand.

Try getting your agent or manager to find out the best time to call your grandmother in her nursing home, taking into account when all her friends will be around and she can show off your name on her caller ID, essentially making her weekend. I dare you.

That same phone rings now, which triggers a feeling of dread in my gut, like I'm one of Pavlov's fucking puppies. Only one person calls the house phone here rather than my cell, and it's not someone I possess any desire to talk to, ever. Unfortunately, I can't exactly ignore her, either. I snatch the phone and drop onto my bed, answering it without bothering to glance at the screen.

"What is it, Marsha?" I ask, already bored with the conversation that hasn't started yet.

"For the billionth time, Joshua, it's Yvette. Or Mother, if you're feeling novel."

I roll my eyes. Yvette is the fucking stupid name she chose when she first started auditioning a billion years ago and landed on *Time Goes By*, the absurd soap that's been her baby for longer than I have. As if she's fooling anyone into thinking she's exotic and French instead of a one-time diner waitress from Oklahoma.

Sort of like how she pretends she's thirty-four, even though she's got a nineteen-year-old son who's more famous than she is.

"How can I help you?"

"You can come to dinner tonight, at the house," she says coolly, referring to the thirty-room mansion she and my father occupy in Bel-Air, although they reside in different wings. "I thought it would be nice to eat together, as a family."

We have never, in as far as I can recall, done anything as a family.

Unless it was for publicity.

"Photo shoot?"

She sighs. "No, Joshua, not a photo shoot. I just want us all to eat together. Is that so much to ask? Elaine is preparing those pork chops you like."

"I have literally no idea which pork chops you're referring to."

"Seven o'clock," she says huffily. Then her voice brightens a bit. "I look forward to seeing you then!"

It's hard to say who hangs up faster.

I'm not sure when's the last time I saw both my parents in the same room, but it's obvious there's something behind this stupid dinner, and I won't find out what until I go. Just as well—I don't have dinner plans anyway, unless you count the tequila I expect to be licking out of a belly button later. But I'm not meeting Paz and Hudson until eleven, so I jump in the shower, throw on jeans and a T-shirt I know my mother will hate, and tell my driver, Ronen, to be out front at six thirty—that should get me there about half an hour late.

"I asked you to be here at seven, Joshua," she says tightly when I arrive, her eyes narrowing on my outfit. "And is it so much to ask that you dress like an adult for dinner? If you're old enough to live by yourself in the beach house, you're old enough to put on a button-down. Go get dressed."

"You want me to head back out?" I jerk my thumb toward the door. "I mean, sure, but I won't be back for a couple of hours."

"You have plenty of clothing in your room upstairs. Go change into something presentable and then join us."

"There *is* a photo shoot, isn't there."

"*Harold!*" she calls out impatiently. As if my dad gives a shit what I wear to dinner.

"Do what your mother says, Joshua," I hear, and I look up to see him sitting at the kitchen counter, a bunch of papers spread out in front of him, a pen in his teeth. Clearly, he has no more desire to be here than I do, to the surprise of absolutely fucking nobody.

I'm already sick of this whole night, so I choose the path of least resistance and haul my ass upstairs to get a shirt. It's true I've left plenty of shit in this house. I make a mental note to have Ally deal with clearing it out. The less I have tying me to this place, the better.

It's almost eight by the time we actually sit down to the stupid farce of a dinner, and though I know I've never had Elaine's pork chops before, they're pretty damn good. My mom amps up the small talk, putting her acting skills to maximum use as she pretends to give a shit about my life.

"Have you talked to Calvin about your next project?" she asks me, taking a tiny bite of cucumber, not even pretending she'll be eating more than half a salad for dinner.

"I dropped Calvin a year ago," I remind her dully, though that's not exactly the truth of how it went down. "Holly Bremen's my agent now."

"Right, right. Well, Holly, then?"

"I'm having dinner with her tomorrow." I exhale sharply and take a long drink from my wineglass, even though my mom's preferred pinot noir tastes like ass. "Can we get to the point of this dinner?"

"Joshua—"

"He's right, Yvette," Harold says flatly. "I have work to do. If there's something you need, just say it."

She sucks in a sharp, insulted breath and forces a single tear into her eye. It's her signature move, and you'd think she'd know by now that it doesn't move either me or my father for a second. We know all her soap actress shit backward and forward. "So much for the support of family. I'm really counting on you both in this difficult time."

"Your parents are already dead, Yvette, so whatever it is, just spit it out."

I nearly choke on my wine when I laugh. I forgot just how much of a dick my father can be.

"My show's been canceled," she says icily. "You happy now, asshole?"

Huh. For a second, I think I might actually feel... bad for my mother. Granted, she's a pretty lousy actress, and the show's terrible, but it's her entire fucking life. She was on that show when she met my dad. Her pregnancy with me is actually documented in some sort of terrible borderline-incest storyline. When I was little, I used to think it was cool to watch those episodes and point myself out in her belly. At least until she'd shut off the TV because she hated the way seeing herself pregnant reminded her of having cankles.

Harold must feel the same twinge of sympathy I do, because he actually musters up an "I'm sorry to hear that, Yvette."

"Me too," I mumble.

Just like that, the sugary smile jumps back onto her face. "I'm so glad to hear that the two of you are in my corner, just like I knew you would be. I think you're going to love the idea I have for my next move, now that I'll have some free time."

Some free time? I snort. As if my mother does anything other than the show and get trashed on wine coolers at her favorite spa.

She ignores me and plows onward. "And really, wouldn't it be nice to have some more time together as a family? I think this is really something that will bring us all together."

And just like that, I know exactly what she's going to say. "I am *not* doing a fucking reality show, Marsha."

"Oh, Yvette..." Harold sighs. "Come on."

"What happened to your support?" she demands. "I need you both on board with this. It's important for me to maintain an onscreen presence."

"Why can't you just jump to another soap?" I ask.

"Because that sneaky bitch Laura is screwing Tom and he told her the show was tanking weeks before anyone else found out. She already snatched up the role on *Myrtle's Beach* I would've been perfect for."

"What about that other one?" asks Harold. "The one with the redhead."

"I've had creative differences with one of the producers." Which probably means she's fucked him. Fantastic. "Anyway, I've been on *Time Goes By* for twenty years, and I think it's time to do something different, get my name and face out there to a new audience. We could *all* use that, couldn't we?"

"I'm not exactly hurting for clients," Harold says wryly.

"I'm doing fine, too, thanks for asking."

She glares daggers at me, then turns to my father. "You're absolutely correct, Harold. I didn't mean to suggest you needed any assistance. But I'd love to have you on every now and again."

Funny how she didn't offer me the same option. And I blame the fact that I seem to have drunk the entire bottle of wine in front of me for why it took me so long to realize why. "You need me, don't you? I'm a condition of you getting this show."

She clutches the stem of her wineglass until her bony knuckles turn white. "The studio did mention that they would be interested in featuring my son alongside me, yes."

I shake my head. "Un-fucking-believable."

Harold sighs, but when I glance over at him, he's typing furiously on the ancient BlackBerry he insists on using. He's clearly checked out of this conversation; it's just me and Marsha now.

"Is this really so much to ask?" she all but spits.

"A reality show? Yes, it's a lot to ask."

Her jaw clenches, and then it relaxes and she takes a sip of wine. "Well, then, given that obviously we'll have to be tightening some purse strings around here, I must say, I look forward to having you back here, Joshua."

I roll my eyes. "What are you talking about?"

"Well, now that we're losing my income we'll obviously have to give up some things. And the beach house really is one of our most expensive assets. Considering neither your father nor I ever use it..."

"I'll buy the damn thing from you, if that's what you want."

But of course it isn't. She smiles evilly. "Well, as it happens, I've been approached about the house a number of times. I'd have to consider all offers."

She knows I can't outbid anyone. Hell, I probably can't even pay market value. Modeling and doing appearances pays, but it doesn't pay Malibu-beach-house money. "You're seriously blackmailing me with my fucking house to get me to do your stupid show?"

She takes another sip of wine, then turns to my father. "How are your pork chops, dear?"

He mumbles something under his breath as he continues to send e-mails.

"Well, this has been lovely," I declare, wiping off my mouth and dropping my napkin on the table. "I'll be in touch." Pushing back my chair, I enjoy the way the screech against the hardwood makes my mother wince, and then I pull out my phone and head back up to my old room. Much as I hate to admit it, I need a job that actually pays. I brace myself for a patented Ally "I told you so" and dial.

"What's up, Josh?" She's just out of breath enough for me to know I've interrupted something good. It gives me twisted joy to know Liam probably wants to punch me in the nuts right now.

"A script. Pick one. Whichever one you think will have the highest price tag attached. Fuck, pick all of 'em. Just talk to Holly and set up the auditions."

She's trying not to laugh, but she's a lousy actress. "For real? Will you actually show up?"

"Yeah. Whenever. You know my schedule."

"Better than I know my own," she says cheerfully. "Anything else?"

There's a fumbling, and then I hear, "Yes." Liam's grabbed her phone. "Don't worry, Chester. I'll pass along your very important message requiring Ally to keep making out with me now. I assure you she's doing a fantastic job." Then he hangs up on me.

I sigh and text Ronen to come back and pick me up. I need to get out of this house and into a bottle of Patrón.

Chapter Two

*T*ell me again *why* you're even bothering to try to dig Josh Chester out of his apathetic little hole when you have about a billion better things to do right now?" I slide back into the passenger seat of Ally's car, skinny iced hazelnut latté in hand, and check my reflection in the side mirror. Oof. I need to log some tanning hours, stat.

She gets in the driver's seat and puts her own vanilla latté in the cup holder between us. "Trust me—he needs this. And he *will* step up. Eventually. I know Josh."

"Which is still just so weird." I take my first sip while she starts the car. "I can't believe you've survived working for him for over a year. I don't think anyone other than his driver's done that, and he's Israeli army."

"Josh isn't so bad once you get past the absurd requests, constant slutting it up, putdowns of my wardrobe, the fact that he's impossible when he doesn't wanna do something, and the late-night phone calls I'm pretty sure he times perfectly for maximum piss-Liam-off potential." She makes a face. "Okay, yeah, he sort of sucks."

I laugh as I reach over to turn on the radio and find something fun. "Should I be offended that it's far longer than I lasted as your boss?"

"Considering you've lasted fifteen years as my best friend? I think not."

Taylor Swift. Perfect. I sit back and take another sip of my drink as she pulls out of the spot. "Yeah, but now you're gonna go find a new best friend at *Columbia*," I say sourly, giving the final word extra fancy-voice oomph. "Just watch—in two seconds, you and your new roomie will be total besties."

I'm not sure if it sounds like I'm kidding. I'm not sure I am. I'm not sure I care.

She grins. "Van, *no one* is taking your place. You think Adrienne Hughes from Montclair, New Jersey, would ever act out scenes from my favorite movies to keep me company after I had a root canal? *Or* hire me as her assistant and tutor to help me pay for college when I was in dire need? Please."

Hmph, I suppose that makes me feel a little better. "Adrienne Hughes from Montclair, New Jersey, huh? You already know her name and everything?"

"Just got my assignment yesterday. That's all I know, though. I haven't e-mailed her or anything."

"Good. Don't," I say with a smile, and she laughs.

"I don't know who's more possessive—you or Josh."

"Me or Josh?" My eyebrows shoot up. "Hello, how about your totally smitten boyfriend?"

She shrugs. "Actually, Liam's been pretty cool with...everything."

If I hadn't been best friends with Alexandra Duncan for pretty much my entire life, I would've bought her "isn't that nice?" tone. But I have been and I'm not believing it for a second. "And you wish he were a little less cool with it, huh?"

"It'd be nice to feel like he's gonna miss me a little," she admits sheepishly.

I can't help it—I crack up so hard I actually snort.

"What the hell, Van? You don't get to pry into my brain and then laugh at me."

"I'm sorry, it's just that—you're kidding, right? You don't think Liam's gonna miss you like crazy? Are we talking about the same boy? The one who actually attempted to make you dinner last night? The one who talked to you about buying a place in Manhattan—"

"He hasn't mentioned that in months."

"Oh, *whatever*. That boy's as in love with you as Josh Chester is with himself." I take another sip as I people-watch out the window. I love Ally and Liam and I'm happy for them, but it's hard not to be jealous of what they have. The fact that she still has any insecurity about it boggles my freaking mind. Especially when I compare them to my current dead-end relationship with Zander Wilson, one of the five guys who make up Wonder Boys, a band so cheesy even I don't listen to them.

She mumbles something I can't hear, and then we drop it, listening to the radio instead. Of course, after a minute, we both join in, and by the time we pull up to Fred Segal, we're both hoarse from singing along to the radio at the top of our lungs.

I swear, if my voice didn't suck, I'd be the *best* pop star.

There are a couple of teens hanging out outside, and they giggle when they see me and Ally walking to the store. One boldly steps forward and asks for a picture. I smile for her phone, chat with them for a few seconds, and then follow Ally inside and upstairs.

A cute blond shop girl is admiring Josh almost as obviously as he's admiring himself in the mirror, and immediately, I'm sorry I came. Josh doesn't so much as turn around, even though he'd be able to see us easily if he weren't so in love with his own reflection.

"Josh," Ally barks, and he jumps.

"What the fuck, Duncan—oh." Then his eyes flit over to me. "K-drama. What are you doing here?"

"I really missed being showered with racist nicknames," I say sweetly, taking a seat. Obviously, there'll be no mention of it in front of Ally, but we also have some party planning to do, stat.

He grunts, and we all turn to the shop girl, who's just sort of watching us with interest. Immediately, I remind myself to play nice, because everyone in this town talks, and I've got a "nice girl" reputation I'm determined to keep; my publicist, Jade, would kill me if I ruined it.

Of course, Josh has no publicist, or filter, because Josh doesn't do much of anything. But at least he's mostly minimized his level of asshole-ness in front of Ally, because he knows he'll get an earful if he doesn't. My best friend does not take shit from anybody, even the spoiled actor keeping her in lattés.

"What do you think?" Josh asks her, straightening the cuffs of his jacket. "For that bullshit puppy charity thing."

While they discuss his clothing choices—and what he should and shouldn't say in front of strangers—I pull out my phone to text Liam, so he can distract Ally for long enough to let me and Josh get some planning done.

We're here. Text Ally w/some sort of sexmergency so Josh and I can talk party, please!!

I scroll through my other texts while I wait for him to respond. Most of them are from Jade, who sends quick bursts of ideas and demands at all hours of the night. They've reduced some since she took on an intern, though. Now I get loads of e-mails from "Brianna," who seems to think I'm an illiterate child.

A response pops up from Liam. *I'm on it.*

I grin at the screen, then glance over at Ally, who's demonstrating something to the shop girl on Josh's sleeve. After a few seconds, I hear her phone beep and then watch her pull it out of her pocket...and blush like a mofo.

"Excuse me," she murmurs, stepping away while I hide a snort behind my hand.

I wait until she's out of earshot, and then yank Josh off the pedestal in front of the mirror. "I don't know how long Liam will keep her, so come on—let's talk party."

"Party?" the shop girl asks, and I'm not sure if she's about to try to sell Josh another outfit or get herself an invite.

Of course, Josh wastes no time at all. "Party," he confirms with a sleazy smile. "At my little place in Malibu. Right on the beach—"

"It's a small, private party for a close friend," I say with a trace of apology in my tone as I glare at Josh.

"Hey, if Prince Zander can come—"

"Zander's my *boyfriend*," I remind him impatiently. "Ally's actually spent more than five minutes with him."

"Zander Wilson, right?" the shop girl pipes up, sounding excited now. She's starting to annoy me, though I obviously can't show it. "You guys are so cute."

Josh smothers his laughter with a cough, and I glare at him before smiling and nodding at the shop girl. Finally, he works his face into a normal expression and asks her to get him some cufflinks.

As soon as she's gone, I whack him on the arm. "What the hell is wrong with you, Josh?"

"I'm sorry, but we both know your boyfriend is a total closet case, right? Why the hell are you dating a guy in a *boy band* again?"

"I like him!" I say defensively, even though it's a sort of a lie. I mean, Zander's fine, but it's not like we attend parties and award shows together because we adore each other's company. He's just another one of Jade's suggestions, and at this point, my romantic life is so pathetic that I'm happy to do what she says just because it's easier than finding my own boyfriend. Not that I would ever in a billion years tell Josh that.

"You sure Jade's not the one who likes him?" Josh's smile is so smug I want to punch it off his face.

"Oh, just shut up," I mutter. "You haven't done a damn thing but show off your ass in jeans since last summer. Who are you to even talk about anything?"

"Please, like I don't know all about the dragon lady, especially after everything with Liam last year. How is she, anyway?"

"Ask the bitchy intern she has doing all her dirty work these days," I mutter. "*After* we agree on a band for the party. And remember—this is for Ally, not you, so the answer isn't 'whoever has the hottest chick on sticks,' got it?"

"Man, I can't believe the boys don't come a-runnin' for you, K-drama. With all that natural charm and—"

"Here you go," the shop girl says sunnily, and Josh jumps back into flirt mode as he holds out his wrists to allow her to thread in the cufflinks. A moment later, Ally returns, too, trying to hide the goofy smile on her face following her phone call with Liam.

"Ooh, those are nice," she says, peering over Josh's arm. "Yes, he'll definitely take those."

I sigh as I watch the three of them get chatty and check my phone again. There's a new e-mail from Brianna with a list of interviews scheduled for me this week; a text from Zander, not-so-subtly reminding me of how much the church youth group he volunteers at would love for me to make an appearance; a voicemail from my mother, asking me to pick up ginger; and then a new text from Liam: *Get anything planned?*

I shove my phone back into my pocket and excuse myself to go look at some cute dresses on my own. Suddenly, I find myself in great need of retail therapy.

I have Ally leave me there, telling her I want to shop more and Josh's driver will take me home. She's so focused on getting to Liam ASAP that she doesn't argue, and I make Josh sit down with me so we can finally get things done. She's heading to New York on August twentieth, so we schedule the party for the eighteenth, so her last night can be with her family. As usual, Josh's focus is on how to top his previous parties, and after his third attempt to convince me that his backyard can totally accommodate sword-eating fire dancers, I tell him we're done and I need a ride. Now I'm just hoping to beat my parents home.

No such luck.

"Vanessa, you're finally back." My mother looks up from the newspaper she's reading in the den. "Is Ally with you?"

"Nope, just me." *Sorry to disappoint.* I swear, if my parents could trade me for my overachieving, straight-A-getting, Ivy League-bound BFF, they'd do it in a hot second. "I'm going up to run some lines. I have a table-read tomorrow."

"You don't have time to sit with your mother for a few minutes first?" She folds up *The Korea Times*—her every-weekday read, without fail—and pats the seat next to her on the couch.

Be nice, I order myself and take a seat. Maybe she's *not* calling me over just to talk colleges or what I plan on doing when I'm "done with this acting nonsense." Maybe—

"I just saw Jinsung's mother at the bank, and guess what she told me her son is doing when he graduates college."

Maybe not. "Running for president?"

Mom tsks in annoyance, which is basically her default language with me. "He is going to be an apprentice to an architect. Doesn't that sound interesting?"

"About a tenth as interesting as starring in a network's top-rated TV show." I frown at the slight chip I hadn't noticed earlier in the mint-green polish on my index finger. "But if Jinsung would like to sit in on a taping so you can show *me* off, I'm sure I could help arrange it."

Another tsking. "Yes, your show is doing very well, Vanessa, but do not be arrogant. You are already eighteen. How much longer will you be able to act as a sophomore in high school?"

I know I could drop stats about Bethany Joy Lenz on *One Tree Hill*—twenty-two when the show started—or Gabrielle Carteris on *Beverly Hills, 90210*—a whopping twenty-nine—but there's no point. I've had every argument with her before, and nothing ever penetrates the sleek black helmet of hair covering her skull.

"Maybe you could let me actually *start* failing before you plan for it?" I suggest, trying to keep my voice gentle. "Sometimes, I don't even understand why you let me audition at all when I was younger. I assumed the fact that you did meant you and Dad would get behind me someday, but you still haven't. Why?"

She sighs. "When you were a child, yes, okay, it was a nice hobby and built a solid work ethic. But now? Now you should be in college. Like Jinsung. Like Ally. Your grandparents did not move their families to America so you could play pretend forever. At some point, you must become an adult. This show lets you think you are sixteen forever. That is not the way life is."

"But you want me to go to college so I can get a job, right? So I can learn, and make money?" I press. "That's what I'm already doing. Why can't you appreciate that? I'm like the picture-perfect American dream right here." I gesture at my designer clothes, my expertly done pedicure, my newest clothing purchases bought with my own earnings. "Maybe your friends' kids should be more like me. Maybe they should stop aiming to be doctors and lawyers instead of doing something cool and creative." I tap the copy of *The Korea Times* she just laid down on the coffee table. "How many of your friends have been in this paper? Because I have. At least three times."

But it's clear from the expression on her face that my mother just feels sad for me. Poor Vanessa, who's deluded herself into thinking she's important. Poor Vanessa, who's on the verge of failure, even as she's succeeding. Poor Vanessa, whose being *in* the paper is overshadowed by the fact that she can barely read it.

And poor her, for having only been able to have one child, who turned out to be such an unintellectual disappointment.

I stand up from the couch before this conversation can veer any further into the same familiar territory, my feet moving toward the stairs as if they've got minds of their own. "I'm going up to read."

She doesn't say anything as I head up, and I can hear the flick of her newspaper as she picks it back up, as if I were never there.

Once upstairs, I change into shorts and a sports bra, grab my sides, and get on the treadmill to run lines while I walk. But even in my zone, and even though my parents have been pulling this kind of unsupportive crap for *years*, my mother's words continue to penetrate my brain. Because a big part of me knows she's right. Not about the age thing—I look young enough that I'll probably be able to pull off playing high school well into my twenties—but about the fact that I can't guarantee there'll be another role for an Asian-American actress when *Daylight Falls* ends.

Even this past summer, while my costars (e.g. Liam) were starring in career-making roles, I was stuck playing yet another science nerd, this time in a stupid slasher movie. The fact that I actually suck at science only rubbed salt in the gaping wound of my career.

The only person who gets it—like, *really* gets it—is my costar Jamal. Where I get roles like "science nerd" and "med student," he gets "guy on the basketball team" and "token black friend who bites it first in every horror movie." We're practically our own freaking drinking game.

We both know we're lucky to be on a show with two people of color in the main cast, but just the fact that it *is* lucky feels crappy. Even with good reviews on the show, I still get people thinking I'm only on it to fill some sort of racial quota—as if the role of Bailey

Summers hadn't actually been written for a blonde and given to me because I was just *better* than everyone else.

Whatever.

I read through all my lines a few times, trying some different tones and affects until I feel Bailey fully inhabit my body again, and then I grab my phone. I need to get out of this house. I'm not really in the mood to see Zander, but he *did* ask me what I was up to tonight in his text earlier, and it's not like Ally's free. I reply to his earlier text with, *Having dinner w/u?*

After five minutes of waiting for a response, I give up and go take a shower. When I get out, though, I see I have a reply text.

Sounds good ☺

Zander's really big on smiley faces. He signs his freaking autographs with them. My "nice girl" rep is nothing compared to his "nice boy" one.

We agree on a Jade-approved place—height of trendy, lots of exposure—and then I text Ally. *Need u to pick me a hot outfit ASAP.*

She's always slower to respond when she's with Liam, and I get to work on drying my hair and carefully applying my eyeliner while I wait. When there's still no response and I know I'm cutting it close, I huff out a breath and pull on a pair of black leather shorts and a sheer-ish, sleeveless polka-dot blouse I immediately see makes it clear I haven't logged enough time in the sun this summer. I trade the blouse for a fuchsia one that looks way better against my skin and make a mental note to book a spray-tan appointment—something Ally used to do for me once upon a time without my even having to tell her it was time for another one. It's kind of sucked, watching her be someone else's assistant, but not as much as it'll suck watching her leave.

I glance back at my phone. Still no answer from Ally, but there's a new text from Zander giving me a heads-up that paparazzi will be present at dinner. I smile and go back into my bathroom to add a little more makeup, and swap out my lip gloss for one that makes my teeth look whiter. It's hard work looking this good, and it's always nice to get fair warning there'll be cameras on you. My BFF may have checked out completely, but I still have to be on at all times.

Chapter Three

Josh

"*I*t's your mother. Again." Ally holds out the phone as if the fifteenth time will be the charm. It's been a week since "Yvette" mentioned that dumbass reality show, which means a week of ignoring her calls. She's getting desperate to shove me in front of the sleazy-ass producer she's suckered into this stupid idea.

"Well, you can go ahead and ignore it. Again." I'm sexting with a waitress from one of the clubs I went to last week, trying to get a new topless pic to use as my wallpaper, and I don't have patience for this shit. "Did you confirm my flight to Miami?"

"Confirmed the flight, and that Ronen will be here in time for your pre-flight beauty ritual. I *also* confirmed your audition this afternoon, so please actually show up to this one. I know you don't seem to care about booking anything for some reason, but you *do* realize your personal income flow is pretty lacking, right?"

"You remind me every fucking day," I growl, but I can barely even hear it. The phone's no longer ringing, but the echo of it—and my mother's nagging voice—are bouncing around in my head like a fucking game of Ping-Pong.

"Do you need an Advil?"

"I'm fine. You can go."

"Is this about your mother calling?"

I lift my head from my phone and glare at her. "My psycho-bitch mother is none of your concern."

"It would help if you'd tell me *why* she's suddenly calling you every hour."

"Not much you can do unless you can get her a job so she can get over the idea of me doing a shitty reality show with her."

Ally freezes. "You're doing a reality show? Seriously, Josh?"

"Certainly not planning on it." My phone beeps with another text, and I glance down hopefully, but it's just the waitress being boring and trying to get me to come back and see her first. Fuck that.

"Good, because that's a ridiculous move. I *know* you can land at least one of these jobs. If you start with reality TV, you're gonna be done for life."

"Tell me something I don't know. And tell my mother, too. If you can't do that, keep ignoring her calls."

It looks like she wants to say more, but she doesn't, and I don't ask what she's thinking. She's not usually one to keep her opinions to herself; I'll take the gift of her silence where I can get it.

"You can go home whenever," I add, since she doesn't seem to quite get that I don't need her in my face anymore. What I *do* need is another drink or five, maybe a lap dance, but I've got a photo shoot tomorrow for Aspen, the designer jeans brand that keeps me in first-class tickets to Miami—and on major billboards all over the country—and I need to squeeze in a workout and a decent night's sleep. Contrary to what I tell every blogger and reporter who asks, my cut body doesn't perfect itself.

A few more clicks on the laptop she totes around, and then she closes it with a sigh. "Fine. But you *need* to show up to this audition today. And you might want to think about looking at places closer to LA, anyway. Once you *are* working more regularly, you'll realize what a bitch it is doing this drive every day."

"Subtle."

"If you're looking for subtlety, I think you hired the wrong assistant." She slides the laptop into her bag and stands up. "Go over your lines. Kick some ass today. Land the part. *Then* you can let yourself get disowned."

I shake my head and watch her leave before going down to the gym. One more hour of masochism seems just about right for this day.

★ ★ ★ ★ ★

The audition sucks. It's obvious from the second casting sees me that they have zero expectations, and they're right to. I can't pretend I think the stupid, derivative shit I've spent the afternoon memorizing deserves any effort, so I don't give it any. And then I leave.

I know the first thing I'm gonna see when I check my phone after sliding into the backseat of Ronen's Escalade is a text from Ally asking how the audition went, and of course she proves me right. I don't have the patience to deal with her now, and I know that early night's sleep isn't happening, either. I need to get out—blow off some steam with the guys and get a good drink and a warm body or three. It's still early, though, so I text Wyatt instead and tell him to get TamTam—his favorite bong—ready because I'll be there in twenty.

It takes forty, thanks to traffic, but not long at all from there for me to get completely blitzed. This is exactly what I need to clear my head after the shitshow combo of the audition and my mother's insanity. By the time I pull out my phone to check the time, it's already ten and definitely time to get out of this house.

I still don't feel like going home, though, so I text a few of the guys, including Liam, even though he never wants to go out. He's the first to text back, and surprises the hell out of me by asking when and where. Guess he's not spending the night with Ally, for once. I tell him to pick me up from Wyatt's, and we go to Circuit, which has a comfy VIP section and very accommodating waitresses.

When we walk up to the roped-off section, Royce Hudson, Jeremy Hill, and Paz—don't even know if that's his first name or last—are already there. Royce is sucking a cherry out of a redheaded waitress's belly button, but when he sees us, he whips his head up. "Look who the fuck is finally good enough to come out with his boys!" he yells out, nearly choking on the cherry. "What'sa matter, Holloway? That girl dump your ass?"

Liam snorts. "Hudson, I almost forgot how charming you are when you're drunk." We each fist-bump Royce hello, then do the same with Jeremy and Paz. The waitress sits up slowly, sizing us up and smiling slowly as she does, then slides off the table like water and eases out of the section to make room.

"Hey, you chased away our entertainment," says Royce, nodding toward the waitress.

"I didn't tell her to go," I say with a shrug, grabbing the nearest open bottle and taking a drink without bothering to check its contents.

"Yeah, but Holloway fucking radiates 'taken.' Bitches don't wanna be around that."

"Pretty sure what they don't want is to be called 'bitches,' actually," says Liam. I roll my eyes and take another drink. Whatever brand of vodka it is, it's pretty smooth going down. "Plus, plenty of 'em don't give a shit if you're taken. Trust."

He sounds so damn bitter—getting hit on pisses Liam off even more than it used to now that he's with Ally—and Paz snorts. "Poor Holloway. You getting too much ass? Boo fucking hoo."

"Oh, shut up."

I let them bicker like little kids and scan the club to see if the hot waitress who blew me in the bathroom last time we were here is around. I don't see her, but the waitress who was giving Royce her cherry when we walked in returns, carrying neon-green shots that are apparently on the house. She drapes herself back over Royce and we toast to I don't even know what before drinking them down.

I glance at Liam as we toss the empty glasses back on her tray. He still looks pissed. Stressed. The other guys are distracted by the waitress, so I lean in. "Dude, what's wrong with you?"

He grabs the vodka I hadn't realized I was still holding and tosses it back. "Nothing. I'm fine." He's lying; it doesn't take a PhD to guess he's not taking Ally's leaving as well as he wants to be. "How was the audition?"

"Shitty." The bottle's nearing empty, and the waitress is busy making out with Hudson. "Hey, Hill, you guys got any more booze?"

He looks up from his phone. "We had Patrón... somewhere. Might be under Hudson."

Hudson reaches under what's a little too close to his ass for comfort and pulls out a bottle without breaking mouth-to-mouth suction. I wipe the whole thing off on the corner of his shirt before uncapping it to pour shots for Liam and me.

"Sorry, man," he says with a frown. "Got any more lined up?"

We clink shots and toss 'em back. "Not yet. Going down to Miami for an Aspen shoot this weekend. Having dinner with Holly when I get back. And I have to figure out this shit with my parents."

His eyebrows shoot up. "You've been talking to your parents? About *what*?"

I forget how seriously Ally takes the whole discretion part of client privilege. "My mom got canned," I mutter, taking a swig straight from the tequila bottle. "Now she wants to do some reality shit so she can pretend she was ever relevant."

Liam barks out a laugh. "Your family. In a reality show. Seriously? And your dad is cool with this?"

"My dad was paying attention for approximately five seconds of the conversation. Anyway, he's not the one that network gives a shit about. Lucky me."

"I don't get it. Just say no."

"She's blackmailing me with my house." Man, talking about this shit is really ruining the buzz I've spent all day building. "Fuck this." I yank Royce away from the waitress. "Hey," I say to her. "Is Gia working tonight?"

"You mean Gina?" she asks, wiping her mouth.

"Yeah. Yeah, Gina. Right. She here?" I need a serious distraction, and the bottled variety just isn't cutting it right now.

"I think she's around. I'll check. Can I get you boys anything else?"

Liam holds up the empty vodka bottle. "Another one of these, please."

"Hey, is that Scott Lassiter?" Jeremy asks, keeping his voice low. We all look up, and see that it is indeed. Lassiter's the fastest-rising young director in Hollywood right now, but he's also picky and neurotic as balls. Getting an audition with him is next to impossible. The other guys all sit up a little straighter, like that'll suddenly give them a shot in hell of getting noticed.

"Any of you guys auditioning for his Iraq movie?" Royce asks.

Jeremy snorts. "My agent's been trying to get a meeting with him for months. No luck. He's such a dick."

"What about you, Chester?"

Royce's mouth is curved up just enough for me to know he's actively trying to be an asshole right now; he knows there's no chance Holly could score me an audition. Lassiter's impossible enough, and Holly's a junior agent. If I could've gone with anyone else—and I mean, *anyone*—after getting dropped by Calvin, I probably would have.

"There's not a single hot chick in that movie," I say flatly. "No chance I'm going to sweat my balls off in the desert for that shit."

"The asshole doesn't even return my agent's calls," mutters Paz. "Self-righteous prick."

"Paz, you've got like nine inches to grow in every fucking direction—including your dick—before you can play a soldier," says Royce. "I'm perfect for that shit."

"You'd look like an *actual* dick in a uniform," Paz shoots back. "But Holloway...fuck, man, you'd be perfect. You auditioning?"

Liam doesn't get a chance to answer, because suddenly, the man himself is standing before us.

"Mr. Lassiter." Jeremy jumps up, sticking out his hand like an overeager tool. "Jeremy Hill. I'm a big fan."

Lassiter looks at Jeremy's hand, ignores it, glances around at all of us. His gaze settles on Liam. "You. You look familiar. Who are you?"

"Liam Holloway." I swear, the way he says it, you'd think he was about to tack a "Sir" on the end. He really *is* kinda perfect to play a soldier, all respectful and disciplined and shit. "I was in James Gallagher's last movie, *The History of Us*." Sir.

"Oh yeah. Fuckin' Jim. That movie was all right. Who's your agent?"

"Evan Cooper, Sir."

I knew it.

The rest of us laugh, and so does Lassiter, but he's not walking away. "Lift up your shirt."

Liam's so stunned, he doesn't even respond. Fortunately, I have no such problem with my reaction time, and at least one of us recognizes this for the opportunity it is. I yank up Liam's shirt as far as I can, revealing his eight-pack to the entirety of Circuit.

Half the fucking club stops and whistles, and I grin as some girl calls out "Nice body!" from the front.

"I'm inclined to agree," Lassiter says wryly. "Here, *Sir*. Tell Evan Cooper to give me a call." He hands over a card, gives Liam's abs another quick glance, then walks off toward the bar.

Liam whirls around to see us all gaping at him. "Did that shit seriously just happen?" he asks me.

"That shit *seriously* just happened," I confirm, giving him a bro-five that nearly breaks my palm in two. "Scott fucking *Lassiter*! That's a Fourth of July movie, man!"

Just like that, the goofy, bewildered smile on his face falls. "Right. A Fourth of July movie. Which means filming starts soon."

"So?" asks Paz.

"So it overlaps with *Daylight Falls*," he says miserably.

Which means there's no chance in hell he'll be able to do it.

He sighs and drops back down to his seat. I don't really know what to say him now—none of us do—but it doesn't matter. He pulls out his phone, and I know we've lost him to Ally for the night.

"Chester, this place looks absurd," Liam observes as he walks around the pool area, taking in the last few weeks' worth of planning. "Hasn't Ally told you a million times, no fire?"

"She said no fire*works*. Or fire dancers. She's never said anything about setting the hot tub on fire." I watch one of the burlesque dancers touch up another's makeup, and I wonder how badly it'll stain my pillowcase later.

"And don't you think a Gray's Papaya cart is a little excessive? I didn't even know they *had* carts."

"It's vintage." I was particularly proud of that find. "And this party's for *your* girlfriend. You'd think you'd be a little more appreciative. Especially since you insisted on being painfully boring for your birthday. Which, by the way, if you think you're getting away with for your twenty-first..."

He rolls his eyes. "Don't worry—you've already made it plenty clear that next year we'll be acting out the *Grand Theft Auto* edition of your choice."

"Excellent." We head over to the bar and help ourselves to a couple of bottles of Stella while the guys set up. "How'd the Lassiter audition go?"

"Not sure." He takes a long drink, and I realize this might be the first time Liam's actually looked nervous over a movie role. Even last year, when he scored the James Gallagher part Jeremy Hill had a total hard-on for, he didn't really give a shit. "They said I'd need to gain like ten, fifteen pounds of muscle." He side-eyes the bottle. "This probably isn't helping."

"They always say that shit. Anyway, a little protein powder and you're golden."

"Patchett was there, though. And Gray. And Valenti. Valenti almost beat me out last year for *History*."

"Yeah, but he didn't. Dude, you've gotta get a little more of an ego, or little dicks like Valenti and Hudson are gonna walk all over you. You've got this shit. Trust."

"Doesn't even matter if I do. There's no way I can work it out with the show."

"Man, you really love excuses. Isn't it filming mostly in Imperial Valley? If you got a reduced storyline on the show and basically busted your ass, you could do it. You get a callback?"

"Yeah." He takes another long drink. "Friday."

Ah, fuck. So that's the real problem; he's gotta act his ass off the day after he sends Ally off to New York. "So, that could be cool, right? Channel your pain into some sort of war-torn PTSD shit?"

He snorts. "Yeah, maybe." Then he pulls out his phone. "Still no text from Van. Guess they're still shopping."

"Hey, Josh Chester!" a voice calls out from behind us. We turn, but I don't recognize the guy coming toward us.

"Who are you?" I raise my sunglasses, but I've definitely never seen this guy before in my life. "Are you one of the bartenders?"

He laughs and holds out a hand. "I'm Chuck. Joe Perotti sent me."

Joe Perotti... Why does that name sound so familiar?

"The reality show guy?" asks Liam.

Motherf—

"I didn't realize you decided to do it," Liam says slowly.

"That's because I didn't." I turn back to Chuck, who's finally figured out I won't be touching his slimy hand. "This is a private party. Invited guests only."

"Your mother *did* invite me," says Chuck, his stupid sleazy smile not wavering for a second. "Said this would be a great opportunity for some preliminary footage. Joe loved the idea."

"How did my mother even *know* about it?" I ask Liam, ignoring Chuck completely.

"Um, look at this place, Chester. They can probably see that light-up ice sculpture of the Empire State Building from space. Doesn't take a brain surgeon to figure out you're doing *something* here tonight."

"Well, what I'm *doing*," I spit, half-looking at Chuck now, half-hoping he'll just disappear if I ignore him long enough, "is throwing a party for a friend, and I'd really like for everyone who shouldn't have gotten past security to get the hell out."

"Like I said"—Chuck grins like an asshole—"your mom set this up. And seeing as apparently this is her house..."

"Don't kid yourself, Chucky. I earn more in a fucking day of modeling than my mother earns in six months as a has-been drama queen. If she weren't holding on to this place as tightly as humanly possible in her little ferret paws—"

"Oooookay." I feel a hand on my arm and look down to see Liam pulling me away. "Chester, how many times have we discussed the fact that you cannot just say whatever the hell you feel like?" he mutters under his breath. "Guys like him live to rile you up to get footage like this."

"Well, I'm not signing a damn thing, so good luck to him if he's got a creep filming me from somewhere." I realize right then that I'm still holding a half-full bottle of Stella, and I chug the rest, hoping it'll calm me down, because I know Liam's right.

Of course, it's warm by now, so I basically just drank piss.

I put the bottle down before I can hurl it at the concrete.

"I fucking hate her," I say quietly. "I hate them both."

He frowns. "I know. Trust me, I know all about parental douchebags. But you've got a kickass party set up, and people are gonna get here soon, and that guy's just gonna get lost in the crowd. Let's let the fact that Ally's leaving be the only thing that blows about tonight, okay?"

It's such a childish, Liam pep talk, but it works; his Yoda shit always does. I take a deep breath and look around. "Yeah, let's go get another beer."

Chapter Four

Vanessa

*9*t's so weird to be looking at sweaters," Ally muses for the third or fourth time that afternoon. "I can't believe I'm gonna need *sweaters*." She says it as if it's awful, but there's a reason I'm the actor of the two of us. She can't wait to wear itchy wool and cashmere cable-knit. And she eyed eight billion pairs of boots when we were in the shoe department. Girl's clearly already an East Coaster in her mind.

"That one's cute," I say, trying to get excited about it. It *is* cute—a gray thing with a black Peter Pan collar that'll probably look nice with jeans—but it's hard to get psyched about *why* she'll need sweaters. Not that we don't wear sweaters and boots plenty here in LA, but they're not exactly the wardrobe staples my jean cutoffs or cropped tops are.

"Yeah." She fingers the fabric lightly before moving on, her eyes seven shades of dreamy. "I hope it's nice when I get there. There are so many things I wanna do outdoors! I need to spend at least half a day just sitting and reading in Central Park, obviously. And I didn't really get to see much of the city when I was there for Liam's birthday last summer. I need to just walk around—SoHo, the Village, the Upper East Side..."

I smile and nod and occasionally chime in as she talks about her soon-to-be home, but the more she talks about the things she can't wait to see and experience, the bigger the lead ball in the pit of my stomach gets, and not just because my best friend's going to be in a different time zone.

She just sounds so...*old.* I mean, she sounds like the Ally I know and love—the one who can spend a billion years planning every detail of a trip to the freaking mall—but these things she's talking about doing, she's talking about doing *alone.* Her best friend will be in LA, her family will be in LA, even her boyfriend will be here. So why isn't she freaked out at the prospect of going and exploring all by herself?

I'd be freaking terrified.

Don't you realize you're gonna be living with strangers? I wanna shake her and ask. *Don't you realize you aren't gonna be eating home-cooked food? Or seeing your parents every day? Or grabbing Pinkberry with me just because it's a Saturday?*

But of course she knows. And she can't wait.

"So when do I get to come out and visit?" I ask, trying to get on board with the excitement.

"Whenever you want, Vanny!" she says gleefully, though she keeps her voice down so as not to attract any attention with her mention of my name. I'm wearing a purple wig and (prescription-free) glasses, but that hasn't stopped a few people already today from asking for my autograph. "I mean, as long as I don't have orientation. Or mid-terms. Or finals." God, even those words seem to excite her.

No wonder my parents would swap us in a heartbeat.

As she keeps talking, oblivious to the fact this entire conversation makes me feel like someone is squeezing my ribcage with pliers, I sneak a glance at my phone. Phew—definitely time to text the guys and get us over to that party. I could drink my freaking weight in Skinnygirl strawberry daiquiris right now.

Showtime, I text Liam as soon as Ally looks away to examine another sweater.

Less than a minute later, her phone rings, and she rolls her eyes when she sees Josh's name and face on the screen. "Yes, master?"

"Where are you?" Even I can hear him barking through the phone. Nice touch.

"Shopping with Van. Because you very, very explicitly told me I should enjoy my last couple of days in LA."

I can't hear his response, but then she says, "What happened to the one I *just* bought you?" Judging by her facial expression as she listens to the answer, I don't want to know.

She sighs and hangs up. "I'm sorry, do you mind? I need to get Josh yet *another* black leather belt from Louis Vuitton, because he doesn't seem to understand what should and shouldn't be tied around bed posts."

"Don't mind at all," I say with a grin. Trust Josh to come up with the most ridiculous excuse ever...and for it to probably be true, in addition to convenient.

After a quick stop for the belt, we get in the car and head up to Josh's. Not a minute too soon—I was getting itchy under that wig. I've got outfits for both me and Ally hidden in Josh's guest house, but there's not much I'll be able to do about the fact that my hair looks sad and flat.

It's oddly silent as we approach, despite the mayhem I know is lying in wait back there, and I have to admit that I'm pretty impressed by Josh right now. For someone who can barely keep his own mouth shut, ever, he's doing pretty well at this whole "surprise" thing.

Which makes it extra epic when we walk around back and *bam*.

Ally's face goes from confused to terrified to ecstatic in seconds, and I can't help grinning proudly as I watch her take in the surroundings for all of two seconds before people swarm out of every corner of Josh's house and yard. There are old high school friends, friends from the *Daylight Falls* set, and people I don't even recognize, which of course might just mean they're random girls Josh wants to hook up with.

I watch as Ally hugs Josh, kisses Liam, then turns to me with a suspicious raised eyebrow. I nod guiltily and accept my hug, too, but even with her arms wrapped tightly around me and her voice whispering "thank you" in my ear, she already feels three thousand miles away.

"Wow, K-drama, what number's that for you?"

I glare daggers at the host as he edges me over in my chaise and makes himself comfortable draped over me. "I could ask the same about how many girls you've hooked up with tonight. Guess Ally's already given up keeping you in line."

"My my, what do you know? Jealousy looks pretty good on you," he says with an infuriating smirk.

I don't know how Ally's managed to work for this asshole for a year, but cutting the amount I have to see him in half is definitely the only good part of my best friend leaving. "Don't make me barf all over you." I may have had the tiniest bit of interest in Josh Chester *once*, like a billion years ago, but that ship has wrecked. Hard. "I'm not into downgrading, thank you very much."

"Burrrrrrn!" Royce Hudson reaches over from the next chair and slaps me five. Royce is an even bigger tool than Josh, but I smile around my straw as I take another sip of my coconut-rum thing.

"Oh, please. Downgrade, my ass." Josh snaps his fingers at a passing waitress, making me grimace. "Hey, you!"

"Do you have to be such a dick?" I demand under my breath as I take another sip. This is why everyone thinks all actors are arrogant jerks—far too many of us *are*.

The girl spins around, loose flame-red curls swinging over bare shoulders tattooed with colorful flowers. "It's actually two clicks, then a snap, then a meow," the waitress deadpans as she spins the cork-bottomed tray in her hand. I choke on my drink at the unexpected response, and the corner of her mouth quirks up as she glances at me before fixing her gaze on Josh. "What's up?"

He's too drunk for her sarcasm to compute. "Which of us do you think is the most famous?"

"Oh my God, Josh, what the fuck is wrong with you?" I blurt before I can stop myself. Usually I'm good at remembering that Vanessa Park does not use the F-word, but something about Josh...

I glance back at the waitress. She's biting her lip in an attempt not to crack up, but her dimples are showing and I know this is bad. Not that she looks like the type to run to the tabloids or anything, but—

She cocks her head at me, and I realize I've been staring. God, I have clearly had too much to drink. I tear my eyes away and glance around to see if Zander's shown up yet. "Well," she says, "my ex-boyfriend's obsessed with the *Zombie Camp* movies"—she gestures at Royce—"but I'm a *Daylight Falls* girl, personally."

At the mention of my show, I can't help but look back at her, and I do so just in time to get a wink.

The words "in your face" are on the tip of my tongue to shout at Josh, but they're sticking in my mouth; my lips are too busy smiling. I look away again—fast—and immediately spot Zander walking toward us.

I sigh with what I hope sounds like relief.

"You moving in on my girl, Chester?" he asks, his eyes flickering over Josh occupying my chair. There's a glass of something dark brown in hand, but knowing how good Zander is at the Nice Boy role, I suspect it's exactly the straight Diet Coke it appears to be. He looks cute, his brown hair flopping in his eyes. His outfit makes me cringe a little—I can tell it was picked by his stylist, and it's topped by his favorite gaudy crucifix necklace—but at least it's not a velvet tuxedo; that was a seriously embarrassing night.

"Hey!" I shove Josh out of the seat and raise my face for a kiss. "When did you get here?"

"Just a couple minutes ago." He sits down on the edge of my chair and pecks my cheek. "What'd I miss?"

"Chester was just learning that he's the very bottom of the totem pole," says Royce, and everyone else cracks up, including the waitress. "Your girlfriend and I are superstars, though."

"Tell me something I don't know," Zander says smugly, and now he snuggles in, wrapping an arm around my neck and pressing his lips to mine. Everyone else's eyes are on us, and I can practically feel Josh's laughter, and suddenly I need to get out and breathe. I disentangle myself from the kiss as naturally as possible and mutter something about spotting Ally before climbing over Zander and off the chair.

I'm sure a few people are staring at my uncharacteristic behavior, but whatever. I've obviously had too much to drink, because I've never felt this claustrophobic before. A few gulps of sea air and I'm feeling a little better, though I'd kill for a glass of—

"Water?"

I spin around on my heels and find myself face-to-face with the redheaded waitress. She's holding out an ice-filled glass, and I take it gratefully, tipping it back for a long swallow.

"You okay?" she asks with far more concern than any of the guys at the party would have.

"Fine. Just needed to breathe." I'm genuinely not sure if I'm lying. "Thanks for the water."

She nods. "So, your friend is leaving, huh? That sucks."

With a flash, I realize she's the first person to acknowledge that this is hard for me—not for Josh, and not for Liam. It makes her very hard to look at. Instead, I murmur my agreement and take another long drink, probably crossing my eyes in an effort to avoid hers.

"I'm guessing being surrounded by that boys' club doesn't help."

I snort, then realize again that this girl has seen way too much of Not-So-Nice Vanessa. "They're good guys," I manage, like anyone would believe that. "Sorry you're not really seeing everyone at their best."

To my surprise, she throws back her head and laughs. "Jesus, you have no idea who I am, do you?"

Is that a trick question? "Umm...the waitress? From before?"

"Man, Jade was right. No one *does* notice the help."

And that's when I realize why her voice sounds vaguely familiar, and my stomach drops. "Holy shit. You're her intern. Brianna."

She laughs again, and it'd be a nice sound if it weren't totally at my expense. "She would kill you if she heard you right now, you know. *Remember,*" she says, switching into a dead-on impersonation of my publicist's tone, *"you are America's Sweetheart."*

"Oh God."

"Nice to meet you, too, though feel free to call me Bri," she says with a grin, showing those dimples for real this time. Together with her side-swept bangs and beachy red waves, they should make her look like a cutesy doll, but they're balanced by her tattoos and all-black ensemble—including her fingernails and the plastic frames around her startlingly light green eyes.

Eyes that, I realize now, look exactly like Jade's.

"Are you...related?"

"Yup. Unless anyone asks. Then...nope."

"I appreciate you sharing your secret with me," I say with a smile and feel a little twinge at how sincerely I mean that. Ugh. Clearly too much alcohol. *Clearly.* Where the hell is Zander, anyway? Shouldn't he have been the one to come after me? Why did Brianna?

Wait. Why is Brianna even here at all?

"You're spying on us," I say flatly, my stomach sinking a little with the realization. And here I thought I was the actress.

For a second, she looks taken aback, but just as quickly, she rearranges her face back into the same blasé expression she had when Josh snapped her over. "Basically." She shrugs. "Sorry. Mommy Dearest's orders."

"That's really, really screwed up." I shove the glass of water back into her hands. "You're both really screwed up. This is a private party, you know. There aren't even any paparazzi here."

"No, just a billion cell phone cameras," she says with a roll of her eyes. "You dropped your persona in two seconds in front of me when you thought I was nobody but a waitress. What if I'd gone to the press or even just a little blog with the story of how Vanessa Park isn't the sweetheart they think she is?"

Is it possible to hate someone this early into meeting them? Because that's exactly how I feel. And only part of it is because I know she's right.

"You can tell your *mother* that I'm so sweet, I won't even get you kicked out of Josh's party right now," I say with as much honey in my voice as I can muster, although it sounds more like vinegar when it comes out. "Now, if you'll excuse me, I'm going to find my boyfriend."

She steps away to let me go, and I storm past her, my cheeks burning for far too many reasons to contemplate.

Chapter Five

I'm all for Liam getting the part in the Lassiter movie, but after years of watching him be treated as Hollywood's hottest body when he barely breaks a tenth of the sweat I do to look this good, I have to admit I'm enjoying watching him struggle as he bench presses next to me.

"Holy Mother of God, *what* is happening to me?" he whines as he replaces the barbell.

"Looks like someone was up all night...exercising." I do another couple reps, then replace my own, just to stretch out my hands for a minute. "This is why you always kick the girl out well before dawn."

He scowls at me as he reluctantly removes ten pounds from each side. "The shots from last night aren't helping either. You and your stupid parties."

"Oh, come on. You had fun last night, and so did she. And I bet you got killer head for that present."

He just rolls his eyes at me and resumes the position.

"I had a lovely night, too, thanks for asking," I say coolly, moving into position to spot him, since I'm already bored and half-afraid he's gonna drop it on his face. "Hooked up with that singer."

"Of course you did," he grunts as he lifts, and I smile proudly. She's a pretty damn good get, if I may say so myself. Notoriously picky, especially since she used to bang their drummer steadily for, like, three years. Nice to know I'm probably one of the few guys in the LA area who knows her natural hair color.

"They've got a show tonight. You wanna come?"

"Are you kidding? After I have dinner at the Duncans, I'm passing right the fuck out. I don't remember the last time I felt this tired."

"My old therapist would say you're emotionally exhausted."

"The hot one you screwed on her couch?"

"That's the one."

Loud, high-heeled footsteps have both of us turning our heads. Liam replaces the barbell as Ally lets herself into the gym, protein shakes in hand, with my agent right behind her. Holly's eyes widen for a second at the sight of us, sweaty and in nothing but gym shorts, and I give her my best wolf grin and watch as she sets her face back into stone.

People trying to make Serious Names for themselves in the industry are always the least fun.

Ally's a little less immune to the sight, and I have to snap my fingers to get her attention as she drools over Liam's sweaty, shirtless body like she hasn't seen it a zillion times. "That envelope for me?"

"Shots from the Aspen shoot. You wanna go to your office?"

"Nah, let's see 'em here." We lay them out carefully, and I can see I look pretty damn good. "Don't let them use this one," I order, pointing to one by a palm tree. "I look short." Not that I am.

"Your complex about being two inches shorter than me is getting a little pathetic," Liam says smugly as Ally hands him one of the shakes and me the other.

"So you're not even six feet. So you're basically only half a man. So what?"

"Fuck you."

"Are they always this awful to each other?" Holly asks Ally.

"Yes," Ally responds without hesitation.

"Delightful." Holly turns to Liam. "So, Liam, Josh tells me you have a callback for Lassiter tomorrow. How the hell did Evan Cooper score that?"

Liam narrows his eyes at me. "You didn't tell her Coop had nothing to do with it? What'd you do, Chester, make her feel like crap for not getting you an audition you didn't even want in the first place?" He turns to Holly. "We met Lassiter in a club. And I'm better-looking and a better actor than Josh. That's it."

"And Mickey Davis is gonna let you do this?" she asks, referring to *Daylight Falls'* showrunner.

"I have no idea." He mops off his face with a towel, then takes a long drink of the shake. "Haven't gotten that far yet. You know Mickey, though. Think I got a shot?"

"Depends on their plans for you this season. How's your storyline?"

"I surf. I hook up with Bailey, then cheat on Bailey, then get caught, then hook up with her again. Oh, and I surf some more. It's all very exciting. Clearly, I'm indispensable."

Everyone's quiet for a moment, and then Ally snaps her fingers. "Okay, I know Van's gonna kill me for suggesting this, but I think I might have a slightly brilliant idea." She turns to Liam. "What if you got a guest star to be a love interest for Bailey? Like, a multi-episode arc? Would they let you go then?"

Liam shrugs. "It's not impossible, I guess."

"No, definitely not," I agree, taking a sip from my own shake. "But if you write off or de-bang-ify a show's biggest piece of ass, you have to provide a replacement of equal or greater bangability. So, who?"

Uh oh. She's turning scary, determined Ally face on me. "You."

"Me?"

"You." She turns to Holly. "He doesn't actually have any work lined up right now, does he?"

"No, he does not," Holly confirms, her voice sweet, as if she's not pissed I screwed up that one audition and then refused to go to any others. "But TV..."

"What's wrong with TV?" Ally asks bluntly, cutting a glance at Liam.

"It's a lesser form of entertainment," Liam informs her, rolling his eyes. "Clearly, you're just blind to my pathetic-ness because you like my body."

"Oh, man, this is awkward. I'm not sure if I still want to make out with you after this." She taps her mouth thoughtfully. "No, wait, I definitely do."

Holly ignores them both. "If you'd just read one of the scripts I brought you at dinner—"

"I've read them," says Ally. "Which one of those is a higher form of entertainment, exactly? The one where he'd have to play a prince in a complete crap-fest of a misogynistic Disney-wannabe movie? Or the absurdly pseudo-intellectual one that subtly advocates for eugenics?"

My eyebrows shoot up faster than my dick at the Playboy mansion. Ally must *really* want this for Liam; she never talks that much shit about potential projects on the table.

Holly scowls. "I think you'd better leave decisions about his projects to your boss."

"I don't know; I think I just made my decisions about those." I grin at Holly before pouring half the shake down my throat. Sometimes it's easier just to get rid of all the shit at once.

She smiles tightly. "Okay, then. I'll send you some more tomorrow." She stands, and Ally immediately steps aside, as if removing any obstacles to the door will get Holly out faster. Their passive-aggressive smile-off is a thing of beauty as Holly sees herself out.

"Well, that was unexpected," Liam says, amused. "Thanks for the shake, by the way."

"Is it as gross as it looks?"

"Worse." He takes a final sip and tosses it in the trash, then turns to me. "I gotta go. But are you really interested in a guest arc? I could talk to Mickey."

I still haven't really processed the idea, but I know if it helps him out, I'd at least consider it. Especially since his costar, Zoe Knight, is semi-hot, and I haven't tapped her yet. "You think it'll help you be able to take the Lassiter part if you get it?"

"No clue. I'll let you know how it goes. Can I jump in the shower before I head out?"

"You better. Don't need your car smelling like BO next time I'm in it." I wait until he's closed the door to my personal locker room and run the shower, and then I turn to Ally. "You really think this is a better idea than doing one of those movies? Or are you just trying to make your boyfriend happy?"

"I think you need something to do that'll keep your mom's reality show crew away from you during the day, and you care more about helping Liam than you do what role you take on next," she says coolly. "And, frankly, it's a whole lot harder for you to screw this up. I think it's what you need to ease you back in."

She's right, on all counts. "Fine. Set it up," I say, tossing my own cup in the trash. "And don't let Holly give you shit."

★ ★ ★ ★ ★

"So we'll see you back here Monday morning for a table-read with a draft of a new script." Mickey Davis doesn't stand up at the end of our meeting, but it's hard to blame him since he's got a pooch so big it must be tough to carry around. Instead, he sticks out his fleshy hand, and I shake it as I get up. Liam had warned me Davis wasn't too thrilled he'd landed the Lassiter role, but he seems A-OK now. The Josh Chester Charm strikes again.

"Sounds great. Looking forward to it." I slip on sunglasses and let his assistant lead me outside, checking my phone to see if Ronen's left me a text about where he's at. Instead, I've got one from Holly.

Told your driver I'd be getting you instead. I'm in the lot.

I spot her almost immediately when I step outside by the way her unnaturally black hair gleams in the sun. She's standing up against the car, typing like crazy on her phone, but she looks up when I get close enough to block her sunlight.

"Hey," she says, slipping the phone into her purse. "How'd it go?"

"Great. We're gonna try it out. He's having writers come up with spec scripts to see about fitting me in as a love interest for Bailey while she and Tristan are on breakup number four thousand."

Holly eyes me blankly.

"Tristan is Liam's part on the show. Bailey is Vanessa Park's. Christ, have you not even watched it?"

"I don't watch TV." She turns back to the phone, starts typing again.

"Because it's a lesser form of entertainment?"

"Because I'm busy." She reaches for the driver's-side door handle. "Rob bumped up your interview to five minutes ago, so we gotta—"

"Chester! Hey! Is this your new girlfriend?"

"Hey! Girlfriend! What's your name?"

I hadn't spotted them before, but suddenly, paparazzi come rushing over, and I realize there are some random pedestrians taking pictures of me, too. I instantly put on a smile and wave for the cameras, blowing kisses at an old woman and the aide with her who's eye-fucking me. Then I feel claws on my arm and turn to see Holly's face has gone completely white.

"What the hell?" she whispers fiercely. "We gotta go. Get in the car."

"Chill out." I unclasp her sharp nails from my arm and take the autograph book a little girl's holding out to me, eyeing Holly as I sign my name. "This is part of the job. They're fans. Just smile and wave."

"But..." Christ, she looks so freaked out. For all her trying to be cool and professional, this is clearly an area of the business she hasn't encountered before. Guess that's what happens when your biggest client is, well, me.

I throw my arm around Holly's shoulders and smile for the cameras and reporters. "Please, I think you all know better than to think I've settled down," I announce. "This lovely creature is my agent, Holly Bremen. Remember that name, because you're gonna be seeing it all over *Variety* in the next few years."

And remember mine, too, I think as the flashbulbs continue to go off. *Because if you don't, I am fucked.*

Chapter Six

Vanessa

$\mathcal{G}$ really wish Zander were a better kisser. I mean, he's fine, but we've been making out in my trailer for like twenty minutes, and my mind keeps wandering—to what I should wear to the premiere of Casey Rinaldo's movie this weekend, to what color I should get on my nails tomorrow, to—

"Hey, K-drama, where the hell are you?"

To why the most obnoxious guy in the world is standing in the doorway right now.

I jump away from Zander and wipe off my mouth as Josh approaches, as if that'll cleanse me from this unpleasant moment. Ugh. I knew Josh auditioning was a horrible idea as soon as Ally mentioned it, and now I'd forgo Pinkberry for a year if I could magically get the power to teleport myself out of here.

"Josh, what the hell are you doing here? I thought you were meeting with Davis."

"I met, I saw, I conquered." He grins broadly. "Guess who's gonna be your new costar, baby."

No. "You have to be kidding me."

"Just curious who you'll think is a better kisser," he muses, wedging himself on the couch between me and Zander. "Holloway or me?" We're no longer even touching, but I can still feel Zander bristle.

"How perfect is that gonna sound on the cover of *Entertainment Weekly*?"

I jump off the couch. "No way in hell. You're coming on as my love interest? I did *not* sign off on this!"

Josh laughs. Such an asshole. "Please. Like anyone cares."

"They will," I warn him, crossing my arms, though I have no idea if this is true. Considering what a battle it was to talk them out of putting me in orange leggings, the jerk probably has a point.

"Well, I'm doing it to help Liam get a lightened schedule so he can film the Lassiter movie, so you might wanna think about him before you try—and fail—to get my ass booted from the set." He smiles smugly. "Besides, you haven't even given me a shot yet. Wanna practice before the table-read next week?"

"I am literally gonna hurl all over your overpriced shoes right now."

He laughs. I don't.

"I'm going for a walk," I declare, grabbing my phone from my purse and not even caring that I'm not being subtle about it. Then I march outside and immediately call Jade; she's always the first to know everything.

"Did you know Josh was joining the show?" I demand as soon as I hear a voice on the other end.

"Vanessa?"

My stomach tightens. Of course Brianna's answering Jade's cell phone. "Is your mother there?"

"Jade's at a meeting right now." Brianna's voice is pleasant and professional, smooth and confident, and that only annoys me more. Acting should be left to actors, not to publicists—or their interns—who pretend to be friendly for five seconds. "Is everything okay?"

"As if you care," I mutter, and then immediately regret it. God, this girl is worse than Josh at making me drop my nice Vanessa guard. "I was just looking for more information on something," I add, making sure my voice sounds sweeter now.

"On Josh Chester joining the cast of *Daylight Falls?*" Brianna asks. "It's just a three-episode arc. Shouldn't be too bad. You can handle yourself just fine. I've seen it."

I can hear the smile in her voice as she says this last bit, and despite everything, my lips curve up a bit, too. She may be a manipulative sneak, but there's some actual sincerity in there. It makes me tingle with a little pride.

After a few beats, she asks, "So, should I have Jade call you?"

"Please," I mumble, because it seems way too awkward to admit that she just made me feel better about the whole thing with a few words. "But, um, no rush, I guess."

"Okay." We're both silent again, and then she says, "Come on. Are you really so pissed about me being at Josh's party? I was just doing my job."

"I'm not pissed," I lie, because I shouldn't really care enough to be. "I just think it's weird that you showed up and pretended to be"—*Nice, and funny, and the only person who actually thought to see how I'm feeling about Ally leaving*—"a waitress."

"Of course it's weird. Jade is weird. You know this already."

"I don't like feeling deceived." My voice is stiff, and even I want to laugh at myself. Why do I care what my publicist's freaking intern thinks or does? "Whatever, it's—"

"I'm sorry," she says, cutting me off and surprising me. "I won't do it again."

"Okay. Thanks, I guess." This conversation has definitely taken a turn for the strange, and I don't really know what else to say. "I should go. I left Josh and Zander alone in my trailer, which seems like a terrible idea."

She laughs. "I'll tell Jade you called. And hey, listen, if you wanna take a few bites of an onion or something before your spit-swapping scenes with Josh Chester, I swear, it'll be our little secret."

"I appreciate that," I reply, feeling a full, genuine smile creep onto my lips for the first time that day. "Bye." She says goodbye, and I hang up and stare at my phone for a minute before heading back to my trailer, where Zander and Josh are, unsurprisingly, giving each other shit.

I leave the door open behind me to give Josh easy access to leave and surprise them both by dropping in Zander's lap. "Don't you have *anywhere* else to be?" I narrow my eyes at Josh.

"Nah, I think I'll just watch."

"You know what? Go ahead." I pray Zander's somehow become a better kisser in the last five minutes, and then I press my lips to his. If there's one thing I've learned being an actress, it's to fake it 'til you make it.

And if there's another, it's that sometimes, you'll just have to kiss with an audience.

"It's been one week of filming, and already he's a royal pain in my butt." I put the phone on speaker so I can set it on my dresser while I trade the clothes I wore to the *Daylight* set for the sports bra, tank top, and cropped yoga pants I'll need for my nighttime

Bikram session. "I don't understand how you dealt with him for a *year.*"

Ally laughs. "He's not so bad once you get to know him."

"I *know* him," I remind her. "I still don't like him."

"That's what you thought about Brianna, and you seem pretty okay with her now."

Do I? I hadn't realized I'd even been talking about her to Ally much. But things with her are definitely better. The e-mails that used to be short and kinda formal are way friendlier now. She'd even sent a few texts that week—things like, *It's only 3 eps!!* and *I haven't seen a single news story on the murder of Josh Chester, so I hope that means it's not so bad!* It's been nice having her support, especially with Ally gone.

"Yeah, she's cool."

"Well, given that she's the spawn of Satan, that's actually pretty impressive, isn't it?"

I laugh. It's pretty amazing to think that she's Jade's daughter. Unlike her mother, she's actually sweet, and thoughtful, and she smiles every now and again, dimples and all. "Very. *And* she's a fan of *Sherlock.* Like, every possible incarnation of it."

"Aw, that's cool, Vanny. You guys should hang out. Hey, hang on one sec." There's a crackling sound as her hand covers the receiver and then her muffled voice as she yells something to someone. Whoever it is responds, and as their conversation continues, I let my mind wander.

Would it be weird to ask Bri to hang out? Would she even want to?

I could ask her to come over for a *Sherlock* marathon, maybe. Or go shopping. Ally used to go with me, but now that she's gone, I haven't been in, like, forever. Or maybe to Pinkberry…Would that be sacrilege without Ally? Does Bri even like Pinkberry? Will she think that's dumb?

"Van? Yoohoo! Are you still there?"

Whoops. "Hey, sorry. Didn't realize you were back."

She laughs. "I gathered. Sorry—just trying to figure out what movie we're seeing, but I've got another few minutes. Have you been looking at any apartments since I left?"

"Not really," I admit, feeling a little twinge at the knowledge it's not the answer she wants. I don't even know how to explain to myself, let alone to Ally, why I'm dragging my feet on moving out, now that I'm eighteen. It's not like I have a cute little sister or family movie nights, like she did. But the fact is, I am so, so scared at the prospect of fully leaving my parents. Which I will never, ever admit to another living soul, not even my best friend.

"Did you check out that place in Liam's complex? It sounded good, and they've got such a nice pool."

"Not yet." I pull my hair into a ponytail and determine to change the subject. "Speaking of which, how's *your* new place? Boys walking around in towels everywhere?"

She laughs. "Not quite. Anyway, kind of hard to get excited at the sight of shirtless men, given my boyfriend. I think he's ruined me."

"Pretty sure that's been his plan all along," I tease. "How about the roomie? Is she your new bestie?"

"As if. She doesn't even *like* The Beatles," she replies in a mock-whisper.

"Sacrilege!"

"Right? And she insists on going to this fro-yo place that's *not* Pinkberry, just because it's closer. Like, who cares about a couple miles when it's *Pinkberry*?"

I know she's partly kidding to make me feel better, but it works. And at the same time, I sort of hate that she already has a new fro-yo buddy. When she was here, she barely hung out with anyone but me, Liam, and Josh. Now that she's over there, she's making friends a whole lot more quickly.

Meanwhile, I've got Josh—an actual hemorrhoid in human form—and Liam, who spends every spare moment working out for his stupid new movie role and smells like a walking protein shake at all times. Jamal's great, but when we're not on set, he's with his girlfriend, Theresa, like, a zillion percent of the time. I guess Carly Upton, who plays my best friend on the show, is okay, but she's a little boring. And needy. And okay maybe I don't like her that much.

So maybe I *should* ask Bri if she wants to hang out. Worst that can happen is she says no, right?

"How are classes going?" I ask, because I don't want to talk about her roommate, or the fact that New York City has Pinkberry too, or Liam, or the apartment I'm not renting.

Apparently that was the right question, because she launches into a whole thing about her core classes and how they will or won't matter for her eventual law school applications. I do my best to listen while I put on my bare makeup minimum—essential in case of a paparazzi run-in on the way to yoga, but not enough to turn my face into a melting mess in the sweltering heat of the Bikram Yoga studio.

We chat for a few more minutes and then hang up, promising to talk again this weekend. I still have fifteen minutes before I have to leave, so I quickly check my Instagram and "like" some of Zander's recent pictures, leaving a mushy comment on a selfie of the two of us from a premiere we went to last week. Then I flip through Ally's pictures and "like" a bunch of those, too, even though the sight of her sharing fries and doing makeovers with people who aren't me is more than a little depressing.

On a whim, I check to see if Bri has an account. There are about a zillion Brianna Harrises, though, and I don't have time to look through all the little icons to see if any of them feature light-green eyes behind black-rimmed glasses, framed by red waves. I switch over to Twitter instead, respond to the few tweets from people I actually know, plus a couple from random fans, and then toss my phone into my purse.

My mother's in the kitchen, and I pass through on my way out to give her a peck on the cheek and accept an apple in return. I've told her a million times that I get queasy during yoga if I eat right beforehand, but she's afraid I'll pass out if I don't. As usual, she won that argument, the same way she's been winning every minor battle since she and my father allowed me to go on my first audition when I was a kid, on the condition I prove myself "responsible enough to handle it," whatever that means. The major fight—to continue on this path or to go to college—is still a quiet, passive-aggressive push-and-pull...for now.

But for all that my parents infuriate me sometimes, I know they love me and want to make sure I'm well taken care of. And if I move out on my own, who knows how long it'll be before I find someone else who'll feel that way about me?

★ ★ ★ ★ ★

I show up to yoga a few minutes late for the eight o'clock class, my rolled-up mat stabbing me in the butt as I try to let myself into the chokingly hot room as quietly as possible. Raoul, the teacher, just twitches his nose when he spots me; he's used to me showing up late, even if he's not terribly Zen about it. I roll out my mat and move quickly through the two poses I missed before catching up to everyone else at the tail end of Awkward Pose.

"Calm" isn't exactly the word anyone would use to describe me, but the whole ninety minutes of chill-out time kinda works for me, even if the room is a bajillion degrees. I like having to clear my head of all the drama and obligations that fill it during the week. And as attached as I am to my phone, I'm even kinda glad Raoul would kick my ass if I so much as favorited a tweet under his watch.

So it's pretty unsettling to look up during Standing Bow and see a familiar pair of light-green eyes making contact with mine in the mirror.

Unsettling enough that I break pose and nearly fall on my butt.

In the mirror, I can see Brianna struggling not to laugh as I literally bend over backward to avoid crashing to the ground. I suck a curse back into my lungs, knowing that while Raoul will forgive lateness, he'll throw a total fit if anyone dares disturb the quiet sanctity of the studio. We're not even allowed to wipe off our sweat under his watch. He's almost as psycho as Jade.

Almost.

I get narrowed eyes from Raoul, but he'll never get truly pissed at me because I once snuck him an old sweatband of Liam's. (Our little secret, of course.) I force myself back into position and close my eyes, shutting out the rest of the world, including Brianna Harris.

But I swear, I can still feel her eyes on me.

It's easy enough to look away through the next four poses—they all involve looking in directions other than forward anyway—but when we shift into Tree Pose, our eyes meet again, just for an instant, and I can't help wondering what she's doing here. I've been coming to this class for a year, and I've never once seen her. If she's spying on me again...

I narrow my eyes at the mirror, and now she's the one who startles a little in her pose. *Good.* It's nice to see her be the one caught off guard for once. But the longer I hold my stare, the more I realize she's doing just fine in the sweltering heat, and she knows not to mop up her sweat, and once she's back in pose, she stays put. Actually, she looks a whole lot more graceful than I do. And is that an Om tattooed on the back of her neck, partially concealed by her ponytail?

Maybe she's not just here to spy on me.

Forget about her, I order myself as we drop into toe stands. *Clear your damn head, Vanessa Park.* So I do. For the rest of the ninety-minute class, I forget about Brianna, and that Josh Chester is a pain in my ass, and that my best friend lives across the country, and that my parents want me to be someone I'm not, and that my career has an uncertain future, and that I need to get my own place. With the exception of the occasional superfast water break, I do nothing but pose, breathe, and sweat.

When it's over, I avoid all eye contact as I give myself a thorough wipe-down. I love the class, but afterward, I always feel gross. It's liberating, sometimes, getting to look that disgusting without worrying about cameras or whatever, but now, of course, Brianna's here, seeing me bathed in sweat, my face a freaking tomato.

I kinda hope she'll just walk out, but no such luck.

"Fancy meeting you here," she says as she walks over, taking a long sip from the bottle of water in her hand. "And no, before you ask, I'm not here spying for my mother."

My lips twitch. "I wasn't thinking that," I lie.

"Oh, yes, you were. But I'm not. I used to go to the five o'clock, but I had to change it up now that I've started the internship with Jade." A trickle of sweat slides down her forehead, and she swipes it away. "Well, that, and my ex-girlfriend still goes to the five o'clock," she adds sheepishly.

Ex-girlfriend? "I thought you had an ex-boyfriend," I say, then realize how stalker-y that sounds. "I just mean, you mentioned him at the party. The *Zombie Camp* fan."

"That too," she says with a grin, then takes another sip of water. "I'm an equal-opportunity leave-relationship-destruction-in-my-wake kind of girl." She says it like she's just informed me she has no preference between vanilla and chocolate fro-yo, but there's a hint of a challenge in her eyes, like she's waiting for me to judge her. Which just reminds me that she doesn't know me any better than I know her.

"I hope the girlfriend had better taste in movies." I pat down my face and neck one more time with my towel, then take a long drink.

Her lips quirk up in the corner, and I feel like I've passed some sort of test. "So, is this your usual class?"

"Yup. Raoul and I are buds."

"I'll bet. What do you usually do afterward?"

"Um, shower?" I gesture down at where sweat has seeped through my...everything, basically.

She laughs. "Probably a good plan."

It's a good opening to ask if she wants to hang out, but before I can figure out how, she says, "Well, unless you're showering all day tomorrow, too, are you up for a shopping trip after filming? Jade says you need something new for the exhibit opening Friday night, and I need to buy something that's *not* business-casual. I swear, I've never worn so many pantsuits in my life."

"Jade has you wearing pantsuits?" It's impossible to imagine punky, quirky Brianna in something so straitlaced, but then again...Jade.

"Jade would have birthed me in a pantsuit if she could have." Brianna rolls her eyes, which are actually kind of warm in their makeup-free, glasses-free state. "We're talking about a woman who insists I call her by her first name at all times, so that I never slip out of being 'professional.'"

"Huh. So she really is like that twenty-four hours a day."

"Seven days a week," she confirms. "So, are you up for it?"

I think about my conversation with Ally. And I think about the fact that I'm still not sure how much I trust Brianna. And then I think about the fact that, if I say no, I'm gonna have a very long night of stressing ahead.

And I say, "Sure, why not?"

Chapter Seven

Josh

*B*y the end of my first three weeks, we've got two episodes in the can and I can't remember if I've ever worked this hard in my life. I've had to wake up at seven almost every day, and it's killing me. I've barely gone out because I can't stand the hangovers anymore, not to mention that my beer gut was getting a little out of control. I'll be damned if Holloway maintains his rep as the show's "body" while he's basically on vacation in the Valley.

I let myself into Holloway's trailer–which he barely even uses these days–and let out a long, loud groan. I'm tired as balls, and all I want is a shower and a nap before I go out with the guys again tonight. I groan again as I drop onto his couch. Feels like it's been fucking *hours* since I've gotten off my feet.

A frantic knocking sounds at the door, and then I hear, "Liam, are you okay? It sounds like there's an animal dying in there."

Pushing myself up off the couch, I realize K-drama's on the other side of the door. I swing it open. "Just the party animal that once resided within me," I say dramatically, leaning against the doorpost. "What's up?"

"What are you doing in here?"

"I need a shower, and the guest stars get lousy digs," I inform her, raking a hand through my hair. "They really don't appreciate where the true talent lies."

She rolls her eyes. "How strange of them. But just as well I found you—your agent's lurking around here. I assume she's looking for you to tell you she's had enough of you."

More likely she's looking for me to nag me to pick a script for once this guest arc's up. "Lemme just shower, and—"

"Is that him?" I stifle a groan as Holly joins Vanessa. "There you are. Did you get that script I sent over? *Wings of Phoenix?*"

"That's filming in Philly, right?" asks Van. "Aren't you banned from there after that whole incident at City Hall?"

"I swear, people have no sense of humor. You'd think they'd be more immune to innocent actor shenanigans, given that *Transformers* filmed there. I'll read it anyway—I'm sure they're over it by now. Probably. I paid for the fire damage, anyway. Or maybe it was the water damage. Whatever it was, I threw money at it."

Holly exhales sharply. "Meanwhile, everyone seems to think I'm also your publicist and manager. Have you thought about getting an actual publicist?"

"And suppress his natural charm?" Vanessa says sweetly, laughing when I give her the finger.

"Whatever gets me fewer e-mails. Dylan Mackenzie wants to make sure you're still in for the celebrity golf thing next Sunday."

"Tell him I wouldn't miss it, and ask if his girlfriend will be back in that little argyle skirt."

"I'll be sure to. Glory Thompson called to confirm your radio interview tomorrow—"

"Reschedule for Thursday. I'm back on set tomorrow."

"And I confirmed your dentist appointment for Thursday as well."

I shudder. "Can we reschedule that one for never?"

"Joshua." Vanessa fixes me with a *look*. "She's not your assistant."

"Neither are you," I remind her, "so unless you're going to be helpful..."

She rolls her eyes and leaves, and Holly walks in, closing the door behind her. I still need a shower pretty badly, so I'm hoping we can wrap this up soon. It's hard to get whipped into a frenzy about picking up yet another job with early call times or...anything having to do with Philadelphia, really.

"Any word from Val at Aspen on the fragrance shoot?" I ask.

"I called her this afternoon. She says they're still looking for a female model to pair you with. The one who did their last denim campaign has a fragrance non-compete."

"Anything else?"

"Yes. Your mother called. Twelve times. Which is why I'm here."

Shit. "My mother called you?"

"Apparently at least one of you thought it was relevant to tell me that you're signed on for a reality show."

"I'm *not*," I assure her. *Not until I get desperate.*

"Well, she seems to think that you are, as long as you're living in their beach house. You *are* still living there, aren't you?"

I don't say anything. She already knows the answer.

"Why didn't you tell me about this, Josh? I'm your *agent*. Dealing with your work is my job."

"Because I'm not doing it, and this doesn't count as work. She's just desperate for attention now that her show's been canceled, and this is the only way she can get it. They won't give her the show unless I agree to be on it."

Holly raises an eyebrow. "Really."

Statement, not a question. Which means she definitely has a very bad idea brewing right now.

"Don't even think about it, Holly."

"*You* need to work, Joshua. If you can line something else up, fine, but until you start taking your auditions seriously, I don't know what else to do with you. If you want to keep me on as your agent, you're going to need something to show for your efforts. Even if it's reality TV."

"Seriously?"

"Seriously. Or, you know, you can just read the *Wings* script and call me when you're done. You nail that audition, there's nothing to worry about."

Ugh, so *that* was her plan—blackmail me into the stupid audition. I should've guessed. "Yeah. Fine."

She heads out, but stops in the open doorway. "And Josh?"

"Yeah?"

"Get a publicist."

It's always been one of my biggest fears that one night I'd be out at a club and realize I'm completely over this shit. I'm not quite there yet, but right now, buzzed on drinks I've had a billion times before, chick in my lap who looks exactly like the last three who've been in my lap, I'm pretty fucking bored.

I have to adjust the girl to reach the phone in my pocket, but I'm pretty sure she's too blitzed to care. She's been alternating between touching my junk and tossing back shots for I don't even know how long, and if she's noticed that I'm not paying her any attention, I can't tell.

Of course, Holloway's not even here. He's off at James Gallagher's in-fucking-credible estate in Napa, getting wooed for yet another huge-budget movie. Because locking in the Lassiter role wasn't enough. For someone who hates attention, he's getting a shitton of it all of a sudden; I can't even remember the last time I saw him for more than five minutes. I know he's just keeping himself busy to keep his mind off the fact that Ally's gone, but fuck, where did my best friend go?

I whip out my phone and text him. *R u back yet? Bored.*

His response comes back thirty seconds later. *No, I'm not back. I'm in the Gallaghers' guest house, hiding.*

Well. Whatever's going on there sounds more interesting than my night. "Sweetheart, time to go," I tell the chick in my lap, pushing her up lightly. Then I flag down the waitress, tell her to surprise me, and text Liam back. *Imma need more than that.*

He's got a 25yo wife w/busy hands. Groped me @ dinner, grabbed my ass on the way out, and now she wants to meet up in the hot tub.

Yet another thing to hashtag #LiamProblems. The guy gets more unwanted potential ass than anyone I know, and it's completely wasted on him. *She hot?*

Yup.

So *stop hiding*, I write back, because I know there's no shot in hell he'd ever screw around on Ally, and I like being a dick.

Don't be a dick.

I laugh. He's so fucking predictable.

The waitress returns with a flaming shot of I don't even know what. I stick a twenty in her bra, hold up the glass for her to blow out the flame, and toss it back.

"Good?" she asks, her voice low.

I hadn't noticed one way or the other, but it doesn't stop me from saying, "You tell me." I pull her down to me and let her taste my tongue, and when I sit back, she looks a little dizzy.

"Pretty good," she blurts out, and even in the dark lighting of the club, I can see her blush.

Too easy.

"Josh Chester." The smug way the voice says my name makes my skin crawl, and I watch a tall, skinny, vaguely familiar-looking guy make his way toward me. I have no recollection of who he is, and the drinks I've already put away tonight aren't helping.

"Do I know you?"

"Chuck. We met at one of your parties a little while ago."

"If you were at one of my parties, shouldn't I have already known you?" I ask, raising an eyebrow.

He laughs. Fearless prick. "I'm the guy who works with Joe Perotti. You weren't so thrilled to see me then. I'm hoping you've got better feelings about it now."

I've always been able to hold my liquor, but suddenly, I feel sick. "And why would I be any more excited to see you now? I didn't want you or cameras in my face filming my life then, and I don't want it now."

He hands me a small, sealed envelope, which I'm tempted to ignore, but have a feeling I'd be sorry about. I open it up and see one of my mother's personal notecards. *Joshua,* it says. *I have locksmiths set to arrive at the Malibu house at 9:00 a.m. You will not be given a copy of the new key unless Chuck returns to me with these papers—signed—tonight. Love, Mother.*

"Love?" I mutter aloud. "Really?" I look up at Chuck, wondering if he's banging her. "What papers?"

He reaches into a pocket on the inside of his cheap jacket and withdraws a folded-up package that I see is a contract, complete with waiver. This is so, so fucked up. "You're serving me?" I ask as I flip through.

Chuck grins, his crooked teeth flashing neon colors in the light of the club. "See it however you like. But sign them."

"Are you doing my mother?"

His smile doesn't falter; he just waits patiently. I decide he probably isn't. Even my mother would never bang a lowly hired hand.

"I have an agent," I tell him. "I can't just sign these without her taking a look."

"So call her," he suggests.

This is getting exhausting. I love my house, and a reality show would be easy money, and it'd be nice to stop having this guy ambush me every second. Plus, then I could skip that stupid *Wings of Phoenix* audition I have no desire to go to. But Holly would probably chop off my balls, and she's already my fourth agent. I'm not sure I'll get a chance at a fifth.

"There's no way she'd agree to me signing this without her seeing it," I say flatly.

"Then don't call her."

"You've got really stellar business sense." *Shit.* What do I do? If I don't sign on and then I don't get the movie, Holly's gonna drop me. "Give me a minute."

I hop off my chair and storm out back, which is quieter and decently well hidden. Liam's clearly a little too busy for me right now, so I call Ally for advice instead.

She picks up immediately, her voice hushed. "Liam?"

"Your caller ID sucks, Duncan."

She exhales slowly. "Sorry, Josh. I didn't even look. What's the big emergency? Is Liam okay?"

"He's fine, as far as I know." *If you don't count that he's trying to fend off a hot older woman at a private estate, which apparently you don't know and I'm not going to tell you.* "I just needed your opinion on something."

"Josh. It is 4:00 *a.m.* in New York. What the hell is wrong with you?"

Whoops. "Well, you answered."

"Yeah, because I was waiting—never mind." She sighs. "What is it?"

"Remember that reality show my mom wanted me to do?"

She laughs. "Seriously? You're still thinking about it?"

"You've seen my house, right?"

I know she's rolling her eyes, but I also know she hears what I'm not saying, which is that I don't have anything else lined up. And it's not like I've got a ton of savings. Yes, my parents own my house, but they're also the ones who pay the bill on my black AmEx.

I'd last maybe a month on my personal finances without it.

Not to mention that I'm on my last-chance agent.

Ally's quiet for a few seconds and then says, "Okay, I have an idea. What if you don't let them follow you around to film, but you agree to appear for your mom's filming once an episode? Like, sign the waiver and drop in while...what would they even film your mom doing?"

"Well, there's the million-dollar question." I turn her idea over in my head. It does make me look a little less like a raging tool, but it creates the new problem of having to see my mother way too often. Still, it might buy me some time. "But yeah, I think I can do that."

"Anyway, they're probably just gonna cancel it after, like, three episodes, right?"

"It'd be a fucking miracle if she actually managed to last that long." Suddenly, my chest feels a little lighter. "And it's not like she can hold it against me if the show tanks. I just have to keep her on the air long enough to get her to sign the house over. Once she does that..."

"Yup."

I can do this. A few episodes of a stupid show, done on my terms, if it gets me my house, keeps me in the lifestyle to which I've become accustomed, and retains Holly whether or not I land the *Wings* part? Ally's right—no chance this show's gonna last a minute longer than I want it to. All I need is the deed to the house in my hand, and then I'm free. "All right, I'mma go deal with this now. Thanks."

"I'd say 'anytime,' but apparently you're already well aware of that."

"Glad to see the Ivy League hasn't made you any less of a ball-buster. Now go to sleep."

I hang up—I've never been much for good-byes—and text Liam. *Call your girlfriend, you asshole.*

Then I go back inside, sign the waiver, and somehow find myself with plans for yet another family dinner tomorrow night.

Chapter Eight

Vanessa

C ome on, Bailey. Monroe's too much of a douche for you anyway, and you know it."

"Cut!" I yell and slam my fists into my hips as I turn to Josh. "The line is, 'Monroe's not right for you anyway.' Will you stop with your stupid frat boy ad-libs?"

Becky Kempler, who's directing that week's episode, sighs. "Vanessa, it's fine. We're allowed to say douche on network TV. Can you please stop yelling 'cut'? That's for Bryce to do."

Of *course* I'm the one who gets yelled at when Josh screws up. He's been doing this for weeks, just inserting whatever he feels like, whenever he feels like it. He did an entire scene shirtless that wasn't supposed to be that way at all, and he's somehow found a way to get Liam cut out of even more than the few meager scenes he was already.

I exhale sharply. "Fine. Sorry."

"All right, everyone, back to your places!" yells Bryce, the first assistant director and an inexplicable Josh fan. "Scene twenty-four-A, take twelve. Action!"

"I *said* I wasn't interested," I say to Josh's character, Luke. He's cornered me at Layton's Surf Shop, one of the main sets on the show and the spot where Liam's character, Tristan Monroe, works. "I tried, Luke, but I'm just not over Tristan."

"Come on, Bailey. Monroe's a dick, and you know it."

My entire body bristles when Josh changes the line *again*, but I think Becky's probably going to kill me if I say a word about it, so I don't. Unfortunately, *my* line is, "He's right because he *feels* right," which of course makes no sense with the way Josh has reworded it, and all that comes to mind in that moment is, "No, he isn't. You are."

I expect Becky to scream "Cut!" but she doesn't, instead letting us play out the scene with our new, nastier ad-libs. I can't decide if it's because she wants to bang Josh or just likes the added layer of drama that comes with us sniping at each other, but neither one would surprise me.

"Then how come I'm here and he's giving Grace private surf lessons at the beach club?"

Finally, we're back on track. We go back and forth for the rest of the scene, snapping at each other in a way that doesn't feel all that much like acting. It feels good to get some rage out and to know that it's making my performance better. When we actually wrap the scene, it's such a relief I can literally feel my shoulders getting lighter.

I march off to get a water bottle and a makeup touchup without so much as a glance in Josh's direction, but as Toya swirls on more bronzer, I can feel someone watching us.

"Nice job over there," says Brianna.

"What are you doing here?" I ask, being careful not to get a mouthful of brown dust. She and I have plans to go shopping, but not for another few hours.

"Fun fact about Jade: she doesn't believe in formal higher education. She thinks I just need to see more aspects of the industry to find what I wanna do and then jump right in. Apparently, Hollywood's in my future, because it's in my blood." She sighs heavily and drops into the chair next to me. "After two days of fighting about it, she finally convinced me I might enjoy an afternoon of watching a cute girl bitchslap Josh Chester."

In the mirror, my cheeks are reddening, and it's not the same shade of golden brown Toya's sweeping onto my skin. I wouldn't have thought twice about "cute girl" before that "ex-girlfriend" mention she dropped at yoga. Now I can't help but wonder if she means... something by it.

But no, of course she doesn't. She knows I'm with Zander, not to mention the far more important fact that I'm straight. I mean, it's totally cool that she's bi. But I'm not, and she knows that.

The flush goes down, and Toya grunts in a way that lets me know she didn't miss it. I swallow, hard, then realize I've been silent a little too long. "So, was it everything you dreamed it would be?" I ask her.

"And more," she says with a grin. Then her face grows serious. "Listen, I'm really sorry to do this, but is it okay if we reschedule our shopping trip? My friend got us tickets to tonight's Foo Fighters show months ago, and I didn't realize I'd double-booked."

I hadn't realized I was particularly looking forward to going out until just now, but after a day of dealing with Josh, the idea of having nothing to do but sulk on my treadmill tonight is beyond depressing. "Yeah, of course," I lie. Unfortunately, I say it as Toya's patting on more lip gloss, and she makes an annoyed noise at me.

"Zander's probably getting tired of me monopolizing your time, anyway," she says with a laugh, and I force a smile, too, even though it comes out kinda grimace-like. If Zander minds that we haven't been spending much time together, he hasn't said a word. And I certainly haven't been missing him.

Maybe that's the problem. I've been so desperate to find a new *friend* to make up for the fact that Ally's gone, I haven't been paying any attention to the *boyfriend* right in front of me. Making plans with Zander is exactly what I should be doing for tonight. And tomorrow night. And maybe the night after that.

So what if we didn't exactly get together because of "feelings"? Doesn't mean we can't start working on it now.

"Zander's been a trooper," I say, "but you're right—he'll definitely be happy to have a little more 'us' time. And actually, one of his bandmates is having a party tonight"—one I'd made a zillion excuses to avoid because they always turn into really cheesy a capella sing-alongs—"and he'll be happy to hear I can make it now."

"Perfect! Well, we'll just do it another time then." She glances at her watch. "Actually, I should probably head out now. If Jade asks, I was here until four." She readjusts her messenger bag, then meets my eyes in the mirror. "Will I see you at Bikram on Thursday night?"

I debate saying I might be busy with Zander then, too, just to show her how much I don't care about her blowing me off, but lying feels a little pathetic. "I never miss it," I say neutrally instead.

"Well, then, I'll see you there."

I watch her wave in the makeup mirror, and then I watch her walk away.

★ ★ ★ ★ ★

"Well, somebody's in a sunshine-y mood," Josh observes when I return to set to try the scene again.

Trust Josh to observe my crankiness the second I drop the fake smile I'd pasted on for Brianna's sake. "Somebody wishes she didn't have Hollywood's biggest sociopath trying to move in on her show," I correct him. "And if you think I'm okay with the fact that I have to subject myself to your diseased mouth for this next scene, you're out of your freaking mind. I hope you at least had the courtesy to gargle mouthwash during this break."

"Funny, I didn't see you gargling anything but your drool over me," Josh says casually, "so let's call it even."

Have I mentioned I loathe Josh Chester?

"All right, everyone, places!" I force myself to re-inhabit Bailey's body and let her inhabit mine as we get into places for the next scene, an infuriating one in which Josh's natural smugness will be quite the asset. In fact, he's pretty spot on with his character, Luke— an egomaniacal jackass who gets everything he wants. The difference is, Luke and Bailey are totally into each other.

Josh and I would rather die.

I practiced these lines a thousand times on my treadmill at home last night, and they come back to me with ease now. "You need to stop chasing me, Luke. Accept that I'm not yours and I'm never gonna *be* yours."

"Accept that?" Josh-as-Luke spits, his amber eyes flashing. "Why should I accept that when deep down, *you* haven't?"

For some reason, Brianna pops in my head just then. I quickly replace the image with Zander, and realize that's no better. I just need to clear my mind and stop letting Josh get to me.

"You have no idea what I think," I return, letting my voice quiver a little. Bailey's a bit of a drama queen—nothing like me in real life. "You have no idea how I feel."

"Oh, I know how you feel," Josh-as-Luke says, stepping closer, close enough that I can smell the cinnamon gum on his breath that proves he did prepare for this scene, at least a little bit. He reaches out and strokes my cheek, his fingertips caressing my jaw. "I know *exactly* how you feel."

And then he pulls me close and kisses me, just as the script demands. I tell myself to imagine it's Zander's mouth on mine, but that's not helping me muster up the enthusiasm I need. Especially since I'm all too aware of Brianna's laser-green eyes on me, imagining those lips in their naturally smug curve—

I don't even realize I've opened my mouth until I get the strong, sharp taste of cinnamon on my tongue, and I shove him away. I'm grateful we're still in mid-scene, because I know Josh would be grinning at me like a wolf if we weren't, sure I'd succumbed to his charms, ignorant of the fact that I'd forgotten I was kissing him at all. But he's Luke now, not Josh, and his face flashes with hurt and confusion and heat instead.

"You want me," he says determinedly. "I know you do. And you may think you want Monroe, but he'll never kiss you like I do. So before you decide to toss me aside for that surf bum, you better be sure you're okay with losing what you're giving up." One more hard kiss, and then he walks out.

Cut.

Everyone seems pretty pleased with the scene, but of course, we have to film it again. We get back into place, and as we do, I catch a glimpse of Brianna standing next to an empty chair, thumbs tucked into the belt loops of her denim miniskirt, jaw clenched tight until she notices me noticing her.

If I didn't know better, I'd say she wasn't all that thrilled with that scene.

And for some reason, that gets me excited to do it all over again.

"You and Josh have some pretty crazy chemistry," Carly observes as the two of us walk back to the trailer we share once filming is done for the day. "Is this one of those things where you guys pretend to hate each other when you're actually totally in love?"

I snort. "Trust me when I say there are no positive feelings between me and Josh, unless you count that he throws good parties. That, I'll give him."

As if just talking about him summoned the devil, I feel a hand clap me on the shoulder, and turn to see another one land on Carly's. "Ladies," Josh says genially.

"Lord Douchington," I reply with a nod of my head. "Don't you think you've touched me enough today?" I pry his fingers from my shoulder. "What do you want?"

He grins, not remotely affected by any of my insults, which doesn't surprise me in the slightest. "Actually, I have a question for you." He nods toward my half of the trailer. "May I?"

"If the question is whether I'll sleep with you, the answer is going to be vomit on your shoes. I'm warning you now."

Carly laughs and flutterwaves goodbye as she disappears into her half, and I reluctantly let Josh in to mine. "What is it?" I sit down at the mirror and douse some cotton balls in makeup remover, anxious to get this crap off my face.

He coughs. "I...I need your help with something."

"If you think I'm gonna run lines with you right now, after all the ad-libbing you did in there, you're crazy."

"Oh, please—like my lines weren't a thousand times better than the cheesy shit they write for us. But no, this has nothing to do with the show. This is more assistance of the...parental-pleasing variety. As in, I have no idea how to, and I kind of need to. At dinner. Tonight."

He looks so convinced that this is something I actually have vast experience in that I almost feel bad laughing at his face in the mirror. Almost. "Oh, you're serious," I say after a minute, wiping my eyes. "Josh, if I was capable of pleasing parents, trust me, I'd be doing it. My parents think I'm just as much of a waste of space as yours probably do."

"You?" He snorts. "What's your parents' issue? Were you five minutes late to church on Sunday?"

I whirl around in my seat. "Has anyone ever told you that when you ask a favor, you're supposed to be nice to the person you're asking?"

"Yeah, but you know I never listen to Ally."

"God, you're the worst." I shake my head at his stupid grin, but curiosity at why Josh suddenly wants to be a parent-pleaser wins out. "So, what do you need and why?"

He hesitates, and I think it might be the first time I've seen Josh Chester look...embarrassed.

"Um, did you think you were gonna be able to ask my help *without* telling me what it was for?"

"No, I'm just bracing myself for how big of a bitch you're gonna be about it."

"A pretty huge one, now," I say sweetly.

"I knew this was a mistake." He turns to go, and I let him; I know he'll be back in two seconds. Who else is he gonna ask?

Unsurprisingly, he turns around and walks back in before he can even close my trailer door behind him. "Okay, fine. Just...keep it to yourself, will you?" He shuts the door and makes himself comfortable on my couch while I return to tending to my face in the mirror. "My mother's pressuring me to do this reality show thing in order to keep my house, and I need to please her until I can get her to sign over the deed. But every single thing I do seems to piss her off, starting with how I dress. So can you please come over and help me find something that screams 'let's mutually cooperate'?"

Again, this seems ironic, since my mother's response to me upon leaving the house this morning was, "Shouldn't you wear a real shirt over that shirt?" But I'm pretty sure that Josh's mom at least lives in this century, so this should be easy enough.

The question is, what do I want in return?

"I have plans with Zander tonight." I say it to inform him that I'm busy, but as I do, I realize that maybe he can help me after all. Not that I would ever admit to Josh that our relationship is every bit as lame as he thinks it is. Or that we've barely done more than make out. But while meaningful relationships aren't exactly Josh's thing, getting them to move faster certainly is. If anyone can tell me how to kick this whole thing with Zander up a notch, sadly, it's Josh Chester.

Of course, Josh rolls his eyes at the mere mention of Zander's name. "Not to worry. I'll get you to your date at a proper hour. What time *are* the kids eating the early bird special these days? Wouldn't want him to miss out on any of his beauty sleep. How *would* his hair stand up that way otherwise?"

"Your jealousy is so cute. Sorry my boyfriend has a fan club of a zillion while you can barely get your agent to remember your name." I examine my skin in the mirror, and, satisfied it looks makeup free, I rub on some moisturizing sunscreen. "But, yes, if you get me back on time—and do something for me—I'll help you."

"And what would you like me to do for you, K-drama? Lie down in the lot while you reverse your car over my face?"

"I'm not sure yet," I admit. "But I'm reserving a favor. Right now. You are in my debt. Say it."

He narrows his eyes.

I shrug and put my focus back on rimming my eyes with black liner.

"Fine. Ronen's already here. Finish putting on your face, and you can follow us up."

"Hey, you want my help, then you can drive me up and back to my car. If I'm sitting in the traffic up to Malibu, I'm not doing it behind the wheel." The truth is, I hate driving long distances by myself, but that's yet another factoid to file under "Things I Will Never Tell Josh Chester."

"Fine," he says with a huffy sigh. "Two minutes. And take it easy on the eyeliner—we're going to my house, not your second job at the strip club."

"You're leaving now."

He rolls his eyes but lets himself out, calling out "One minute!" behind him.

Chapter Nine

Josh

*Y*ou can't wear that," K-drama declares the second I step out of my walk-in closet.

"Oh, come on."

"Josh, you *asked* me here to help you pick an outfit. I'm telling you it's not gonna be that one."

"It's just dinner with my parents," I remind her, even though she's right that this is exactly the reason I asked her over. Which was obviously a huge mistake, much like I can already tell this entire night is gonna be. "Who gives a shit what I wear?"

"Your mother does, from what you've told me, and if you wear a T-shirt and jeans to dinner–again–you're not gonna get what you want."

"What I *want* is for her to get off my back."

"Well, your passive-aggressive clothing decisions aren't going to make that happen." She crosses her arms and nods toward my closet. "Pick something that actually requires a hanger. And make it designer. In a calming shade of blue. It'll go a long way."

I know she's right, but I don't need her knowing she's right. "What I'm wearing is fine. I look good, don't I?"

I do, but she just rolls her eyes and does her best "Vanessa Park is not impressed." It's pretty much her default reaction pose to anything I do. Ally would be proud. "Don't say I didn't warn you," she says, and then she turns and walks out.

Goddammit. I wait until she's gone and then I change into decent pants and a blue button-down. If I could avoid her seeing I've taken her advice, I'd do it in a second. She's such a pain in my ass. But I know wearing this crap will make my mom feel like I'm actually listening to her and is my best shot at getting her to listen to me in return.

I take a shot of Patrón from the minibar in my bedroom, then brush my teeth until the smell of tequila is gone. There's no way I'm making it through this night on no alcohol, and the fact that I don't do my own driving means I never have to think twice about it. If I still did any of the harder stuff, now would be the perfect time to whip it out. But my dad can tell that shit from a mile away—it's one of his only interpersonal skills—so alas, all I can do tonight is get good and liquored up.

"Ronen's here!" Vanessa calls up, and I debate taking another shot, but I don't have time to mask the smell a second time. I head out into the car with her on my heels—I'd avoid her completely if I hadn't promised her a ride home in time for her to get ready for some bullshit date with her bullshit boyfriend—and make the mistake of glancing at her just long enough to catch her annoying smirk.

My nerves are jacked up the whole ride. Sending dirty texts to a bunch of different standbys doesn't help, even though I've got plenty of offers I know will help alleviate the awfulness for a few hours after dinner. Everything else is more of the same—Paz trying to get me on a double-date in the hopes he'll get some ass; Royce lauding some club we gotta go to; Jeremy sending me pervy pics of some chick he got with last night; no word from Liam.

By the time I reach the mansion, I'm in an even shittier mood, and I head straight for the bar as soon as I let myself in. I'm about to help myself to the Snow Queen—my dad's favorite vodka—when I hear steps behind me and remember that I'm being fucking *filmed.*

"Hey, Josh!" By now, Chuck and I are apparently old friends. "We actually missed your entrance, but were hoping you could do it again and ring the doorbell this time, let your mom answer. Get a whole 'prodigal son returns' kind of shot."

I have no idea what the fuck he's talking about, but I need this night over with and I need *not* to be filmed drinking, so I do what he says and force myself not to throw up all over my mother's Manolos.

"Josh, honey, it's so nice to have you home." She's careful not to leave lip prints on my cheek, though her face is so heavily made up I'm sure she's left some trace of it somewhere on me anyway. "I made your favorite. How was filming today?"

I assume I'm supposed to pretend I'm the busiest fucking worker bee in Hollywood, so I make some shit up, let them make us reshoot it a hundred times, and then we're sitting at the table, a team of strangers watching us eat and filming asinine dinner conversation.

"This is so nice," my mom says at some point. "I'm so glad we've decided to have these weekly family dinners."

Weekly? There is no fucking way I'm putting myself through this pain weekly. "Me too."

"Maybe next week you'll bring a girl with you," Mom teases playfully, as if that's a natural tone for her. And as if I've ever brought a girl to meet them, ever.

"Doubt it." I stuff a dinner roll into my mouth, hoping it'll keep her from trying to get me to talk for a few minutes. It works, and she switches to gushing about her busy day to my father instead.

All of this only reinforces Ally's point—there is no way in hell people will watch this shit. We're boring as balls as a family, and even having me here doesn't change that. If they were hoping I'd start some shit at the table, they're gonna be sorely disappointed. Being docile and boring is even worse than not participating at all, I realize. I think my mom might even have been disappointed about the fact that I showed up in an outfit she couldn't trash in front of the cameras.

Just then, the doorbell rings, and when my mother says, "My, who could that be?" I *know* there's some sort of setup ahead that's going to piss me off.

Sure enough, when my mother returns to the dining room, Shannah fucking Barrett is walking in behind her.

"Joshua, look who's here!" Marsha gushes. "You could've told me you invited your girlfriend."

"My girlfriend?" I glare at Shannah. "You've gotta be fucking kidding me. What the hell are you doing here?"

"I've missed you." My ex-fuckbuddy strolls over and drops a kiss on my cheek before taking a seat in the chair next to me, where I realize, like an idiot, there's been an extra place setting all along I hadn't noticed. "I was so happy when you called to invite me."

"Like there's a flaming chance in hell I would've done that. I prefer my pork chops without a side of crabs via Garrett Morgan, thanks very much." I look straight at one of the cameramen and narrow my eyes. "Are you seriously filming this shit?"

"Don't worry," Chuck assures us. "The final version will be very different."

"As in, you'll edit it so it looks like I've actually spoken to this skank in the last six months," I clarify.

"Joshua!"

"Christ, Marsha. You really scraped the bottom of the barrel looking for additional on-air 'talent.' What the hell were you thinking?"

"Wow, Josh. Rude much?"

I turn to glare at Shannah. "This is seriously pathetic, even for you."

She just smiles sunnily at me, and I know she's getting paid more than I am to be here.

"Oh, look, the main course is here." One of my mother's many house minions—I can't even keep track of them by name—comes in with a huge platter of steaks, and finally, this night is looking up. I can't even imagine Shannah touching one, and she doesn't disappoint—just ignores the woman and points at the salad instead.

"So, Josh," Shannah says when we've all got food on our plates, a quiet process I'm sure they'll be cutting out, especially so the minion doesn't get any airtime, "I'm really excited about your party next weekend."

"You're not invited to the party," I inform her, cutting a huge piece of steak and shoving it into my mouth as I eye the wine bottle near my mom with envy.

"What party, honey?"

As if my mother gives a shit. I can already tell there's a reason she's asking I'm not gonna like. "I'm having a party at my—at the Malibu house for the *Daylight*

Falls cast and crew. As a wrap-up for the show. A show you're not on," I add pointedly to Shannah.

"Zoe invited me," she says sweetly, as if I like Zoe any better. She's not even as hot.

"What a lovely idea." Marsha looks pleased, and I can practically feel her winking at the cameras, as if there's a chance in hell I'd let them near the party.

"You know not a single person there would sign a waiver letting them be on a reality show, right?"

"Oh, I'm sure a few would be okay with it," Shannah says airily, and I wonder if I could get away with kicking her under the table.

"Well, it's something to talk about." Marsha's voice is the sweet-with-an-edge she's perfected over years of soap work, and normally it rolls off my back, but today it reminds me I've actually got something at stake. She's got my back against a wall—again—and it needs to end. She needs to stop having any semblance of control over my life. And apparently, the only way to make that happen is to give up control over the one thing she's got.

Which means it's time for me to find a real job and a new home.

Chapter Ten

Vanessa

*H*ow's your salad?" Zander asks me for the second time. He has a bit of cilantro on his cheek, but I've already told him about it a couple of times, and I've gotten bored of watching him try to get it. His fault for not realizing cilantro is terrible.

"Still good," I say, trying to sound cheerful. We've been at Giunio's for twenty minutes, having exactly this kind of boring back-and-forth, both of us just kind of poking at our food. How is it possible that I can have lengthy conversations with Brianna and even Josh, but I can't talk to my own boyfriend? "This place is cute."

"Jamie and Robin came here last week and said it was swarming with paparazzi." He frowns, but only for a second, because Zander Wilson never frowns for longer than that. "Doesn't seem to be the night for them, but at least the food's good."

"It's kind of nice to have some privacy for once," I offer, because that sounds like how I should feel. I wish it was. Not that I love posing for the paparazzi all the time, but at least when Zander and I are in a conversational dead zone, they kick us into action, get us holding hands and flirting. And it's fun. I like those parts of being in a relationship.

I just think it'd be nice to have the feelings behind it, too.

Not that I'm trying very hard. I hide a sigh in my mineral water. I suck at this. And if I want things to be better, I have to make more of an effort.

Taking a deep, cleansing breath that would make Raoul proud, I reach across the table and rub the piece of cilantro from Zander's lip, letting my finger linger there for a second too long. His lips really are nice and soft; if only I didn't know it's because he has an intense lip-care regimen.

He smiles, and I know I've made the right move.

"Yeah, I'm glad your plans changed tonight and you were able to come out." He takes my hand and squeezes it, then places it gently back on the table. "I feel like we haven't spent much time together lately."

"It's true." I spear a piece of calamari and take a bite. "It's been hard for me with Ally leaving, so..." I'm about to tell him I've been hanging out with Brianna more, but for some reason, I don't want to bring her up with him. Not like he cares who I'm shopping or working out with these days, anyway. "Um, yeah. You still wanna go to Beyoncé's concert next week, right?"

"Of course. And the Wonder Ball is coming up next month. Did I mention Jamie's having a party beforehand?"

"You didn't, but that sounds great." I push some extra warmth into my smile and take his hand. "We should also just...hang out more. It was nice when you came by my trailer the other week. Maybe I could come by the studio for a rehearsal sometime?"

"I'd like that." He strokes the back of my hand with his thumb as he says it, and it feels nice.

I can totally do this.

"And I haven't been to your house in...I don't even know how long," I add. "Remember when I used to come hang out with you and the guys?" I drop my voice a little. "And...just you." Not that we did anything more than make out when I did—mostly, we just watched recordings of the Wonder Boys' earlier shows—but I hope it'll stir something in him. And that whatever it stirs in him will find its way to me soon. Because I'm getting really freaking tired of being so...unstirred.

I'm eighteen. I'm hot. He's hot. Shouldn't we...stir? Shouldn't we at least *want* to?

"That sounds nice," he says, but his voice has gotten a little funny. He's still holding my hand, though. And then he smiles, and I remember exactly why he has over a million Twitter followers. "Actually, as long as we're talking about this, I had something I wanted to discuss with you. I think you're gonna like it, and we may as well take advantage of the fact that this place is quiet."

"I'm intrigued." I say it teasingly, but I really am. I can't remember the last time Zander and I talked about...anything. My first thought is that he's going on a huge tour this summer and wants me to come with. I'd been hoping to be filming a movie, but auditions outside of the typical bit parts have been pretty minimal. It *would* be nice to have something to keep me busy... "What's up?"

He takes my other hand in his and looks me in the eye. "Vanessa Park, will you take a purity pledge with me?"

My fists instinctively curl up in his hands, and he yelps as one of my sharp nails nicks his palm. "Whoops, sorry!" I blurt, relaxing my fingers. "You just...surprised me a little there." I drop my voice to whisper-level. "You want to take a purity pledge? We're not even having sex."

"Which is exactly why it's perfect. I never thought I'd find another virgin in Hollywood," he says, his eyes and smile warming as he squeezes my hands. "You mean so much to me, Vanessa, and I think this is the perfect journey for us. You're pure, and I'm pure, and what better way to express that than with a public pledge? Think of what role models we'll be."

Role models. Zander's found my magic words. I've always loved the idea of people looking up to me, the way I look up to women like Lucy Liu and Maggie Q– fellow Asian-American actors who paved the way for girls like me to believe they can actually do this acting thing, who let us see characters who look like us. I'd kinda always hoped kids would see me the same way someday.

Could they now? For this?

Did I want them to? For this?

It's not like I'm not a virgin by choice–I am. I want my first to be someone I'm really, truly in love with, and I don't care if that's cheesy or even if everyone else thinks it's naïve. And I've always liked that Zander's a virgin, too. I know he'll never push me to go too fast or do anything I'm not ready for.

So, really, isn't this kinda, sorta perfect?

"What exactly does this entail?" I ask. "We just make a statement to the press that we're committing to not having sex?"

"Well, and obviously we'd need to get rings," says Zander, his smile widening. I can't remember the last time I saw his eyes glow like this. He's clearly thought about this a lot, and though I don't really know what it means, I like that he cares. But...rings?

"Don't rings seem a little marital?"

"That's the point," he says patiently. "They're a symbol of purity until marriage. Then you replace them with wedding rings."

Wedding rings? "Zander, we're so not old enough to get married, or even think about marriage." *We don't even love each other.* "Doesn't this seem a little fast?"

His patience is dimming. "Not really. We've been together almost six months, and neither one of us believes in premarital sex. We should share that with the world. Besides, we're not *that* young. My parents got married at twenty."

And now they hate each other and only stay together because they don't believe in divorce, I think but don't say. Instead, I try to remember what conversations Zander and I have had about sex. We definitely shared that we're virgins, that we think other people jump into bed quickly...but I don't think I ever said I didn't believe in premarital sex. I mean, I don't really think about it in terms of marriage. I think about it in terms of love. When Ally slept with Liam, she was in love with him, and it was right for her. And even if she hadn't been, I wouldn't say I didn't *believe* in it. It's just...not for me.

But if I'm that in love with someone that I'd want to give him my virginity, I guess I'd wanna marry him, right?

Suddenly, Giunio's feels like it's about a zillion degrees.

"I mean, right?" Zander's seriously turning up the smile wattage now, and he looks so sweet. And he has a point—it could be a great thing for kids to see that not *everyone* is doing it. Instead of being peer-pressured into sex they're not ready for, maybe we could help them see that waiting is something to be proud of.

"Zander! Vanessa! Over here!"

We turn to see paparazzi gathering right outside the glass front of the restaurant, huge cameras in hand, encouraging smiles on their faces. Zander and I are still sitting there with our hands clasped together, undoubtedly making exactly the kind of genuine, sweet, romantic picture our fans die for.

Because we mean something to them. We matter. They admire us, and they want to be like us. The enormity of that has never struck me the way it does right now.

So as we wave and smile and kiss for the cameras, I sneak in a whispered, "Yes."

I'd been feeling good about the decision when I agreed to it at dinner, but one lousy night's sleep and a 5:00 a.m. call time later, I'm suddenly not so sure. The hot water with lemon I'm forced to drink so I don't stain my teeth with coffee is totally not cutting it, either.

On top of that, I woke up to several grumpy e-mails from Ally about the fact that Liam's barely been calling her and still hasn't been to New York to visit. I'm not exactly thrilled with him these days, either, since he's essentially dropped off the planet to film the Lassiter movie. Not that I'm fuming about the increased airtime or anything, but it is exhausting, and I could do without ever having to share it with Josh.

Liam doesn't roll on to set that day until two, and when he does, he looks like complete and total crap. "Yikes, are you okay?" I ask. The circles under his eyes are dark and deep, and I know Toya's gonna be working double-time.

"Fine," he bites out. "I gotta get to makeup."

He certainly does. "You talk to Ally this weekend?" I ask to his retreating back.

He freezes. "What the hell is up with this conspiracy of people telling me to talk to my own girlfriend? Yes, I talked to Ally this weekend. Happy?"

"Don't mind him," Josh says, walking over. "This is what happens when you work two jobs and don't get laid."

"Oh, shut up," Liam mutters, even though Josh is obviously right. "I don't need shit from both of you. Hell, I don't need it from either of you." He stalks off toward his trailer, and Josh and I exchange looks.

"What's wrong with him?" I ask Josh. "I can barely get anything out of Ally, but she sounds pretty miserable. But of course, 'It's fine. Everything's fine. He's just busy. And so am I.'"

"Yeah, I talked to her, too. She sounds shitty. But he had a rough weekend—give him a break."

I roll my eyes. "Yeah, I heard he spent his weekend up in Napa, with James Gallagher practically begging him to take the lead role in his next movie. That sounds *terrible*."

"Hashtag LiamProblems," says Josh, and I crack up. "I think he just needs to bail on filming for a weekend and get his ass out to New York. He's barely had a minute to breathe. He won't even commit to coming to my party tomorrow night."

"Well, I for one am very much looking forward to it," I admit. "I could use a little more fun."

"Not having enough with your boyfriend? Sure seemed like it on CelebriTeens this morning."

I raise an eyebrow. "I wasn't aware you read gossip blogs. Does Holly sound out the words for you? Or do you just like the pictures?"

"Hey, no need to be a bitch." He holds up his hands in surrender. "I was just gonna say that the two of you look very happy. It's truly adorable. I hope he's coming to the party. I look forward to getting to know him better."

Like I trust that for a second. I wonder what Josh would make of the whole "purity pledge" thing. He'd probably die of laughter.

For the billionth time since Ally moved to New York, I wish I had my best friend back.

"He'll be there," I tell Josh firmly, even though I never actually told Zander the party was happening. It's a cast-and-crew party, and it never really occurred to me to bring a plus-one. Nor would I have thought Josh would be open to my doing so—especially one of the boy-band-member variety.

"Excellent. I was thinking just a casual thing, but maybe he and the rest of his superhero band can perform. You know how I love my ballads."

I'm tempted to snap back, but it's not worth it. Josh and I can go on like this all day, and none of that will help with what I really want and need—a way to clear my head and really think this through so I can be confident I'm making the right decision. No doubt Jade will have some epic date planned for us for Saturday night, and I need to know if I'm all in *before* I let Zander put that ring on my finger.

"I'll mention it," I lie instead.

Josh actually looks a little disappointed for a second, but he covers it up quickly. "Good. If my mom keeps being a bitch about the house, this may be my last party there. I still may need to get a new place. One that's actually *mine*."

Huh. Now there's something Josh and I actually have in common. Not that my parents are blackmailing me to stay home or anything, but the way they have me freaked out that *Daylight Falls* may be the very last well-paying job of my career definitely makes me think twice about leaving. Even if our situations aren't exactly the same, it's kinda nice to hear someone else have this problem. Maybe Josh and I aren't such total opposites after all.

"I know what you mean. I need to get out of my parents' house, but it's so hard to make myself. I'm not sure I'm ready."

He laughs. "Christ, K-drama, you still live with your parents? What are you, twelve? Man, you need a new place even worse than I do."

When he walks away, he's still laughing, his shoulders shaking.

Asshole.

I go straight from filming to the gym. I'm early for yoga, but I'm eager to get some of my aggression at both Liam and Josh—and myself—out on a punching bag. (Plus, I'm planning on wearing strapless to the Wonder Ball, and I love what it does for my arms.)

This one's for making my best friend doubt you, I think as I give it a series of punches for Liam. *And for getting movie roles thrown at you every second while I'm still struggling.*

And this one's for being a general pain in my ass. I throw a right hook, imagining Josh's smug smile. *And for calling me K-drama, you racist prick. And for laughing at me about my house. Even though I sort of deserve it and am sick of being a freaking child.*

After half an hour, my muscles are screaming, and when I hear a familiar voice behind me calling my name, I give it a rest, taking a deep breath and a long chug from my water bottle as I turn to face Bri and wave with my free hand.

"Having an angry kinda day, huh?" she asks with a smile. Her hair is pulled up into a high ponytail, and she's wearing short black shorts and a matching Nine Inch Nails tee. Clearly, we do not share taste in music.

I pull back the water bottle. "How'd you guess?"

"The full workout before yoga's even started was kind of a clue. Or are you skipping tonight?"

"Nope, I'm going." The workout helped, but I need the total brain-clearing that only yoga provides. Plus, the idea of going back to my house right now holds zero appeal. I like being surrounded by people, even if we're just sweating in dead silence.

"Good," she says with a dimple-highlighting grin. "I've gotten spoiled, having you there."

I feel the same way, but I feel silly saying it. I like knowing she'll be here on Thursday nights, that we have a sort of standing date, even if it's not really on purpose. I like knowing I'll see a friend at least once a week. It feels especially good to see one tonight.

"Do you wanna talk about whatever's bugging you?" she asks, her eyebrows knitting together in concern far more genuine than I've seen in a long time.

The thing is, I do. But she seems so comfortable... sexually. It's cool that she's out and proud. And of course, being bisexual doesn't mean that she's actually *had* sex. But I can't help feeling like she'd laugh in my face at the idea of a purity pledge. Or at least she'd want to.

"Nah, thanks." I force a smile back. "But I appreciate you asking."

"Of course," she says, linking an arm through mine and tugging me in the direction of the stairs up to the studio. "What are friends for?"

★ ★ ★ ★ ★

Though we obviously don't talk during yoga, it's nice just to see her there, to know I've got a friend in the room. When she makes a face at me in the mirror during Awkward Pose, it's all I can do not to crack up. Which, considering the day I had, is no small feat.

I can't help wondering if maybe I'm wrong, and she'd be understanding about the whole purity pledge thing, or at least be willing to let me talk about it. Normally, I'd make Ally hash it out with me for hours, but with all her Liam drama, I'm not sure she's got any room for mine.

Clear head, I admonish myself. *Deep breaths. Let the heat draw out all the stress.*

By the time we pause to sip water after finishing the first round of poses, I'm actually feeling pretty Zen. And sweating like a pig, as usual. I yank my tank top over my head before we start again.

In the mirror, I swear I can see Bri watching me out of the corner of her eye.

I stand up a little straighter as we get back into the Standing Deep Breathing Pose, but when I glance in the mirror again, her eyes are closed. She looks focused. Determined. Her face gleams with sweat, but she looks calm—so unlike the Bri I know, who's constantly joking and smiling. There isn't even a hint of her dimple now.

She keeps her eyes closed even when we shift into Half-Moon Pose, and it's weird, watching her. It's like seeing her transform. I think of the first time I saw her here, when I thought she was spying on me again. I feel stupid about it now; she's obviously into this. It looks so natural on her, like she was born in Rabbit Pose or something. Her ponytail's pulled high enough that I can see the entire Om just underneath her hairline, and when she stretches upward, her T-shirt rises just enough to show that there's more, colorful ink just north of her hip.

It's only when I catch Raoul's gaze on me that I realize how long I've been staring. We're almost halfway through and I haven't taken my eyes off her once. Nor has she opened hers. His scrutiny is totally mild, but I feel myself blushing under it anyway. I tear my eyes away and finish the rest of the poses, alternately watching Raoul and counting the tiles on the ceiling.

When everyone's done, she and I take our time hydrating, wiping ourselves down, and getting our stuff together, until we're the last two in the room.

"Don't you get hot in that thing?" I ask, gesturing at her sweaty cotton tee. "I can't even stand my tank top anymore by the first water pause."

The corners of her lips quirk up. "You realize we don't all look like that in a sports bra, right?" She lifts her chin in the general direction of my torso.

Instinctively, I look down. "What—flat as a board?"

She snorts. "Yes, but I meant in the ab area."

I glance at the same area on her. Okay, so there's the *slightest* curve of tummy there, just a cute little nothing. "That's your issue?" I point with my water bottle, then take a sip. "Please."

"I didn't say I have an *issue*," she says defensively. "I just...don't need it on display. Especially next to..." Now she's the one gesturing. Apparently, words aren't really our thing. "It's not like I think I'm fat. I'm just...St. Louis thin. Not LA thin. I like food."

"You think I don't?" I roll my eyes, thinking of all the burgers I used to put away with Ally at our favorite diner. "I work out every freaking day so I can eat and still be 'LA thin.' Or almost LA thin, I guess." I pinch at the tiny bit of love handle I can never seem to get rid of.

She whacks my hand, making me yelp. "Stop that," she demands as I rub my injured paw, making sure she didn't chip a nail. "You're crazy if you think your body is anything less than perfect."

I open my mouth to argue, but something about the look in her eyes makes me shut it. Like...she believes what she's saying. About every single part.

Instead, I say, "Well, I think the same about you."

And the thing is, I mean it. I like that she's built that way, all gentle curves. In a town of zero percent body fat, it's nice to see a little softness.

"Oh, shut up," she says, but her voice falters a bit. Because without meaning to—without even realizing I was doing it—I've placed my palm on her tiny little tummy.

What the hell am I doing?

"It's true," I say, quickly pulling my arm back, though it does nothing to dissipate the heated tingle on my skin.

"Thanks," she mumbles, stretching her lips into a thin, grim smile for just a second. "Um, I should go shower. I'm pretty gross right now."

She isn't, but I don't think my being an even bigger creeper is a great idea right now. "Yeah, me too." I hitch my yoga mat higher on my shoulder, but I can't let her go just yet. I need to get my stupid, embarrassing tummy touch out of her head. "So, um, got any fun weekend plans?"

"Not really." She shrugs. "Maybe hanging out with some friends from high school. But probably just helping my mom. She doesn't believe weekends are days off."

I already knew that well about Jade. In fact, I have a meeting with her and Zander bright and early on Saturday to discuss the whole purity pledge thing, how it would go down, whether we'd be giving any exclusives on the story.

I really, really hope Brianna knows nothing about that meeting.

"Cool," I say with a nod. And then an awkward silence descends, and I know it's time to let her go. "So, I guess I'll see you next Thursday."

I hope she'll say something about hanging out before then, but all she says is, "Same time, same place. And probably the same T-shirt. Washed, of course."

All I can do is nod again. God, I'm pathetic. I even debate mentioning Josh's party tomorrow night, but inviting her out after that seems even weirder. She clearly wants to get away from me right now, and I don't blame her.

So I step back and watch her go.

Chapter Eleven

I thought this was a small party." I turn around to see Holly sizing up the packed bar. The crowd at my wrap party for *Daylight Falls* is admittedly a little bigger than I was expecting, thanks to everyone bringing a few guests, but I've always been a "the more, the merrier" kinda guy. Especially when "more" refers to the amount of cleavage being shown off by Carly Upton's roommate.

"This is like half the number I had here for my last one," I tell her for no good reason other than I'm already a little drunk.

She sighs and grabs a flute of champagne off a passing tray.

Whatever. She's always been a little bit of a killjoy. But the food smells awesome—I'm having it catered by my favorite Korean barbecue place—and I'm looking forward to the fact that it'll be a pretty chill evening, as far as parties at my place go. Not that I'd ever admit it to anyone, but I actually liked working on *Daylight Falls*, being surrounded by people all day, even hanging out with K-drama. It was almost worth getting up at the ass-crack of dawn not to spend every day hanging out by myself or with my idiot friends.

Speaking of my idiot friends. My phone buzzes with a text from Liam that he'll be late. Shocker. The guy's barely surfaced to breathe, let alone party. I don't know how the hell he went from doing a couple of modeling gigs to being in every project under the sun, but suddenly, he is *everywhere*—on every entertainment website, blog, show, and front page, the new fucking golden boy of Hollywood.

And, predictably, he hates it.

Ungrateful bastard.

He's missing out now, though, if I may say so myself. The pool area is full, the music's playing, and the sounds of meat sizzling on the grill and drinks being poured are all combining with it to make my perfect soundtrack. If I were the sentimental type, I'd think I was actually a little sad about the fact that this would be the last *Daylight Falls* gathering at my place, at least until hell freezes over and Liam wins an Emmy for playing Tristan Monroe.

It's definitely smaller and more chill than my usual parties, but it's nice, just relaxing and eating and drinking and talking with our feet dangling in the pool. I'm actually enjoying myself for what feels like the first time in a really long time.

Which is, of course, when Chuck and a couple of cameramen come fuck it up.

I jump up the second I see the scrawny bastard and rush up into his face. "I told you already. Nobody wants to be on your piece-of-shit show. You may be able to set foot on my property because of my psycho-bitch mother, but you're not getting any of my guests on film. Unlike that famewhore, these people are on a show viewers actually give a damn about."

Chuck just grins. "Why don't we ask them?"

And people think *I'm* a douche. But fine. Chuck wants to have his ass handed to him by Jamal and the other guys—let him. Maybe that'll get rid of him once and—

"Dude, what the hell?"

I whirl around and see Grant Rabar and Marco Barone glaring at us. The scent of pot is heavy enough in the air that I can tell exactly why they're not thrilled to see cameras on them. *Fucking Marsha.* "You're filming us?" Grant spits.

"No." I know if I put a hand on Chuck or any of the cameramen, they'll sue the shit out of me; that's exactly what bloodsucking motherfuckers like them do. "These guys were just getting out of here. *Now.*"

The camera guys, of course, are loving every second of this, and my blood boils in my veins at the thought of them airing it, even with everyone's faces blurred out. I turn back to Chuck. "Dude, you *seriously* need to get out of here before I call the cops."

He snorts. "For what? We've got permission from the *owners* to be here." He motions for one of the camera guys to come even closer, and I can hear the rest of the crowd starting to take notice of their presence now. Bottles are quickly being tossed by the underagers, and I'm sure baggies of all kinds are being shoved into pockets. All I want is to physically drag Chuck out on his ass, and then have Ronen run over him a few times for good measure before driving me to my parents' house to blow up at my mother.

"Dude." Royce walks over, shaking his head.

I'd thrown out a few extra invites to the guys, but they're the last people I want to see right now, especially because I'm pretty sure they're all high.

"Can you call Liam?" I ask him impatiently. "Tell him to get his ass over here. I don't care what shit's clogging up his schedule today." I need someone who's more level-headed than I am. I'm just barely sober enough to keep from losing my shit completely.

"Everything okay, sweetie?"

What the—oh for the love of Christ. I look down at the bright-red talons digging into my arm and the long, tanned fingers they're attached to. I used to know that hand very, very well, and now the sight of it is just pissing me off. "Jesus, Shannah, you're like a walking STD—we fucked and now I can't get rid of you."

"Wow, charming much, Josh?" Even with her snotty tone, Shannah's still latching on like a viper. Her career must be going even shittier than mine for her to reach desperation levels like these. I'd heard rumors the family sitcom she's been on for years is ending this season, and this is as good a confirmation as any.

"Why would I bother being charming with you, Shannah? Been there and very literally done that. I can't believe you've actually sunk this low."

"Are you kidding?" She flashes chemically whitened teeth that glow against her orange skin. Did I really find this chick hot once upon a time? "I'm getting paid to make your life hell," she says, covering up the mic I now see wired into her bikini top. "What more could I possibly ask for?"

I slide my hand on to hers, letting it look like a gesture of affection for just long enough to ensure the cameras will zoom in to catch it, and then I yank her hand off the mic. "You're the one who screwed around on *me*, remember?"

Seeing her cheeks turn bright red is pretty gratifying, but she doesn't give up so fast. She never has. "I know we've had our problems, but I'm willing to work on them. You know that."

Christ, I can't even with this shit right now. Meanwhile, the people I actually *want* to stick around are bailing at warp speed, and I'm feeling like the biggest douchebag in Malibu right now, which is always an accomplishment.

My eyes dart around, and I'm relieved when I finally spot someone I know will be on her best behavior as long as there are cameras around. "K-dr—Vanessa!" She looks up, completely confused. At least I know she's not high. "C'mere."

She casts a quick, annoyed glance at Shannah—pretty sure she hasn't been a fan since Shannah was a total bitch to Ally at one of my parties last year—and walks over. She doesn't even have a drink to put down first. Such a good girl.

"What's up, Josh?" She looks at Chuck, the cameras. "What's...happening here?"

I wrench out of Shannah's grasp and pull Vanessa at least far enough away that they won't catch our voices on camera. Shannah might be wearing a mic, but I'm not. "My mother's been so kind as to invite these gentlemen to my private party. I will give you a billion dollars to get them the fuck out of here."

She raises an eyebrow. "What makes you think I'd be able to do that?"

"I have no idea. But Ally would be able to, and you're the closest thing I've got since my asshole best friend checked out on me. Come on. I'm sure some men find you vaguely attractive, in a boy-chested kind of way. Go charm them." Sparks shoot from her eyes. Whoops. "I mean..."

"Oh, shut up," she mutters. "God, I can't wait to figure out what you can actually do for me so I can collect on all the damn favors you ask." Then she steps away from me and walks over to Chuck. Miraculously, in under five minutes, they're gone.

"What the hell did you say to them?" I demand, keeping one eye on Shannah, who's dancing over to Zoe Knight rather than leaving with Chuck and Co. "And was it too much to ask to get rid of her, too?"

"I'm not a miracle worker," she says dryly. "I told them if they left, I'd make sure they got a *much* better show tomorrow night, with complete cooperation from you and everyone who came with you, to whatever club they choose. And yes, I'm sure you can expect to see Shannah there, causing even more drama. If you let her, and you actually let them make an insane episode for once, they'll start listening to you a whole lot more than your mother." She shakes her head. "Of course it never even occurred to you to play ball with them, you idiot. It's not like *they* care about your mom. You're the reason she got the show in the first place."

"So now I'm going to a club tomorrow night, but I can't drink anything?"

"They don't care if you drink, Josh," she says, like I'm a total idiot. "They won't show that if you make the rest good enough. Just...put on a show. It's what you love doing, anyway."

"Not the worst point in the world," I concede. "Thanks, K-drama. Now I'm actually feeling kinda glad I was a nice guy and invited your little friend."

Her mouth twists into a frown. "You invited Zander?"

"No, not him. You told me he was already coming. Which..." I turn and look around the pool area. "He doesn't seem to have done."

"Then which friend?"

Guess she doesn't wanna talk about the boyfriend. "Mini-Jade. You guys are friends, right?"

I hadn't thought she'd had anything to drink yet, but suddenly she looks like she's gonna puke. "You invited Bri? Here? Tonight?"

"Yeeeeah. Is that bad? I thought I was being nice. I bumped into her at the Coffee Bean on Sunset earlier and mentioned that you'd be here. Haven't seen her, though."

She presses her lips together in a thin line, and I have no idea what's going through her head right then, but she looks...pissed?

"Can you just *not* interfere with my life for five seconds?" she spits. "You don't have to go around inviting *my* friends to stuff, okay?"

"What the hell? How are you possibly twisting this into my being a dick? I didn't realize you apparently hate the chick. So sue me." Christ, I've had enough drama for the night. Now that Chuck and the cameramen are gone, I need another drink.

"Whatever, Josh. Next time, just...mind your own business. I only came so I wouldn't be the only one from the show who was obviously missing, but since even your 'best friend' doesn't wanna be here, I don't see why I have to be." She flags down a passing waiter, grabs an appletini shot from his tray, and tosses it back. "If you'll excuse me, I have to...talk to anyone who's not you." She thrusts the glass into my hands, and, completely and totally speechless, I just watch her disappear.

Chapter Twelve

Vanessa

*G*od, Josh Chester is so infuriating. I wish he didn't throw such good parties; I swear I'd never find myself around him otherwise. Although, now that his run on the show is over and Ally's completely free of him, I probably never have to.

It's a nice thought.

I ask the bartender for something stronger than the shot I just drank way too fast, and he hands me something with a cherry and way too much alcohol. I accept it anyway. The idea of facing Bri again this soon after the inexplicable tummy-touching incident demands a little altered reality.

"Can I have a mineral water with lime?" a girl asks from behind me, and I hold back a groan. I know that voice, and I know exactly who likes her water that way. Hopefully, she doesn't know the back of my head, because I haven't had nearly enough alcohol for this encounter.

No such luck. "Hey, I was wondering when I'd bump into you."

I turn around, plastering on a smile. No T-shirt today. Instead, Bri's wearing a cute handkerchief-print maxi dress, her hair twisted messily on top of her head, a guitar pendant hanging from a thin silver chain around her long neck. I've never seen her in red lipstick before, but it works on her, especially with her face framed by the wild red curls that've escaped her knot.

She looks beautiful.

"I was wondering the same about you. How long have you been here?"

"Just a couple minutes. Long enough to catch the shitshow with the reality guys. Never a dull moment around Josh Chester, is there?"

"Only when he's speaking." I take a sip of my drink as I watch the bartender hand over hers. The water is cool and clear and looks so refreshing next to my mystery drink, I sort of want to swap. Except I need to escape my head after yesterday, just a little bit, and can't help feeling a little annoyed that she doesn't need to do the same. "Just water, huh?"

"For now," she says simply.

She's showing no signs at all of feeling weird, and I'm starting to wonder if maybe everything was entirely in my head. I know that's a good thing, but for some reason, it's only making my annoyance grow. I need to take my drink and find a little peace and quiet.

"Okay, well." I make like I'm looking at someone else over her shoulder and need to go say hi; let no one say acting skills don't come in handy off set. "I guess I'll see you around."

I do in fact spot a bunch of people I could and probably should say hi to, and normally I would. But right now, I want to be alone more than I ever have before in my life.

No, that's not true. I don't want to be alone. As I walk away from Bri, putting purpose into my step until I'm pretty sure she's no longer watching, I think about how badly I miss my best friend. Ally would tell me that I'm being a complete idiot and reading far too much into a new friendship. In fact, maybe that's exactly what I need to hear.

Now that the reality show guys are gone, the party's picked back up, so I duck inside Josh's house to make the call to Ally. It rings four times and goes to voicemail. Of course.

I get as far as "Hey, A," before I realize I don't even really know what else to say. I don't want to talk to a machine. Why is it so impossible to have a normal freaking conversation these days? I sigh. "Just wanted to say hi. Guess I'll talk to you later." I hit End and then stare at my phone, willing her to call me back, hoping she just needed to find a quiet space or something.

After four minutes, which I spend downing my drink, I'm contemplating calling her again, and of course, that's exactly when I hear, "You still PMS-ing, K-drama?"

I whirl around to see Josh double-fisting beers. "Do you just troll around coming up with the most offensive statements possible?"

"Would you believe it actually requires zero work on my part?"

"Oh, go away."

"Seriously, Park, what crawled up your ass and died? You in a fight with Mini-Jade?"

"Stop calling her that," I spit. "She isn't anything like her mother."

"Then why are you so pissed I invited her here? I thought you guys were cool. Do yoga and stuff."

And stuff. I grit my teeth, feeling them grind, and then loosen my jaw again. "We're fine. We're friends. But you didn't have to invite her here."

He shrugs. "Well, too late now. Anyway, I thought she was gonna be hanging out with you and your boyfriend. So, why'd he flake?"

"He didn't flake," I say flatly. "I decided it'd be nice to be with just *Daylight* people tonight. I didn't realize you'd be inviting Bri or your gross friends."

"What gross friends?"

I jerk my head toward the French doors leading out to the pool, and the group of guys sitting beyond it—Josh's usual posse of guys who get either the "Bad Boy with a Heart of Gold for the Right Girl" or "Dumb Stoner" roles. "What are they even doing here?"

Another shrug. "It's a party. They're my friends. They show up."

"Well, they're not friends with any of the rest of us. Royce Hudson tried to stick a hand up my dress at the VMAs last year."

"He's a dick when he's drunk," Josh says, like that's any excuse. "Besides, they're friends with Liam, too." He walks over to the door and peers through. "See? He's hanging out with them now. He's—oh, for fuck's sake, Shannah."

"What?" I jump over to the door and follow Josh's eyeline. Sure enough, there's Liam, practically passed out on a chaise by the pool. And draped over him is none other than his and Josh's shared former bedbuddy.

I swing the door open and storm out, even as Josh yells at me to calm down. But there's no way in hell I'm calming down. I'm too worked up—about Bri, about Josh, about Ally not being here when I need her—and right now, Liam's looking like a perfect target. "What the *hell*, Liam? Are you kidding me?"

His head jerks up from where it had been bent way too close to the low neckline of Shannah's halter top. "Vanessa. I...what?" He blinks dumbly, and I think about how many girls have fallen hard for those ocean-colored eyes, including my best friend, who'd probably answer his call at any hour. I look at his dark circles of exhaustion and remember that they come from working two movies on top of our show, and how much I struggle to land even a bit part in one.

I think about everything that's falling into his lap right now—how much he's taking for granted and how stupid he's being, letting Shannah near him while Ally's away—and I want to scream.

My rage must show on my face, because he pales considerably and pulls away from Shannah so fast she almost falls off the chair. "This is so not—I mean, you know this isn't anything. You *know* I was just sitting here, and there's nothing weird going on."

He grabs for my arm, but I jump out of the way, nearly stumbling on a wayward beer bottle. I can't even see straight with the rage clouding my vision. It's one thing for *my* relationship to be bullshit—my relationships are *always* bullshit—but not Ally's. Not theirs. What they have is real—not staged hand-holding and kissing for the cameras and purity pledges, but actual love.

Or at least I thought it was. But I don't know the guy begging me for my silence right now. He sure seems a whole lot like more bullshit.

As if to further prove my point, the voice he uses to say, "Vanessa, you know me," sounds like it belongs to a stranger.

"I did," I say bitterly. "Back when you were actually around instead of ceding your airtime to Josh, and making my best friend happy instead of forcing her to wait for your phone calls every night so she winds up missing the parties and study sessions she *should* be going to. Somehow, I don't think 'cheater' is that unbelievable a new role for you. Hell, you should tell

James Gallagher how good you are at it. He'll probably write a whole movie centered around it just for you."

"Jesus, Vanessa. Is that why you're being like this? Because you're jealous?"

"I'm not *jealous* of anything, you jerk," I spit, but we both know it's a lie. Of course I'm jealous that he's getting roles and *Daylight Falls* might be all I ever have. Of course I'm jealous that he's been in a relationship with someone for a year and all I've had since we publicity-dated is a string of irrelevant setups. Of course I'm jealous that he's on his own, with his own place and an established career, and his best friend still in town. "Just leave me alone."

"Not until you promise you're not going to call Ally with some crazy story. You're just gonna upset her over nothing."

"He's right, K-drama," Josh chimes in. "Frankly, you're being a little crazy tonight. Maybe you *should've* brought Wilson to the party. Have him around to keep you in line."

"I can't even deal with this right now," I say on a sharp exhale, turning away from the guys and walking toward the beach.

"Van—"

"I won't call Ally," I yell over my shoulder. "But you should." And then I quicken my pace until I hit the sand, and the sound of crashing waves drowns out everything around me.

I haven't been on the beach more than five minutes when I hear Bri coming up behind me. "Hey, I've been looking for you everywhere. Are you okay?"

Closing my eyes, I breathe deeply, willing myself not to snap. *I don't want you here*, I think, wishing I could push the words out the back of my skull so I could get rid of her without turning, without speaking.

And I wish they were true.

"I'm fine," I bite out, keeping my gaze fixed on the reflection of the moon in the Pacific.

"No, you aren't."

I squeeze my eyes tight, as if it'll help me emit the necessary "go away" vibes, but my heart's not in it. I don't want to be alone. And what's more, Bri's company feels like exactly what I need right now.

"I saw you blow up at Liam," she adds, her voice soft, like she's afraid to wake a sleeping beast.

"I don't want to talk about it."

She sighs. "Fine. So we won't talk about it." I hear a shuffling of sand, and I'm afraid she's turned around to go, but then I feel the warmth of her presence at my side. "We'll just stand here. Or sit here. Can I sit?"

I chew on my lip as I contemplate my response, and finally, I give up and shrug.

She drops onto the sand next to me. "So why are you out here if all your friends are up there?"

"I wanted to be alone."

"You hate to be alone."

For the first time, I turn to her full-on, meeting her seaglass-green gaze. "How do you know that?"

She shrugs, but I think I might see a hint of a blush in the moonlight. "How don't I? You've told me you hate shopping by yourself, and driving by yourself. And even on set, you're usually hanging out with Carly or Jamal. Other people separate themselves to get into the zone or whatever, but you never do. Even the exercise you do is always something with other people around."

"God, are you always that observant? Or just when it comes to me?"

I'm embarrassed by the words as soon as they come out of my mouth–they don't sound quite how I mean them–but I'm also really curious about the answer.

"I don't know," she mumbles, looking out at the ocean, the bangles on her wrist jangling as she draws a spiral pattern in the sand. "I'm perceptive, I guess."

"Apparently." I watch her trailing fingers, the way the sand flows around her black-painted nails. It's the first time I notice yet another tattoo–a tiny heart on her hand below the bridge between her thumb and index finger. "I didn't know you were coming tonight. Why didn't you say anything?"

She shrugs. "I wasn't sure I was. Josh just mentioned it this morning, and you hadn't said anything, so I didn't know if I should or not."

"You don't need my permission to come to a party," I say, making sure she can hear the teasing in my voice.

"Yeah, well, I came, so."

I'm about to ask why, when I realize two things: 1) that's sort of rude; and 2) there's only one possible reason. She doesn't care about anyone else here. She isn't even trying to talk to anyone else–not Liam the Golden God, or Josh, who for whatever reason a million girls find irresistible. She's here for me, even after last night, even after the...touching.

And I don't know how to process why that makes my entire body fill with warmth, despite the breeze rolling in off the ocean.

"I'm glad you did," I admit, and it feels like a weight lifting off my shoulders. Next to me, she visibly relaxes too. "I'm sorry if I've been...weird."

Her fingers keep tracing, spirals giving way to other shapes—lightning bolts. Fish. Hearts. "You wanna talk about it?"

I do, but I don't. I'm embarrassed to even mention the purity pledge, and for whatever reason, I don't wanna talk about Zander with her, anyway. As for the rest...

"You can trust me, you know." Her voice has the slightest tinge of annoyance. "I'm not my mother. I promised I would never spy on you again, and I meant it."

"I know that."

"I thought we were friends."

"Of course we're friends. I just...I don't know." I bite my lip and meet her gaze. "You ever feel like you just have *no* idea what you're doing? Ever? Like, I constantly rely on people telling me what to do, what to wear, how to deliver a line, where to be, and I don't have to *think*. And I know this makes me sound dumb, but I've always kinda liked that. I don't really wanna think."

"It doesn't make you sound dumb." She scoops up a pile of sand and lets it filter through her fingers. "Not any dumber than me doing whatever my mom tells me to do."

"Yeah, but that's only because she's withholding your tuition right now. As soon as this year's up, you're gonna get some job or go off to college, doing...I don't know what. Important college-people things."

She laughs. "Except that she's right that I have no idea what I wanna do with my life. I haven't exactly taken to her career, and spending a few days on set didn't really make me want to do anything other than hang out with you more. So I'm no closer than I was a couple months ago. I just keep hoping that she knows what she's talking about and eventually I'll stumble into something I love."

"Is that the worst thing?" I ask. "Just...not having a real direction right now?"

"It's not the *worst* thing, but it's not the best thing either." She digs up another pile of sand and lets it sprinkle onto my fingers, which are splayed out between us. "I mean, look at you. You're eighteen and you've been working for...how long? Seven years? Eight? You know exactly what you're doing, and you love it. You can take care of yourself. That's so cool."

The bark-snort combo I emit involuntarily is an unfortunately dead-on imitation of a seal. "Are you kidding me? Yeah, I love what I'm doing, but I have *no* idea where I go from here. You know how many roles there are out there for an Asian-American actress? Me neither. At least you have a real education and will end up going to a decent college if you don't figure out the job thing. My parents are afraid I'm gonna wash up with the show in a couple years and end up unemployed, broke, and living in their house forever. And you know what? They're probably right."

"Of course they're not right." The anger in Bri's voice surprises us both, if her slight jolt backward is any indication. "Van, you're smart, talented, and gorgeous. You're *good* at this. I don't know what it's like to be a minority in Hollywood, but I know you're not even close to done. You're gonna be whatever you wanna be."

I love her idealism and her faith, even if it's misplaced. The truth is, *Daylight Falls* has been a great ride and probably will be for another couple of years, but I've been doing this—and been best friends with Alexandra Duncan, Mistress of Hollywood Cynicism—for far too long to believe in miracles.

"That's not true for girls like me," I tell her, trying not to sound as bitter as I feel. "Life's different for someone like Liam."

"Ah, Liam." Bri laughs. "He really is pretty, isn't he?"

I roll my eyes. "No comment."

"Oh, right. I forgot you've been there, done that."

"You know that was all your mother's idea, right?"

"Of course I know. Those kinds of plans are Jade's specialty." She stretches her arms out in front of her, which makes her bangles jangle again. "Can't really blame me for not wanting to follow in her footsteps, can you?"

"Never."

"But still, Liam always seemed to me like a decent guy. You really ripped him one tonight. I thought you guys were friends."

"We are. We were. I don't know." I inhale the calming salt air. "I thought we'd hang out more with Ally gone, maybe, or at least chill on set, but I feel like ever since she left, he's just throwing himself into this whole world that doesn't have a place for me or anyone else in it. And that includes Ally, which in turn makes *her* more distant, which sucks."

"Maybe he's trying to keep himself distracted from the pain of his girlfriend being three thousand miles away. Speaking of things that suck."

"Yeah, I guess," I mutter.

"Hey." Her hand covers mine. "It's okay if you're not a hundred percent sure what you'll be doing in five years. I mean, it has to be, right? If you're screwed, I'm *beyond* screwed."

I laugh, squeezing her fingers. "Then, yes, it has to be. Because we're both gonna be fine. We just need to make some actual plans, or something."

"And to move out of our moms' houses!" she adds triumphantly. "Definitely a solid goal for both of us."

"I will if you will."

"I will, so you will." The confidence in her voice is unwavering, and it makes me smile. It's infectious. More than that, it's the first time I've actually felt like maybe I can make it happen, especially if I have someone trying to dig out of the same hole at the same time.

"We could do it together, even," I say, growing excited now. "Get our own cute place. Something close to both the set and Jade's office."

"Could we get a shaggy purple rug? I've always wanted a shaggy purple rug."

I burst out laughing. "Of all things, *that's* what you want? Sure, we can get a shaggy purple rug. As long as there's enough space on the hardwood for our yoga mats."

"Obviously. And fish—we should get fish. One of those really cool fish tanks they have in fancy hotels and whatever."

"I'm pretty sure those are like a billion dollars," I tell her sadly.

"Oh." Her face falls. "Well, maybe just a dinky little goldfish bowl then. I've always wanted a pet."

"I thought you've always wanted a shaggy purple rug."

"That too. Shockingly, Jade wouldn't let me have either one."

"I *am* shocked. I bet you'd make a great fish mom, too."

"I totally would, right? I'd spoil those babies rotten."

"I believe it," I say sincerely. "You are a very excellent caretaker." I realize then that her hand is still on mine, and I hook my pinky around hers. "I really am glad you came."

She swallows hard, but doesn't respond.

For the second time in two days, I feel like a complete and total idiot, and I quickly slip my hand out from hers. "I'm sorry, I didn't mean...I'm sorry."

"You know, you don't flirt like a straight girl," she murmurs, the words rolling right through my body to curl my toes.

My skin prickles with heat as a guilty flush steals over me, and I'm grateful it's hidden by the dark. I guess I *was* flirting, but...why? I mean, yeah, there's no ignoring that she's attractive, but it's not like she's the first girl I've ever noticed that about; I work in freaking Hollywood. And of course I like hanging out with her, and feel like I can talk to her—she's a friend. Period. That's all girls are to me.

Isn't it?

"I'm sorry," I rasp again, and mean it. "I'll stop."

She's silent. And then fingertips, soft and cool as they sweep through my hair, rest on the base of my neck. "No," she says, softer now, her touch tingling my skin. "Please don't."

Oh God. The prickle of heat blazes brighter, lower, and there isn't any ignoring what it means. I don't understand how, or why, but I am turned-on beyond belief.

By a girl.

And I really, really don't want to stop flirting with her.

"I should go," I say, forcing myself to stand. "We're drunk, and..." I don't know how to finish that sentence. I'm not even really drunk. Neither is she. But I don't want to start anything I don't know how to finish. Hell, something I don't even know how to start. What *could* even happen? My mother would go ballistic. My fanbase would revolt like crazy. I don't even know which of us Jade would kill first. And Zander...

Her jaw ticks, and I realize I've definitely said the wrong thing. "Yeah, okay. Have a good night, then." She jumps up and starts to stalk back to Josh's house, and even though I know I should let her, I can't let the night end like that.

"Bri, wait."

She turns back, silently.

"It's not...I mean, it's not you, or that I don't want... It's...ugh." I'm not making sense, which is to be expected since it doesn't really make sense in my brain, either. "I'm with Zander, and your mom is my publicist, and things are just crazy." I take another deep breath of cleansing salt air. The look on her face—a combination of hurt and anger—is clawing at my gut, and I know I have to say what I'm really feeling, even if it's too weird to process. "But...I'm not trying to confuse you." I drop my voice to a near-whisper, even though no one else from the party has trickled onto the beach. "*I'm* confused. About you, and how I feel, and why for some reason I am still thinking about the fact that you called me smart and talented and gorgeous."

For a second, her full lips curve into a smile, and I think, *I love your mouth.* Never have I looked at someone and thought, *I love your mouth.* But I do love hers. Then the smile vanishes, and she says, "You're right. You should go. Or I should go. Going should happen."

I smile sheepishly. "Yeah, exactly." Hopefully both of us will think more clearly in the morning, because this is a train wreck waiting to happen on infinity levels. "We'll talk soon, or something."

"Yes. Definitely. G'night, Park." She wraps her fingers in the chain of her necklace and takes off, leaving me staring after her, trembling, every inch of my skin on fire.

Chapter Thirteen

Josh

I feel like shit when I wake up in the morning, or maybe it's afternoon. It takes a minute of squinting to see the numbers on my clock, but no, it's only ten thirty. My instinct is to go back to sleep, but my mouth feels like I've chewed off the ashy end of a cigarette. After a minute, I know nothing's happening until I get a bottle of water.

Halfway to the kitchen, I freeze. There's a voice floating out of my kitchen. I'm pretty sure I didn't nail anyone last night, thanks to Chuck the Walking Cockblock, so who the hell is in my house?

I edge closer and hear, "I'm sorry, A. I was just having a really crappy day. It wasn't anything." She pauses, presumably waiting for a response, and when I hear none, I realize I'm eavesdropping on Vanessa talking to Ally on the phone.

Right. I completely forgot I let K-drama stay here last night. I've never seen her get too drunk to drive herself home, but she was definitely in no condition by the end of the party last night; she's a shitty enough driver sober.

I walk into the kitchen just as she's hanging up. Her back is to me, her elbows resting on the granite countertop of the island, and she's wearing the clothes I lent her last night—an old Clippers T-shirt and a pair of boxers. I don't usually give a crap about legs unless they're wrapped around my neck, but I have to admit, hers are pretty nice.

She turns and casts an irritated glare at me. "Must you be such a creeper?"

"For your information," I say, sailing past her to the fridge, "you're in my kitchen, in my clothes, at ten thirty on a Saturday morning. If anyone's the creeper…"

"It's too early for this." She rolls her eyes, then nods at the cappuccino maker. "How do you make that thing work?"

"Fuck if I know." I nab a bottle of water and take a huge gulp, swishing it around my teeth. "Ally used to be here to do it by now."

"And of course you still haven't bothered to learn," she mutters.

"Hey, you wanna do it? Be my guest."

She scowls but makes no move toward it. I snort. Why am I not surprised?

"Do you have anything a little…simpler?" she asks impatiently.

"Not in here." I love the look of the machine, but I think coffee tastes like ass. Even when Ally used to make it, it was usually just for herself. Anyway, it's bad for the pearly whites. "There's a Keurig in the guest house, though."

She looks at me like she's waiting for the punchline. When it doesn't come, she looks helplessly at the cappuccino maker, sighs, and turns on her heel.

I follow her out; apparently, she doesn't realize the guest house requires a key. She taps her foot as I unlock the door, but she doesn't seem impatient, exactly. More like she's filled with nervous energy or something. As I watch her dive for the coffee machine,

I can't help thinking caffeine is probably a bad idea. Too bad she'd probably rip my balls off for saying so.

"What do you even do with this place?" she asks as the machine rumbles to life under her fingertip. "It doesn't look like anyone's ever slept here. I *know* Ally only pretended to when she was staying at Liam's."

The place *is* a little sparse. "I dunno. My parents used to have people here, back when they came more often, but they both prefer to stay in Bel Air as much as possible. Anyway, it's really just a bedroom and bathroom."

"Still, it has cool potential." She slides one of the mugs on the table into the coffeemaker, presses another button, and little by little, the scent of coffee fills the air. "You should do something with it."

"Like a sex den?" I ask, just as she says, "Not a sex den."

I grin. "You gonna move out of your parents' place anytime soon?"

She mutters something under her breath that I don't catch, and I have a feeling I don't wanna ask her to repeat it. Then she grabs the mug, sprinkles in some sugar and one of those creamer things from the little hostess tray, and takes a long, deep sip without even waiting for it to cool.

"Oh God," she groans in appreciation, sounding so orgasmic there's a shift in my shorts. "That's perfect."

"Hit it a little hard last night, did you? I don't think I've ever seen you drink so much. Sorry Mini-Jade missed it. She left pretty early."

Her eyelids flutter shut. "Will you stop calling her Mini-Jade? It's creepy. You know her name."

"I know yours, too, but K-drama's just so much better." I hop up onto one of the stools lining the breakfast bar. "Is this about your boyfriend skipping out on last night?"

"For the millionth time, Joshua, he did not skip out. And for your information, I'm going straight from here to see Zander, so don't get any ideas into your over-gelled head."

A vague memory from last night stirs in my brain. "I thought you said you had a meeting with Jade. Didn't you say you needed to get back to LA by noon for that?"

She wrinkles her nose, and even through my hungover haze, I realize what's happening here. I throw back my head and laugh. "Seriously? Haven't you learned your lesson from the whole thing with Liam last year? Don't you get tired of this endless publicity fauxmance shit?"

"This is *not* the same thing," she insists, her knuckles whitening around the mug. "Liam was a stunt, obviously, but Zander and I...it's not the same."

"So you're genuinely into him?"

She takes another sip of coffee, and I smirk, recognizing it for the time-buying tactic it is. K-drama's a halfway decent actress, but that doesn't mean she's a good liar. By the time she says, "Yes, I am," I already know without a doubt it's complete bullshit.

"So what's the meeting about?"

"Just event stuff," she says stiffly, leaning against the island. "It's really not a big deal."

"You're meeting on a Saturday and it's not a big deal?"

"It works around my filming schedule, thank you very much. Some of us still have regular jobs."

Ouch. "Not that I'm dying to go back to a life of ass-crack-of-dawn call times with you any time soon, but for your information, you're not the only one who has meetings today," I tell her. I take a swig from my water bottle. "I'm coming in with you. Meeting up with Holly to discuss some more options."

She raises her eyebrows. "More...*acting* options? For you?"

"For your information, I'm testing fabulously well for my work on the show, so, yes. Acting options. Hopefully less lame ones this time."

"Oh, please. You loved every minute of working on *Daylight Falls*."

"Only the ones where I got to torture you."

"Like I said," she says wryly. "Every minute."

I smile around the neck of the water bottle and let a little more trickle down my throat. "You're funny, K-drama. Don't worry—one of these days you'll get your own boyfriend, without Hollywood help."

"And one of these days, you'll die single and alone. Probably in your own vomit."

"That *is* how all the best celebrities go," I say, stroking my chin thoughtfully. Which reminds me that I need to shave. And shower. And brush my teeth. "You gonna be ready to leave here in half an hour?"

"Mmhmm," she murmurs, already diving back in for another sip. I swear, you'd think that shit was laced with bourbon.

I start to walk out, leaving her to worship at the altar of caffeine, but I can't help noticing her nervous energy hasn't settled at all. She looks stressed as hell, and as much as I don't wanna give a shit, she helped me out last night. I feel like I owe her one.

"Are you sure you're okay?" I ask, scratching the back of my neck. I'm not used to being sincere, and it's uncomfortable as hell just listening to myself. "You seem...not."

She purses her lips. "Are you, Josh Chester, seriously showing some sort of caring right now?"

"For Christ's sake, K-drama—"

"Sorry," she mutters. "No, I appreciate it. I just—I don't know. I'm a little off."

"Does this have to do with your meeting today?"

She shifts uncomfortably and takes another sip, but this time I'm pretty sure she's just hiding behind the mug.

"I promise, I won't say anything. Or make fun of you."

I can tell she's contemplating telling me, but man, does she not want to. And now, of course, I'm dying of curiosity. Finally, she says, "We're talking about something I'm not sure I'm really behind, is all. But maybe I am. I just need a little more time to think about it. And Jade isn't exactly the most patient."

"So maybe Brianna can convince her to chill out a little. She works with her. Get her to come up with some reason you guys need to slow down on whatever this mystery plan is."

A funny look crosses her face, and she looks like she might puke. I thrust the water bottle in her face, but she waves it away.

"I need to take a shower," she mutters. She drains the rest of the mug, then walks it over to the sink and rinses it out. "You said half an hour?"

"Yeah. You gonna be okay?"

She shrugs, and we head out the doors and back to the main house, where we part for different bathrooms. It's driving me crazy, not knowing what's eating at her, which is dumb; who cares? Anyway, she'll probably bitch and moan about it in the car, whatever it is. Nothing that's my problem.

I brush my teeth and use my other hand to turn the shower to scalding hot, just how I like it. I need to rinse off this hangover, and my weird concern for K-drama. All I should be thinking about right now is my meeting with Holly and what the hell I'm gonna do next. Because tonight may belong to my mother and Chuck, but I need to find a way to make it the last night that does.

Chapter Fourteen

Vanessa

*D*espite Josh's having been weirdly nice-ish this morning, I couldn't bring myself to say much to him in the car ride down to LA. The mention of Brianna in the context of the meeting I'm about to walk into completely threw me. Somehow I hadn't really put together that, as Jade's employee, of *course* she would find out about the whole purity pledge thing. Hell, she'll probably have to help plan however it goes down.

The coffee that'd been so welcome this morning gurgles in my stomach as I push open the front door to the building that houses Jade's office. She insisted on meeting here because she has a policy against bringing clients to her home (presumably because she's pissed off enough former ones that she doesn't wanna be stalkable) and she doesn't trust waiters. This place has always kinda given me the creeps, though. There's too much glass; everything's transparent. Even with the office mostly empty, as it is now, I still feel like there are eyes on me everywhere.

I take the elevator to the second floor, praying with everything in me that Bri won't be there when the doors open. After what I said last night—never mind the fact that I can still feel her hand on mine—the very idea of making eye contact with her right now fills me with even more queasiness.

I am really, really sorry I had that coffee.

The doors open, and I see her immediately. She looks up at the sound of the dinging elevator, and for a second before she puts on her phony PR-girl smile (which still looks pretty grim), I see that she looks hurt as hell.

And I feel like shit.

You have no reason to feel bad, I tell myself as I step out of the elevator, moving at molasses pace. *She knows you have a boyfriend. And of course she knows you're just friends. You don't like girls like that. Things have just been getting a little confusing because you miss Ally and things maybe aren't where they should be with Zander. You'll have this meeting, you'll establish where you and Zander stand, and that'll be the end of this. You can go back to being friends.*

I paste a smile on my face that's every bit as phony as hers. "Hey. Didn't realize you'd be here. Funny seeing you again so soon."

"Yeah, well, didn't know you were coming in until this morning." Her voice is tight, and if I hadn't been sure she was pissed before, I am now. "Jade and Zander are already in." She steps out from behind the desk and leads me to the office. "Can I get you a drink? Water?"

"I'm fine," I lie. My tongue feels like it's sticking to my mouth, but I can't bring myself to make Bri run errands for me. Having her hold the door open for me right now is bad enough. "Thanks."

She nods curtly and turns, but then Jade calls her name, and she turns back. "Yes?"

"Why don't you sit in with us?" Jade suggests. "You might learn something here, or even have a helpful suggestion of your own."

"I highly doubt that," Bri mutters under her breath, but she follows me in anyway. She takes a seat across from Zander, which leaves me two options—sitting next to him or sitting next to her. I do the former, and he immediately leans over to give me a peck on the cheek.

I pretend not to notice that Bri looks away when he does.

"So!" Jade says sunnily. "I'm glad you guys could make it in on a Saturday. I know we're all busy, so let's make this quick. I'm thinking we make this happen tonight at—"

"Wait," I interrupt. "I can't do tonight. I have plans. I promised."

Jade raises an eyebrow. "What does that mean, you promised?"

I look helplessly at Bri—I know she was there for the Josh disaster and can back me up—but she's staring at her fingernails like the secret to perfect lowlights is reflected in the black lacquer. "I was helping Josh out of a tricky situation, and I promised I'd go to a club with him tonight for his family's reality show. It's not a big deal. But I did say I'd be there and I did say tonight. Can we just do this tomorrow?"

Zander and Jade exchange a glance. "You're going out with Josh Chester tonight?" Zander says, his voice practically a squeak. "How's *that* gonna look?"

"Josh *and* some other people," I reply. "And it's gonna look like I'm hanging out with a friend and costar." Okay, "friend" might be a stretch, but Zander's tone and question are bugging me. I don't tell him not to hang out with his annoying bandmates; he shouldn't be doing that to me. "You should come, especially if you're concerned."

"To a club?" says Jade. "No. Zander does not go to clubs. And neither do you, missy."

Bri snorts, and I'm so relieved to hear her make a happy sound that it totally bolsters me to bite back. "I do tonight."

"Vanessa," Jade says seriously, "you cannot be seen—and *filmed*—at a club with Josh Chester and his friends. Remember, we're going for a wholesome role model image. That's the point here. You're going to have millions of girls looking up to you and wanting to *be* you. Being consistent is extremely important."

"But what if I don't consistently feel like Miss Purity Pledge?" I blurt out.

Zander reaches over and takes my hand. "Vanessa, sweetheart." (He has never, ever called me sweetheart, except in front of cameras.) "I know you're nervous, and I understand—this is a big step. But we love each other. This is the right thing."

We love each other? How on earth does he sound so sincere? Why is he even bothering in front of just Jade and Brianna? Did I miss some sort of memo?

"Zander..." I start to pull my hand back, but he just squeezes it. I can feel Bri's eyes burning lasers, cutting through his palm to mine. "I don't...I'm not...I need more time to think about this. But I *am* going to the club with Josh tonight," I say, quietly but firmly. It's not even really about Josh now, or about the promise I made; I need more time to think about this, and this is the perfect way to buy it.

Besides, I'm sick of being told what to do.

"I'll go with her," Bri says suddenly, and all heads swivel in her direction. "I'll make sure everything looks on the up-and-up, that it's clear Vanessa and Josh are just friends and she's there for moral support. No drinking—nothing."

Considering I'm still feeling sick to my stomach, the idea of drinking tonight doesn't really hold much appeal for me anyway.

The idea of Bri in clubwear, sitting by my side all night, however, holds way too much.

"I still don't like this," says Zander, scrunching up his nose like a bratty little kid. "We're supposed to be committing to each other, Vanessa. How's it gonna look if you go out tonight with another guy?"

"I'm not going out *with* Josh." I shudder at the thought, and Bri cracking a grin next to me might as well be the hand squeeze I could totally use right now. "I'm going out with a group of people that happens to include Josh. And like I said, if you're that concerned, just come with me. Bri can babysit us both."

Under the table, though, I'm gripping the rim of my chair with both hands, praying he'll say no. *I don't want him there*, I realize with a clarity that scares me. I want to party with my friends and hang out with Bri somewhere other than a mall or yoga studio or Josh's house. And I want to do *all* of that more than I want to spend time with the guy who's supposed to be putting a ring on my finger for the world to see.

What kind of role model does that make me?

Jade's eyes flash. "You may be determined to tank your image, missy, but that doesn't mean I'm going to let you take Zander down with you. You think you know better than me and you want to go to a club tonight? Fine. We can spin this whole thing into tonight making you realize just how much you're no longer interested in this lifestyle." She exhales noisily, and I know she thinks she's just done me the world's biggest favor. "But Bri, you *are* going to supervise, and after tonight, Vanessa, you *will* cooperate. Understood?"

Or what? hovers on the tip of my tongue, but I don't dare say it. For one thing, my parents have drilled "Respect your elders" so far into my brain I don't think I could talk back to anyone over thirty if I wanted to.

But mostly, all I heard was that tonight I'm going to a club with Bri. And though it makes every hair on my body stand on end to think about why, I can't remember the last time I was this excited for anything.

If anyone asks me tonight how long it took me to get ready, I will blatantly lie. I can't even remember when I last spent so much time on my hair and makeup when there weren't any shiny statuettes being handed out on stage. But by the time Bri texts to tell me she and her Jeep are out front, I'm feeling pretty damn good about the outfit Ally helped me pick out over Skype. I know I look hot in this shade of purple, and given that I've been too anxious all day to eat a single bite, I look extra thin in a dress that's wrapped around me tighter than a bandage. My hair's so shiny I can see dimensions of my reflection in the mirror, and third time was the charm for finally nailing sexy beach waves the way my hairdresser, Isaac, has tried to teach me a zillion times.

I don't even know what I hope will happen tonight, but it *does* feel like my very last night of freedom, and for that, I wanna look good.

Thankfully, my parents are at my aunt and uncle's tonight—I can't deal with my mother eyeing me like I've dressed for Satan worship—so I let myself out of the house slowly, giving Bri time to appreciate me from tousled head to sexy-sandaled toe. But there's no reaction at all—no whistle, no admiring once-over, not even a "Looking good." Just a slightly impatient-sounding, "Ready?"

"Yeah." The word sticks in my throat, all excitement rapidly draining out of my system.

She pulls the car out of park and starts off toward Sugar, a club I'd never go to if it hadn't been arranged by the reality-show clan. It's the first time she's ever driven me anywhere, and I wonder if maybe she's just a nervous driver, like I am. But her clenched jaw doesn't look particularly fearful, and her eyes don't dart around anxiously or anything.

I'm pretty sure she's just avoiding eye contact.

I take advantage of that to do my own once-over, but I can't see much. She's wearing a leather jacket that covers up her outfit, and the combination of the night's darkness and the brightness of the neon lights makes it hard to see her face in any detail. Finally, I feel pathetic for staring, and I sigh and look out my own window.

But when we pull up to a red light a few minutes later, I can't help it anymore. "Did I do something?"

"Nope." No eye contact.

I bite my lip while I wait for more, but more never comes. The light turns green, and she hits the gas.

"You're really just going to sit there being passive-aggressive all night?"

She snorts. "No. I'm going to be passive-aggressive for the length of this drive, and then I'm going to get wasted at the club and find a nice young man to drive me home."

For some reason, the "nice young man" part feels like the sharpest stab wound of all. "What the hell, Bri?"

"What?" she asks innocently.

"Don't 'what' me! You're the one who came up with the idea to supervise me tonight. Why'd you even say that if you were gonna be so pissed to be here?"

"Because I'm an idiot," she mutters. "A complete fucking idiot who will never, ever learn."

"Learn *what*?"

We hit another red light, and then she turns to me, her gorgeous eyes blazing with fury. "To stop taking straight girls seriously who get off on flirting with the queer girl but really still want the boyfriend security blanket. Do you have any idea how shitty it felt to hear from my *mom* that you're letting Zander put a fucking chastity belt on you? Pretty sure you had ample opportunity to tell me that yourself last night."

"It's not a chastity belt," I mumble, as if that's any sort of defense. She's right. I know she's right. But telling her just seemed so...*meaningful*, like I was looking for permission. "And anyway, it's not like you don't know I'm with Zander, or that your mom comes up with crazy stuff like this."

"Are you 'with' Zander?" Bri's voice is even more acidic than Josh's when he asks the same question, and makes me feel a thousand times worse. "Because I saw the two of you in that meeting, and I saw the way you looked like you were gonna hurl when he said you guys love each other. Do you even know him?"

"Of course I know him. We've been dating for months. He's a nice guy, Brianna."

She laughs and turns back to the road as the light turns green. "Christ, listen to you. You *know* how much his 'nice guy' act is manufactured by my mom and it still gets to you. He's not a nice guy, Van. He's using you to keep his name in the news before the Wonder Boys go on tour. And you're letting him because you're scared."

I've never heard Bri sound so cruel, and more than anything I want to jump out of this car and run. Tears prick at my eyes, but I refuse to cry in her presence. Instead, I inhale sharply through my nose, grip the door handle, glare out the window, and pray we'll hit green lights all the way to Sugar.

Which is, of course, when we hit another red.

Bri pulls to a stop, and we're both silent for several of the world's longest moments. And then she says, "Dammit. Vanessa, I'm sorry."

I don't say anything, don't turn, just bite my lip. If I do anything else, I know I'll spend the next ten minutes cleaning smeared eyeliner from my cheeks.

She sighs, and out of the corner of my eye, I watch her drop her head into her hands. Her hair is straight tonight—a rarity for her—and the long strands splay over her arms, calling to my fingers. I turn to face her, but keep my hands where they are. A second later, she picks her head back up and meets my gaze head-on.

She doesn't say anything, but her eyes are filled with genuine regret that hits me low in my stomach. For endless moments, neither of us moves, but then the light turns green, and she doesn't have a choice.

"I'm sorry," she says again, her voice raw as she puts her foot to the pedal again. "You're right. You're with Zander, and I have no right to question why or what the two of you do. I'm sure he's crazy about you." The right corner of her mouth curls up, just a little bit. "How could he not be?"

The flip in my stomach at those words is intense and immediate, and I tear my eyes away from her mouth and force them back on the road. For someone who wanted me to stop flirting with her last night, it sure sounds a lot like she's doing it right now.

Or maybe she's just messing with me because she can. "Don't mock me," I say stiffly, watching her reflection in the windshield.

"I'm not mocking you," she says softly. "But okay, yeah, maybe I'm mocking him a little bit. I'm sorry, but I just don't buy this. At all. Why would either of you *want* to take a purity pledge? You really don't want to have sex until you're married?"

"What if I don't?"

"Then I respect that. If it's *really* what you want. But is it?"

The billion-dollar question. "I don't know," I admit cautiously. "I believe in saving myself until I'm in love. Is that really so different?"

"Um, yes? Like, immensely different."

"Okay, well, it's not like I have the ring on my finger yet," I remind her. "I still have time to think about it."

"What is there even to think about? How can you say yes to this if you're not sure it's what you want?"

Is it really any scarier than saying yes to this when I'm not sure it's what I want? The words are on the tip of my tongue, but saying them aloud...that's a whole Pandora's box I'm just not ready to open. Besides, I'm still not sure what "this" *is*. Hanging out with Bri doesn't feel like hanging out with Ally, but it doesn't feel like hanging out with Zander, either. I just know it's never *enough*. But what is it I even want? And what does *she* want?

"Hey, Van." Bri snaps black-painted fingertips. "Where'd you go? We're here."

"Just thinking," I mumble as I unbuckle my seatbelt and pull down the visor to check my makeup in the mirror. "Look, it's not that I don't get what you're saying, but Zander did make some good points. Kids look up to us."

"Yeah, and that's great, but shouldn't they look up to you for who you are and not who you're pretending to be? Don't you want to be someone they admire for ideals you actually possess?"

I dab on another coat of lip gloss, but my hands are shaking. She's right. I know she's right. My idols are actresses who persevered against racism in Hollywood and got themselves great roles against all odds. I have no idea what their policies are on sex, and I don't give a damn. Why would I? How did I let Zander talk me into thinking that matters?

Bri doesn't make me answer; I'm pretty sure she already knows exactly how I feel. Instead, she opens her door as I cap my makeup, and then she slips out. I toss my lip gloss back in my bag just as the valet opens my door and focus as intensely as humanly possible on not flashing anyone in my micromini as he offers his hand to help me slide off the seat.

"Ready?" she asks as she hands her keys over.

"Ready," I confirm, smoothing my dress down over my thighs. "Do–"

"Oh, I should just leave my jacket with the car, right?" Before I can answer, she slides it off and hands it to the valet. "I'm sorry–do you mind?"

I don't hear whatever he responds. I don't hear much of anything at all. Because the only thing my brain can process at the sight of Brianna in tight jeans and a dangerously low-cut black lace top is *holy shit*.

And just like that, I know she's right. I'm not cut out for chastity. And I'm sure as hell no role model.

Because right now, looking at her, my mind is on nothing but sin.

Chapter Fifteen

Josh

$\mathcal{I}$ can't even believe I'm doing this right now. I only half-listen to Chuck as he gives me my dialogue for the night; I'm too distracted by all the people here, about to watch this pathetic farce. It doesn't help that Royce thinks this is hilarious and, since he's twenty-one, has absolutely no problem showing up and being in these shots, getting plastered. I can see him out of the corner of my eye, probably trying to convince the blondes he's flirting with to join him in the bathroom, and it only makes this more unbearable.

And then there's K-drama. I look up at where she and Mini-Jade are cracking up at something in the corner, holding glasses of soda because they've both been expressly forbidden by Jade to drink anything harder. There are those fucking legs again. And the rest of her isn't looking too bad, either, I have to admit. It's nice to see her laughing. Happy. Not giving me shit or sulking over work or that Ally's gone. Just...her. I don't know what they're dying over, but I feel a weirdly strong desire to get in on the joke.

I shudder and refocus on Chuck just as he says Vanessa's name. "Be sure you draw attention to the fact that Wilson's not here, all right?"

Wilson's never here, I think. Not last night, not tonight. I know whatever he and K-drama have is every bit as bullshit as she and Liam were last year. What the hell does she want, anyway? She's a good-looking girl, smart, occasionally even funny. What's up with all the fake boyfriends? It's not like she's not the girlfriend type; she is *definitely* the kind you bring home to mom—if your mom's not an insane, self-centered drama queen. Why does she settle for such shit?

"Hey, Chester. You listening?"

"Yeah, yeah," I lie. Chuck's a pain in my ass, and just because Vanessa signed me up for this doesn't mean I'm gonna be his bitch. "Wilson. K-drama. Got it."

Chuck sighs. "I'm not sure it's a great idea to call her K-drama on TV, between you and me."

"Your irrelevant opinion is duly noted, boomlicker. Can we get this over with now?"

He just grins, which might be the most annoying thing I've ever seen. He has one of those chin dimples I wanna fill with my foot. "Sure," he says cheerfully. "Just get your friend Hudson over here so we can get this going."

Ugh. Right. This shit is so scripted, and scene number one requires some salivating over the girls. Of course. "Hey, Hudson!" I call out, and Royce dutifully excuses himself from the blow-up twins and jogs over with his beer. "Let's do this shit."

We let Chuck position us at the bar, and I'm grateful Royce isn't drunk or high enough yet to laugh through this entire thing. The last thing I wanna do is multiple takes. They flip on our mics, get the cameras rolling, and...

"Dude. Vanessa's looking pretty hot tonight," Royce says, just as he's been instructed. "You gonna tap that?"

"Of course not." Tonight, I'll be playing the role of Josh the Chivalrous. "She has a boyfriend."

"Her boyfriend's not here." He takes another drink from his bottle, and I know the cameras are focusing on the sleazy way he smiles around it. "Go for it, man. I'll take her friend. She's pretty hot."

I glance over at Mini-Jade. She's a little too Punk Rock Chick for my taste, but apparently she's been hiding some great tits. "I'd like to see you try."

"I will if you will." He drains the bottle, puts it down on the bar. "Come on—everyone knows you guys have been all over each other on the *Daylight Falls* set."

That's our job, I know I should say, but the truth is, on set, when she was kissing me, digging her nails into my shoulders, it sure as hell felt like she was pretty into it. She's not a bad kisser, either. She may be annoying, and it's completely ridiculous that she still lives with her parents, and I'm almost positive she's a virgin, but if she did wanna get sloppy and make out a little tonight, I wouldn't say no.

My eyes shift from Mini-Jade's tits back over K-drama's legs before returning to Royce. "Dude," I say instead, because I don't really feel like getting into all the Vanessa shit. Plus, Chuck's already given me my transition out, much as it makes me wanna hurl. "Shannah's coming tonight. She'd go nuts."

"Oh, yeah," Royce says dully. For a guy who pretty much carries a successful movie franchise, he can't deliver five stupid scripted lines for shit. Makes sense, I guess, since he's used to playing a zombie. "Uh, we should at least go say hi." As if Vanessa and I both chose to come to this absurdly shitty club independently. *What a coincidence!*

I glare at Chuck until he has the cameras cut so I can get a fucking drink before they follow us over to flirt with the girls. As I wait for my Jack and Coke, I look over and see that there are already a few guys gathered around the table, hitting on both girls and trying to get them to dance. One guy picks up his shirt; I'm pretty sure he's asking K-drama to autograph his abs.

What a fucking tool.

She's laughing, though. Mini-Jade isn't quite as amused; clearly her mother has her trained to be a possessive pit bull around her clients. Or at least one client. Funny how she always seems to be babysitting K-drama. I wonder who's watching Zander tonight.

I expect the guys to bolt at the sight of us when we approach with our drinks, but the guy with his shirt up just nods and says, "Hey, Chester, Hudson," as if he knows us. If I'm supposed to recognize him from somewhere, I definitely don't. Normally I'd just ignore him, but I'm on camera and feel like teaching him a lesson in being a presumptuous dick.

"Hey...you," I say cheerfully, making patently clear I have no idea who this asshole is. Vanessa shoots me a look, but Mini-Jade cracks up, spitting out whatever she'd been drinking. I decide I might actually like her. Then I move in close enough that he has to pull back the arm he'd been using to brace himself over Vanessa's seat, and slide in across from them, ignoring his annoyed protests completely.

"Fancy meeting you here," I greet the girls, air-kissing with both like complete tools, as if we do this every time we see each other. Royce does the same with Vanessa, though I'm pretty sure he air-kisses with tongue.

"We heard this is the place to be," Vanessa responds dryly. "I hope you boys are staying out of trouble."

"Never." Hudson's eyes drop right back into Mini-Jade's cleavage. "I don't believe we've met. I'm Royce."

"Brianna." She shakes his hand, looking like she wishes there were a bottle of hand sanitizer on the table. Good thing the girl's not going for an acting career. "We met at Josh's goodbye party for Ally, actually."

No sign of recognition, but that doesn't bother Royce. "Can I get you a drink?"

"Thanks, but I'm eighteen."

Next to her, Vanessa laughs and takes a sip of her own drink. Then her eyes widen over the rim of her glass. "We've got company," she murmurs as she puts the glass down. I know without even turning around that Shannah's walking up to the table, yet another condition of this whole stupid night.

"God, this is so many kinds of hilarious," Brianna says from behind her hand. Then she pulls a pen out of I don't even know where and scribbles on a napkin, *We should be having way more fun with this.*

I raise an eyebrow and grab the pen; all our mics are still on. *I don't think your mother would like that, Mini-Jade.*

She rolls her eyes, just as I hear Shannah coo, "Hey, Josh."

Turning, I see Shannah's not alone. How she managed to get two more of her stupid friends to join in for this train wreck, I don't even know, but there they are—Kaia Daniels, who's fresh off a stupid lip-synching scandal on *American Idol*, and Natasha Rivers, who once gave me surprisingly good head in an alley about a mile from here. "Ladies."

I'm pretty sure Natasha's eyeing me and considering a repeat performance—to which I definitely would not object—but then Shannah crosses her arms and says,

"Didn't think I'd see you here with her," jutting her chin at K-drama like she's caught me cheating.

"We just bumped into each other," Vanessa says in the fake-innocent voice she uses as Bailey on the show. "The guys were just offering to buy us drinks. I'm sure they'd be happy to grab you something."

"Make sure mine has cherries with stems," Brianna adds, giving Royce a flirty smile. "I'm a little rusty on that whole 'tying a knot with my tongue' thing, but I wouldn't mind the practice."

Royce bows as he gets up to follow orders, as if she hadn't shot him down just two minutes earlier. Can't blame him for playing along. On top of the great tits, she and K-drama are also clearly pissing the crap out of the other girls.

"Who are you?" Kaia sniffs at Brianna.

"Me? I'm Josh's tailor."

If I'd been drinking anything at that moment, I would've choked.

"Excuse me?"

Brianna shrugs. "Yeah, ya know, if he pops a button or something, he needs me here to fix it. What, you don't have one?"

Kaia eyes her weirdly, trying to figure out how to respond, as Royce shows back up, double-fisting clear drinks I'm guessing have a lot more alcohol in them than the glasses currently in front of the girls. Three cherries bob in the one he places in front of Brianna, and he winks at her and says, "Go to town. Practice makes perfect."

She winks back as she purses her lips around the straw, and Kaia looks like she wants to shove those cherries down Brianna's throat. Even though she herself is completely talentless and almost definitely slept her way onto *Idol*, nothing bothers Kaia more than other talentless people getting in her way. That I suspect Mini-Jade would've tossed that drink in Royce's face if the other girls weren't here only makes it more fun.

What the hell—if the girls can enjoy this, so can I.

"You ladies gonna sit?" I pat my lap. "There's plenty of room for everyone."

Shannah wrinkles her nose—as much as she possibly can, given it's her third. "I don't share," she says coldly. "Are you gonna get me a drink?"

"I wasn't planning on it," I say honestly. Van and Brianna crack up at that, and the fact that they're both a few sips in to whatever Royce brought them probably helps. "You should totally get something, though. Actually, could you get me another Jack and Coke?" I glance at the camera guy. "And, by that, I mean a Coke. Because I am nineteen. And drinking alcohol is both illegal and irresponsible."

Van and Brianna crack up again, and I can't help grinning as Shannah fumes. "God, you know, this is why I broke up with you for Garrett," she snaps. "You're so freaking immature."

"Garrett got arrested for wagging his dick out of a limo window," I remind her. "Pretty sure I'm still winning this contest."

She shoots me a disgusted look and turns on her heel, with Kaia following her to the bar. Natasha winks at me and licks her lips before following.

"That's so great that your friends could come join us!" Bri gushes, taking another sip of her drink and settling into the arm Royce drapes around her shoulder. "They seem really sweet."

"Shannah's great," Van says enthusiastically. "Remember how nice she was after she got caught yelling at that fan? So sweet."

"And she seems to really like you, Josh." Bri covers my hand with hers, which is cold and damp from her sweating glass. "When she's not being a little jealous of this one over here." She nudges her shoulder into Vanessa's side, and Van laughs and nudges her back harder, almost spilling both their drinks. They crack up, and I'd think they were hammered, but they still haven't had all that much.

"Well, how could anyone not be jealous of K-dra—Vanessa? I mean, look at all that natural grace right there."

She sticks her tongue out at me.

"See what I mean?" I wrap my hand around her glass and help myself to a sip. It's a vodka tonic, light on tonic.

"Of course, this one's taken," Royce points out, tipping his own glass at K-drama. "Where's your boyfriend, anyway? How come he never hangs out with us?"

Oh, shit. I'd completely forgotten I was supposed to mention Zander. Though, watching the way her face screws up at the mention, I'm glad I didn't. Bri looks a little weird about it, too, and I wonder if Jade'll be pissed that her golden boy client was mentioned around the likes of me.

"He's got a tour coming up—needs to protect his vocal chords," Van says after a minute, then nabs her glass back and takes a long drink, bypassing the straw. Around us, the song changes, and she laughs. "Speaking of which..."

It wouldn't surprise me in the slightest if Chuck was behind having the Wonder Boys' newest hit, "My Girl, My Woman," play at this exact moment. Even when he's not here, Zander Wilson is everywhere.

"We should dance." Royce tosses back the rest of his drink and holds out a hand to Bri. "I think Park's boy toy would appreciate it."

"I bet he would," says Bri. She takes one last long drink and then plucks a cherry from the glass, sliding it between her lips as she follows him out to the dance floor.

I watch K-drama watch them go, and I wonder if she really is down about the fact that her boyfriend isn't here. She definitely looks...something.

And I definitely need more alcohol.

Reaching up the back of my shirt, I flick off my microphone and gesture for Van to do the same. Chuck starts to protest, but I hold out the mic and say, "I think you guys got enough for now, don't you? Why don't you all take a break and let me get a fucking drink or twelve."

To my surprise, Chuck agrees, though instead of disappearing, they just focus on Shannah whispering in a corner with the other chicks. Whatever. I don't give a shit what they do; I just know I need a drink, and I'm willing to bet K-drama can be convinced to do a shot with me.

It takes even less urging than I expect, and we grab Royce and Bri from the floor and do a round of shots—to Zander, despite Vanessa's eye-rolling—before finally just dancing and chilling out.

I'll say one thing for K-drama—the girl's pretty damn good on the dance floor. As the Wonder Boys' track transitions into Beyoncé, she lightens up, and before long, she's filled with just the right amount of tipsy energy. People start to crowd around and watch as she rolls her body against mine, waves her hands in the air, and sings along to the music. Her voice is pretty terrible, but she's having so much fun that no one even cares.

It's kind of awesome to watch her letting go like that. Not that I've never seen her have fun before, but right now, she looks...like she's glowing or something. Royce has nudged Bri closer to make the two girls dance up on each other, and if she minds being sandwiched between us, it doesn't show. I'm certainly not complaining about the view down Bri's top, but the truth is, I kinda want them to disappear. I kinda want everyone to disappear. For weeks I've been feeling like everything is spinning, and right now, Van's hips beneath my hands, even as they rock to the music, feel like exactly the stability I need to keep myself grounded, just for a night.

Doesn't hurt that her hair smells really fucking good. Sweet. Like strawberries or something.

Fingers brush mine, and I look down to see that Bri's now got a hand on Van's waist, too. She's pulling her closer, and I'm doing the same, and we end up merging like an Oreo while Royce whistles. I'm pretty sure the cameras are on us, but I don't give a shit. I don't give a shit about anything. Right now, all I want is the scent of strawberries in my nose, the sound of her crappy singing in my ear, and her little body beneath my hands.

I don't wanna think about Chuck. I don't wanna think about my mother. I don't wanna think about my shitty future.

And I don't wanna think about what it means that I don't wanna let go of Vanessa Park at the end of the night.

Chapter Sixteen

Vanessa

$\mathcal{I}$ don't even know how many songs I dance sandwiched between Bri and Josh, watching the flashing lights and singing along. I feel drunk on pure adrenaline, though I know there's some vodka mixed in there. There are flashbulbs going off, and I know I'll see myself on websites tomorrow if I spend two seconds looking, but I don't care.

Zander would hate this.

Jade will kill me.

I don't care. About either of them. Any of it. In front of me, Josh looks like he's having every bit as much fun as I am. Behind me, Bri seems to be enjoying herself, too. Every few seconds, I feel her hair or breasts graze my back, her breath on my ear, and my brain short-circuits.

Royce must be saying something to her I can't hear because she cracks up laughing, unconsciously tightening her grip on my waist and pulling me close. My mouth goes dry, and I grip Josh's shoulders and say, "I need to grab some water."

"I'll come with—"

"Aww, were you leaving?" Shannah swoops in like she has some crazy radar detector. "Make sure you send my love to Zander." There's so much insincerity dripping from her voice I have to walk carefully to make sure I don't slip in it.

"Wait up," Bri calls, and I do. "Didn't even realize how thirsty I was until I saw you heading to the bar."

I glance at her, wondering if I'm imagining the extra meaning that seems loaded into that sentence. She's not looking at me, but the quirk of her lips suggests that I'm not.

The adrenaline is back, working its way through my system double-time. My heart thuds against my ribcage as we near the bar, and I force myself to focus on the singular goal of getting water. Thankfully, the bartender practically dives over to us, ignoring everyone else demanding his attention. We get a couple of icy glasses and sip them as we make our way back to our seats.

Neither of us says a word for a couple of minutes, instead watching the guys get down and dirty with the other three girls. I think about Bri laughing at whatever Royce had said, and I wonder again if I have things all wrong.

"You don't actually have to babysit me, you know," I tell her. "It's cool if you wanna go back and dance with Royce."

She snorts. "Thanks, but I think I've spent enough of my night being poked in the back by unwanted objects. I'll stick with you, if you don't mind."

I inexplicably feel a little weight lift off my shoulders, and laugh. It's not like that means anything. It's not like I want it to.

Do I?

"This is probably at least a little more fun than having some sort of ring ceremony with Zander tonight would've been, no?" she asks, plucking an ice chip from her glass and slipping it between her teeth.

"Oh, shut up," I say, shaking my head.

"You don't want to talk about it?"

"I'd rather talk about nuclear physics. Or Shannah's hair. Anything. Please."

Those perfect lips curl into a smile around the ice, and then she sucks it into her mouth. I swallow and look away.

It's too late. A hot, buzzing ache is already snaking its way through my body. I try to remember the last time I felt this way, but I know the truth—I never have. I've never *wanted* this badly. I've kissed Liam Holloway and Josh Chester and Zander Wilson—hell, I've hugged Brad Freakin' Pitt—and never have I felt lightning striking me from the inside out the way I do right now, with just Bri's cool breath on my skin.

"Are you down for another shot?"

Her voice is playful in my ear, promising, knowing. My brain is already swirling; one more shot and I'll be unconscious, despite the fact that I haven't had that much to drink. I don't want to be any foggier, though. I don't want to come down off this feeling at all.

I shake my head. I don't have any words other than ones too dangerous to speak aloud. Instead, I simply slide to the end of the banquette, tugging my dress down to cover my thighs, and squeeze her wrist once before getting up and making my way as calmly as possible to the restroom.

My heart is pounding so hard that I'm trembling in my stilettos as I push through the crowd. I have no idea whether she's following me, but I want her to so badly, my skin feels too tight for my body.

And just when I'm sure she won't—that I've misunderstood or misread or *something*—there's a warmth at my back, a "hey" holding a hint of question.

I barely even glance around to make sure no one's watching before I swing open the door to the bathroom and yank her inside.

"Jesus, Park." She takes a deep, slow breath. "What are we doing here?" Her voice is faint, and I almost miss it over the blood rushing through my ears. She's backed up against the door, and she grips the knob like she wants a way out. Only she doesn't take it.

"Go if you want to," I say, my voice equally quiet. I can't muster any more than that. I'm straining too hard to keep my body still, to keep from doing something I shouldn't.

"I don't." Her thumb presses the lock on the knob, but she continues to grasp it. "You know I don't."

"I don't know anything." My pulse is racing and my palms are sweating and I truly don't know—how this is happening or what comes next or any of it. "I just..." I can't say it. I can't. But I want it. I do. "Help me," I whisper.

Soft hands cup the nape of my neck and then her lips are on mine, or my lips are on hers. She made the move but somehow I'm the one in control, pushing her up against the door, gripping her wrists. Beneath me, she's warm and pliable, and when she parts her lips, I don't hesitate for a second to accept the invitation.

She tastes like vodka and lip gloss, sweet with the tiniest bit of bitterness, and it's perfect. All of it. I know it should be weird, and I should *feel* weird, but I just feel...good. And so does she. Her lips are soft and her skin is smooth and she is one hundred percent girl, but there is no one on earth I'd rather be kissing.

And I really do love her mouth.

My hands slide from her wrists to her hips, thumbs seeking out the soft skin just above the waistband of her jeans. Her fingers clutch at the stretchy fabric of my dress as she pulls me closer. It's sliding dangerously high up my thighs, and I'm not sure if she notices.

I hope she does.

She pulls back, though, just enough to whisper, "What the hell is happening right now?"

Oh God. "Am I doing it wrong?"

Her laughter is breathless against my lips. "God, no. Not at all. But...you're straight."

"Actually," I say, my voice shaky as my fingertips travel higher, "I'm not so sure about that."

I wait for a jaw drop or a look of shock or *something*, but all I get is a slow grin over her kiss-swollen lips. "I knew it."

I yank my hands out from under her shirt and step back. "Seriously, Bri?" I drop my voice as low as humanly possible, despite knowing no one can hear us over the pulsing music. "I tell you I like girls and your reaction is to be smug about it?"

"Crap, Van, *no.*" She reaches for my hand, and I let her take it, watching as she intertwines her fingers with mine. "I just...hoped. I've *been* hoping, ever since we met at Josh's party. I've imagined this so many times that at some point it just became impossible to imagine it *wouldn't* happen."

Our hands swing naturally, delicate and girly, indistinguishable except for the darker tone of my skin. "You've pictured this, huh?"

"Nonstop," she says sheepishly, her black-painted thumbnail tracing an arc over the back of my hand. "You haven't?"

"If I hadn't, we wouldn't be here."

"Oh, I think we would've ended up here one way or another." She slips her free hand into my hair and rests her forehead against mine. "But now what?"

"I have no idea," I admit. "You're the PR pro. And this is a mess."

"It is, isn't it?" She glances back at the door. "We probably don't have much longer in here, and we can't exactly go back to my place, or to yours. Even a hotel's out of the question."

I've never wanted to kick myself so hard for the fact that I still live with my parents.

Oh God—*my parents*. What the hell would my mother say if she found out I'd just kissed a girl? If she knew I *like* one? I'm a big enough disappointment to her now, choosing my acting career over college and a traditional career path. She's never really voiced her thoughts much about my relationships, but she also hasn't taken them seriously. Pretty sure that, in her mind, I'm still gonna get over all of this and settle down with a nice Korean boy someday.

I look down at where Bri's thumbnail is still caressing my hand, and a little shiver racks my body.

No, I'm pretty sure I won't be getting over this soon.

"You okay?" she whispers, stopping the path of her nail and squeezing my hand instead. "I'm sorry. I didn't mean to joke. I know this is a big deal."

I just nod. I can't say anything else. It is a big deal. I need to talk about it. I *want* to talk about it. But I need to gather my thoughts first, to understand what it all means. All I've really considered is how much I want the girl in my arms right now; I've barely put any thought at all into what it means to be...

Gay.

Holy crap.

Am I gay?

I gulp in a breath of air and step back from Bri, leaning against the sink. I need my own space right now. I need to breathe. I need to think.

Except now that I'm a step back, I'm just staring at her boobs.

I am so, so gay.

"Hey." She cups my cheek in her palm. "You look like you're gonna be sick. Maybe we should just get you home."

Except the thought of going home makes me feel even sicker. I can't see my parents right now. My normal go-to escape is sleeping over at Ally's, but even if I wanted to stay there without her—and I'm sure her mom would be more than cool with it—it's too late to call and ask. The idea of staying in a hotel, surrounded by more strangers, nauseates me even more.

"Van?"

I blink up at her. Her eyes look softer than I've ever seen them—with concern, but also, my stomach flips as I realize, with hurt.

Right. Having someone look like she's gonna hurl two seconds after you've made out with her probably isn't the most flattering.

"It's not you," I blurt instantly. "It's me." *Oh God. I did not just say that.* But it's obvious from the way her face falls that oh, yes, I did. "Okay, that's *not* what I meant. It's just...a lot."

"I know."

I can tell she wants to mean it, but she's wringing her hands, and her eyes won't meet mine. Seeing her in pain, and knowing I'm the one who did that, feels worse than everything else combined. No matter what I'm worried about and how messed up I am, the one thing I know for sure is that I really, really care about her. I can't have her thinking any less.

Sliding my hands into her hair, I pull her mouth to mine for a kiss I hope makes my feelings crystal clear. It takes her a second to relax into it, but only that. As she steals my breath completely, I tell myself that, in the end, this should be what matters—how perfect and right this is—but I've been in this business too long to forget that my life doesn't entirely belong to me. That even the personal decisions I make affect my job and my future. And given how uncertain that future *is* post-*Daylight Falls*, I know this isn't as simple as most people would think it should be.

As I'm sure Bri thinks it should be.

Either way, I know we've been missing for far too long, and I reluctantly pull back. "We have to go," I say softly, hating doing so because I'm not sure when I'll see her again. Not sure when I'll feel like I *can*.

"Oh, right," she says sheepishly. She steps to the side so she can check herself out in the mirror, and I let myself watch her readjust that absurdly hot shirt for just a second before I get to work touching up my own dress, hair, and makeup. "I'll go first, I guess. Keep an eye on your phone, and I'll tell you when it's safe to come out."

I watch in the mirror as she slips out the door, and then I apply another coat of lip gloss to replace the one I just left on her mouth. My hand is shaking like crazy, and it takes three attempts to get it on neatly. I have one eye on my phone the entire time, but it never lights up. I toss the gloss back in my purse and pick up the phone, opening my own text.

I know you're asleep, I text to Ally, *but I really need to talk. Can you call me when you wake up?*

A tiny part of me expects her to respond a few seconds later, as if she'll sense just how badly I need her, but she doesn't. Instead, my phone lights up with a text from Bri that says, OK *go*.

I let myself out of the bathroom and start back for the table, only to see that Josh and Co. have already made themselves comfortable there under the watchful eye of the camera. I don't, however, see Bri anywhere. Then Josh spots me, and I know I can't go looking.

"Hey, where the hell have you been?"

I'm still holding my phone, so I just hold it up with a little wiggle of my hand to imply I was on a phone call and plaster a smile on my face as I join them. "Where'd Bri go?" I ask, keeping my voice neutral as Josh pulls a chair over for me.

"Said to tell you she went home. I gotta say, she's a lot more fun than I thought she'd be."

Tell me about it, I think as a dull ache starts forming in my chest at the knowledge that she's gone for the night. "Maybe now you'll stop calling her Mini-Jade?"

He grins. "Probably not."

The subject turns to what it'd presumably been when I'd shown up—stupid gossip no doubt planted by Chuck and his team—and I return to thinking about where I can possibly go tonight to get some time alone with my thoughts and away from my parents. And then I realize the answer's right next to me. I kick Josh in the ankle, startling him from the conversation he didn't really seem that into anyway.

"Ouch. What the hell?" he mutters at me.

"Can I stay in your guest house tonight?" I ask, taking care to keep my voice out of the range of his mic.

He shrugs. "Sure. No problem."

Huh. Of all people, Josh Chester is the one to come through in my time of need. Just when I thought this night couldn't get any crazier.

Chapter Seventeen

Josh

After half an hour of watching K-drama jiggle one of those ridiculous legs at Sugar, I finally take her hint that she's ready to leave, and announce that we're heading out. I can see everyone's eyes bugging out at the fact that we're leaving together, but knowing that this is exactly the sort of shit Chuck wants implied, I don't explain the guest house bit, leaving it for her to protest.

Weirdly, she doesn't, and I admittedly get a little excited at the thought that the guest house was a bullshit excuse on her part.

At least until we get back to Malibu and that's exactly where she goes, with a yawn that's definitely fake and a "good night" that isn't.

Between the late hour and the alcohol, I don't even have the energy to jerk off. But I don't really wanna lie in bed feeling frustrated, either, so I head into my media room to pick a movie instead. I've just put *The Usual Suspects* in the Blu-ray player when a knock sounds at the door, startling me into completely losing my shit.

Of course, it's just K-drama, wearing the same tee and boxers she borrowed from me the other night.

I hope she's here for sweatpants.

"What's up?" I growl, frustrated to have her reinserting herself in my brain when I'd finally come up with a plan to clear her out of it. She winces, and it makes me feel sorta bad. "There's a toothbrush there, right?" I add, as if being hospitable will make me a little bit less of a dick for practically yelling.

"Yeah, thanks." She presses her lips together, and I can tell that whatever she came here to say, she no longer wants to say it.

I sigh. "What is it, K-drama?"

"I just...can't sleep. Were you going to watch a movie? Can I watch with you?"

An image of those legs draped over me on the couch is not doing good things under the shorts I've changed into, and I make a mental note to sit on the opposite end of the couch. "Yeah, okay." I step aside for her to come in, then close the door behind her. "I'm gonna grab a beer from the fridge. You want anything?"

"Just water, please."

I grab her a bottle and myself one of those noxious light beers that may as well be water. As it is, I'll have to spend hours in the gym tomorrow to work off tonight's drinks. When I get back to the couch, she's already curled up under the furry throw blanket in my favorite corner, but she looks so miserable I don't even have the heart to make her move. I take a seat on the opposite end and pop the cap off my beer.

"God, I love this movie," I say as the opening credits start up.

"Oh, is it good? I've never seen it."

"K-drama." I pause the movie and turn to her. "You've never seen *The Usual Suspects*?"

"Nope. It's old, isn't it?"

"Not exactly a classic—1995. I watch it at least once a year. How can you not have seen it?" I pause. "Wait. You know how it ends, right?"

"He was dead the whole time?"

"Wrong movie." I collapse back into the buttery leather of my favorite couch in the house. "Wow. A person who doesn't know how *The Usual Suspects* ends. How can you even call yourself an actor?"

"The movie's older than I am! That's not my fault."

I sigh. "That's a pathetic excuse. Now watch the movie. It's gonna blow your mind."

"Well, now, because you've said it, I'll know exactly what's coming."

"No, you won't. Trust me." I hit Play.

But apparently she doesn't trust me, because she spends the entire movie yelling out "Is *he* Keyser Soze?" every ten minutes or so. It's both sorta cute and really annoying, and I could not feel smugger than during the final scene when she gasps and I *know* there's no way in hell she saw that one coming.

"Gets me every time," I say as I shut off the TV. "When my uncle showed me that movie, I thought it was the fucking greatest thing I'd ever seen."

"How old were you?"

"No idea. Seven? Eight?"

She levels me with a look. "Your uncle showed you that movie when you were eight?"

"Honey, my uncle took me to a strip club for my thirteenth birthday. It's *still* more time than my dad's ever spent with me, so before you judge—"

She holds up her hands. "I'm not judging. Just trying to imagine how old I'd have to be for my parents to think that movie was appropriate for me. Probably forty. Maybe not even then."

I snort. "They do realize you're an actress, right? Like, they know you know all this shit's just special effects and whatever? Anyway, aren't you a little old to have your parents telling you what to do?"

Her mouth twists into a grimace. "I still live with them, remember? And can we not talk about it?"

"Considering this is the second night in the past week you've stayed at my place, maybe you need to *stop* living with them. It's a good sign it's time to get out on your own when you'd rather be here with me."

At least she cracks a smile at that. "Fair point. Though I'm not the only one who needs to get out. You really think clawing your nails into this house is worth letting your mom boss your career around?"

"What career?" I mutter. "I can't afford to get my own place in which I'll be able to live in the style to which I've become accustomed."

She rolls her eyes. "Josh, you're nineteen. You don't need to live in a massive beach house with state-of-the-art everything. I promise, most of us do just fine without it."

"You don't seriously think I'm going to take real estate advice from someone who still lives with her parents, do you?" I snap. It's not like I don't know she's right; I know I don't *need* all of this. But K-drama's got *Daylight Falls*. So does Liam, on top of his crazy, growing movie career. Royce has got a decent little house in the hills, and he's also got his zombie movie franchise.

This house—these parties and my reputation—they're *all I fucking have.*

But there's no way in hell I'm gonna be telling that to K-drama. Or anyone else, for that matter. Not like she'd understand, anyway.

I expect a fiery response from her, so I'm surprised when she says, quietly, "It just sucks, always being under other people's thumbs, doesn't it? Like, a billion people would kill for what we have, and I'm grateful for all of it. But I don't think other people realize what we give up to maintain these images, you know?"

Or maybe she gets it completely.

I'm about to voice my agreement, to spill the thoughts that have been bugging me for days, when she purses her lips, tosses off the blanket, and gets up. "On that overshare-y note, I think I'm gonna go to bed. It's crazy late."

So much for that. She hands me her empty water bottle for recycling, and then we say good night. It's on the tip of my tongue to ask her to reconsider staying in the guest house when I've got a perfectly good guest room in here—not to mention plenty of extra space in my king-size bed—but it's pretty clear that wouldn't be well received.

Instead, I watch her go. Only once I see through the glass French doors that she's disappeared into the guest house do I finally turn off the TV and all the lights and go to bed alone.

Chapter Eighteen

Vanessa

The bed in Josh's guest house could not be comfier, but after hours of tossing and turning and drifting off for no more than twenty minutes at a time, it's clear a full night's sleep will not be happening. When the first light of the sun starts to peek through the windows, I give up on trying, grab my phone, and let myself out of the house and onto the beach, snatching a couple of towels from the poolside on the way.

It's chilly next to the water, even with both towels wrapped around me, but it's so peaceful I decide to stick it out. I'd go jogging if I had any shoes here other than four-inch Louboutins, but since I don't, I sit and watch the few people who are, amid the seagulls and the crashing waves.

I'm gay. I can't get those words out of my head. I can't stop imagining saying them to my parents, to my friends, to the media. They sound fuzzy enough in my brain; I still haven't been able to force them out of my mouth. I'm afraid to even now. What if instead of getting lost in the waves, they get carried on the water?

I clasp my hands together around my knees, feeling lonelier than I ever remember. I hate that I can't talk to anyone about this. I hate that the person who's become my confidante since Ally left is also the person at the center of my current inner turmoil. All I ever meant to be with Bri was friends; how did that spin so far out of control? And how did it take me this long to figure out what I want? Who I *am*?

Next to me, my phone rings, cutting into my thoughts, and I look down to see Ally's name and picture on the screen. I've been dying to talk to her, but now I hesitate. I don't know how to say this to her over the phone, to tell her I'm not the person she thought I was—not the person *we* thought I was. I don't know if it changes things, but I know I don't want it to. I think of how often we've tried on clothes for each other, swum together, seen each other in next to nothing. Never once did I look at her as anything more than a friend. It would kill me if she thought I had.

Still, I need to hear her voice. I scoop up the phone and answer it. "Hey, A. Guess you got my text."

"I just did," she says, yawning. "How do you sound more awake than I do?"

"I never really went to sleep," I admit. "I'm actually sitting on the beach right now. It's pretty nice first thing in the morning."

"Are you...at Josh's?"

"I stayed in his guest house." I dig my fingers into the sand until I hit the damp layer underneath. "It was a weird night. I couldn't go home."

"What's going on?"

I can't tell her just yet. I can't. But I *can* tell her the other stuff; if anyone would understand iffy feelings on publicity plans, it's Ally. I chew on my lip and dig my nails in deep. "It's about Zander. He wants to...get more serious."

"Like...'ukelele' serious?"

I almost laugh at her mention of our "I-lost-my-virginity" code word, but the fact that she invokes it here when the reality is actually the complete opposite is even more sad than funny. "No, not exactly," I say on an exhale. "He thinks we should wait until marriage. He wants us to make a purity pledge."

"I'm sorry, *what*? Marriage? Are you planning on marrying Zander now? I mean, don't get me wrong, he seems nice, but...I didn't think you guys were quite that serious."

"We're not." I take a deep breath of ocean air as I claw up a clump of dirt and then release it. "He and Jade convinced me to think about it and said I'd be a role model, but I don't think I can do it. Jade will kill me if I don't, and I'm pretty sure Zander would break up with me—"

"Vanny, if you think Zander would break up with you for not wanting to commit to this, then he's definitely not someone you should even be considering doing this for. Please tell me you know that."

I nod, then realize she can't see me. "I do. I just... then what? What—" I break off as I hear the beep of another incoming call, and look to see who it is.

Zander. Definitely not up to talking to him right now. I put the phone back to my ear. "Sorry, just Zander calling. I'm ignoring."

"How romantic," she teases. "You were saying?"

I was *going* to say that I actually like someone else, but now, seeing Zander's name pop up, I realize I can't acknowledge anything about Bri until I clean up this whole mess with him. I need to tell him it's over and that I'm not doing this purity pledge. It's obviously not the right move for me. I never felt about him the way I should, and now that I know why, I know I never will.

"I think I have to rip off the Band-Aid with Zander. Today. I'm pretty sure Jade will fire me, but—"

My phone beeps again, and I glance at the screen. *Speak of the devil.* "I can ignore Jade, too, right?"

Ally shudders. "If she heard me telling you that was okay, she'd probably have me shot."

I glance again and realize I also have three text messages. Make that four. Now six. A cold fist squeezes my gut. "A, I hate to ask this, but...can you check CelebriTeens.com? I have a feeling something's happening right now."

"Hold on a sec—let me get to my laptop." I hear a little fumbling and then the sounds of clicking keys. "Okay, let me see...Oh. Crap."

A breeze floats over the ocean and leaves goose bumps all over my body, even the skin wrapped in the towels. "How bad is it?"

"Um, I don't really wanna answer that."

"A!"

She sighs. "It's a huge story about how you're screwing around on Zander with Josh. There are pictures of you making out—"

"*What?* I have never—oh, God. Those must be from the set. We're *acting.* Our characters hook up."

"And pictures of you guys dirty dancing from last night *and* pictures of you leaving together. I'm gonna guess there are paparazzi waiting for you outside Josh's house right now, too." She clucks her tongue. "There is a *lot* of evidence here, Van. I think you would've told me if you were, but I kinda have to ask— *are* you hooking up with Josh?"

"No! Of course not! God, A, you know me better than that."

"I thought I did! But this...Jesus. I'm still scrolling down this thing. They have pictures and quotes and all this stuff. Even Shannah Barrett's quoted here as talking about how you clearly have a thing for him."

This is such a mess. No wonder Zander and Jade are blowing up my phone so early in the morning. I hop up from the sand and make my way back up to Josh's house, needing to know if he's seen any of this yet. I don't see any lights on, though, which makes sense; Josh isn't exactly a morning person.

Either way, I have to get out of here. I have to talk to Zander, I have to make Jade fix this, and I have to make sure that Bri knows it's complete and total bullshit. Not necessarily in that order.

"I think Josh is still asleep," I tell Ally, "and I have to get out of here. But all I have is the dress I wore last night. It won't exactly help anything if I walk-of-shame out of here."

"What'd you sleep in?"

"Clothes that are obviously Josh's. No better. What do I do?"

I can practically hear Ally's brain working on the other end of the line. "Got it! What about Bri?"

My grip on the phone turns to iron. "What *about* Bri?"

"Ask her to bring you something. She can sneak it in her purse, pretend she's at Josh's house on official business or something. Then you guys can leave together, which at least ups the innocence factor a little, no?"

There's so much irony in that idea, but on the surface, I know this makes the most sense. Bri and I just need to put everything else aside for now. She's on my publicity team; she'll get it. This morning, I need her in a professional capacity. We'll deal with the rest when this ridiculousness dies down.

Plus, this way at least I can get to her early, before any of these lies reach her.

"Yeah, okay. I'm gonna give her a call. I'll text you when I get out of here. Thanks, A."

"Always. Keep me posted." We hang up, and I quickly check the text messages that have gathered on my phone. Most of them are frantic ones from Zander, who unfortunately is a morning person, and a few are seething ones from Jade. Nothing from Bri. I wonder if she's even awake.

I take a deep breath and dial her number, though a part of me hopes she doesn't pick up. If she's still asleep, it means she hasn't been exposed to any of this train wreck yet. I like to think she's still enjoying a good night's sleep, maybe even dreaming of a certain petite Korean chick. But after two rings, she picks up, her voice thick and raspy and sexy as hell. "Hey. Woman of the hour."

"You saw."

"I did. Not really where I thought you were gonna go after I left last night."

I duck back into the guest house and close the door behind me. "Bri, please tell me you know everything in that article is complete crap. There's nothing going on between me and Josh. You've been to the set, and you know that's where the pictures are from."

She takes a deep breath and exhales. "I know. It's just...you really freaked out last night, and then when you didn't call..." She laughs, and the nervousness in it is so cute, my bare toes curl against the slate tile. "God, I swear I'm not usually this insecure. You do weird things to me, Park."

"Not as weird as you do to me, Harris," I murmur, heat rising into my cheeks.

We're both quiet for a moment, letting our weirdness sink in. Then I remember I actually had a reason for calling her in the first place. "So, I actually have a huge favor to ask you."

"I'm intrigued. Shoot."

"I'm still at Josh's, and I need to get out of here so I can deal with things."

"You need new clothing and an escape plan," she fills in.

"Man, you really *have* learned a lot from working with Jade. Anyway, yes. Please. Desperately. I don't know how many more messages from Zander I can ignore. But I need to break up with him in person, like an actual human being."

"Can't argue with that," she says, and the smile in her voice puts one on my face. "I'll be there in thirty."

"Thanks, Bri. And if you talk to your mom—"

"Oh, trust me, I'm avoiding her like the plague. I got read the riot act at 5:00 a.m. for not keeping a leash on you last night. I don't even know if I still have a job."

Crap. I hadn't even thought about the fact that going rogue for a night could put Bri's job with Jade in jeopardy. "Oh, no. Bri, I'm so sorry. I'll talk to Jade—"

"Van, stop. I couldn't care less about this job. The only part of it I actually like is the excuse to hang out with you. And trust me, I'm *not* complaining about any part of last night."

Tingles. Everywhere. God, is this what it's like for Ally and Liam, or Jamal and Theresa? How do they even function? There's a ridiculous storm of crazy happening outside, and all I want to do right now is curl up with this girl and hide away from it forever.

Which is probably another sign this is all a terrible career move.

"I'm about to get into my car, so I'll see you in half an hour, okay?"

"Okay. And again, thank you."

"It's my job," she reminds me playfully. "At least for now. See you soon."

We hang up, and I stick my head back out to glance up at the main house. Still no sign of Josh. Which means I get to ignore all of this for just a tiny bit longer.

I run a hot bath and strip off my clothes. In half an hour, I'll buck up and deal with the paparazzi, and Zander, and Jade, and the tabloids. But for the next thirty minutes, I have much, much better things to think about.

It takes Bri forty-five minutes to get to Josh's, thanks to traffic, which gives me plenty of time to get anxious all over again. By the time I see her walking through the pool area, looking over her shoulder every few seconds, I know I'm screwed. That's definitely the look of someone who's just been accosted by the paparazzi. The fact that I'm the one who put her through that only makes me feel worse.

I jump up to let her into the guest house, and with the doors open, I can hear the paparazzi now. I quickly yank her inside and close the doors behind us. "Are you okay?" I ask, checking frantically to make sure no one's ripped her clothing or anything like that.

"Fine," she says with a dismissive wave of her hand. "I went through worse to bring Lana Malcolm a purse she left in a limo. But man, those guys are human vultures. Are *you* okay?"

"For now." I drop onto the bed. "But then, I've just been hiding out here, ignoring everyone's calls and text freakouts." I look up at her and smile at the sight of her System of a Down T-shirt and cutoffs. I like how comfortably she dresses; it puts me at ease. "You look really cute," I tell her, then immediately blush. It's something I've said to Ally or Carly a billion times, but with Bri, everything takes on a different meaning I'm not used to.

Of course, I've never looked at Ally or Carly and thought about how badly I wanted to kiss them, either.

Bri blushes too. "It's just shorts and a T-shirt. I was still in pajamas when you called, so I had to grab the first things I saw to rush out."

"I appreciate your hurry," I say, swinging my legs underneath my butt. "It still does not negate the cuteness."

Her blush deepens, and I feel that same buzzing I felt last night. I love that I can make her blush. "Thanks," she mumbles. "Though you're one to talk." She gestures at where I'm sitting on the bed, still wearing Josh's pajamas. "I'm not really sure I wanna give you actual clothes. Although, if I'm being perfectly honest, I'd rather see you in my stuff than Josh Chester's."

I laugh at her sour face and grab for the oversize purse in her hand, but she holds it out of reach. "I get thirty more seconds to check you out in those shorts, and *then* you may have the clothing I brought you."

"Bri!" I leap off the bed, but she twists away, laughing, and makes a show of looking me over as she holds the bag behind her back and dances away from my hands. We're both cracking up as I chase her, and I'm just reaching forward to tackle her to the ground when a shadow falls over us both and I stumble over my own feet instead.

Josh is standing at the door.

I glance warily at Bri before going for the handle and letting Josh in. The expression on his face is unreadable, but there's no way he hasn't heard by now. He confirms as much as he drops onto the bed. "So, explain something to me, K-drama. If you and I are hooking up, why do I feel so gosh darn unsatisfied?"

"Well, I'm glad *someone* finds this funny." I glare daggers at him. "This probably only makes you look better, doesn't it?"

"Hard to make him look worse," Bri points out.

"What are you doing in my house again, Mini-Jade?"

"She's here to bring me clothes so I can get out of here," I explain to Josh, reaching for the bag. This time, Bri lets go of it easily. "Who called you?"

"Who didn't?" he says dryly. "Holly's all psyched because apparently it hooked me in to some sort of Bad Boys of Hollywood photo spread. Liam texted me that it better be bullshit or Ally would cut my nuts off."

"Ally knows everything. I talked to her this morning."

Bri raises an eyebrow, and I realize she thinks "everything" means *everything*. A little smile plays at the corners of her lips, and my stomach twists at the thought of having to tell her that, no, I didn't quite get to that part with Ally.

"Oh well. Would've been fun to see her completely lose her shit for a minute, but that's probably for the best. Now I just need to deal with the five billion interview requests that Holly says have been blowing up her phone."

"Isn't Holly your agent?" asks Bri.

"Josh refuses to get a publicist," I explain, "so Holly ends up dealing with all his annoying shit. Lucky lady."

"Very," Bri agrees solemnly.

"If you're looking for a job, Mini-Jade, I'm not hiring."

"Trust me, she's not," I answer for her. "And what are you planning on saying in these interviews, exactly?"

He shrugs. "I dunno, that you're like a six, seven tops? Maybe a seven-point-five when you've had some tequila?"

"Josh!"

"Chill, K-drama. I'll tell them it's bullshit, that you're madly in love with your Bieber boyfriend, and that friends crash at my place all the time."

I try not to wince at the "madly in love" part, especially with Bri standing right next to me. "Thanks," I say, and I mean it. I know it takes effort on Josh's part not to take the jerky route. "And thanks for letting me stay here again last night, even though it turned out to be the world's worst idea and I probably should've seen this coming."

"Eh, this kinda stuff always blows over. I've been in the tabloids a billion times for all kinds of stupid shit, and then someone else does something dumber and no one cares anymore."

"This kinda shit always blows over for *you*," I point out. "Sort of like when Liam and I 'broke up' and everyone was all psyched to see him return to bachelorhood while I was the sad and pathetic dump-ee? This business is a little different when you have a dick. And thanks, but it's already hard enough for me."

"It's hard for *you*?" he says in disbelief. "You realize you're a lead in a primetime network show, right?"

"Um, hi?" I gesture at my face. "How many Asian actors did *you* see on the cover of *Vanity Fair*'s latest Rising Young Hollywood issue? When's the last time you saw an Asian actor carry a movie that wasn't about martial arts? My only shot at being in a rom-com is getting thirty seconds of one of those massive ensemble things like...St. *Patrick's Day*. So, yeah, it's hard for me, and I really don't need anything making it harder."

It's only as the last word of my rant leaves my mouth that I realize I've made up more of my mind than I thought. And when I feel Bri stiffen next to me, I know she realizes it too.

I can't come out. Not now; maybe not ever. Not if I want a shot in hell at making it in this business. Being Korean-American is a big enough strike against me, but Korean and gay? I might as well toss my SAG card in a wood chipper.

"I should get you to Zander," she says tightly, nodding to the bag in my hands. "Come on, Josh. Let's leave her to get dressed."

It feels like an extra dig, watching her walk out rather than teasing me into letting her stay and watch. Not that we're at the clothes-off stage. Or at any stage, really. *I mean, be real*, I lecture myself as I dig into the bag and pull out a denim miniskirt and black T-shirt. *It was a drunken makeout.* I yank off the boxers and slide on the skirt; it hangs low on my hips, but it fits. *Just because I liked it doesn't mean I need to make things worse by imagining it was more than it is.*

I pull Josh's T-shirt up over my head and reach for Bri's. *I'm going to talk to Zander.* I slip it on over my head, inhaling the pleasant scent of detergent. *I'm going to talk things out with him. I'm not going to do this purity pledge thing with him until things between us are stronger, and if that means things are over, then things are over. I'd rather be single.*

As I turn to the mirror, I'm feeling good. I'm feeling strong. Like I can conquer anything if I just play things right.

And then I see that the T-shirt I'm wearing isn't a plain black one after all. The letters "NIN" are clearly visible in the light. It's the shirt she was wearing the night I awkwardly reached out and touched her tummy in the yoga studio.

Seems she really *hadn't* minded.

Just like that, all my newfound self-assurance breaks. I may be an actress, but I can tell the difference between real and fake. And what I feel for Bri is definitely the former, even if I can't do anything about that.

Good thing I'm a pretty solid actress, because I'm about to put on one hell of a show.

Chapter Nineteen

Josh

$\mathcal{I}$ watch from my window as K-drama drives off through the crowd of paparazzi, refusing to get within a thousand feet of that mess while she's around. I feel sorta bad that this sucks for her, but having people banging down my door for interviews isn't the worst thing in the world for me.

Holly wants to capitalize on the interest right away, so I've already got my first interview set up for this afternoon. She's convinced that all people need is to see my face again, in connection with something that *doesn't* have to do with reality TV, and then suddenly scripts will fall into my lap, or something. I'm not sure I even want that, but at least it's something to do.

By the time I'm done getting ready, I'm already running late, but I look so damn good I highly doubt anyone will mind. Holly greets me at the studio and all but shoves me into a chair opposite Gavin Lawrence, Smarm to the Stars. A cute little blonde runs over and powders my face; Gavin's already wearing plenty. Then he smiles, and so do I, and it's on.

"The elusive Josh Chester!" The smile grows even bigger. It's like the fucking Hollywood sign of teeth. "You've been a busy man lately. First, those new Aspen ads—which look great, by the way. Then joining Liam

Holloway and Vanessa Park for an arc on *Daylight Falls*, and now a reality show..."

"I like to keep my fans guessing," I say smoothly, using a line Holly fed me on the phone this morning. "I get bored easily. What better way to shake things up than playing the field?" Aaaaand wink at the camera.

"And that you certainly are! Just when rumors seem confirmed that you and Shannah Barrett are back together, this story breaks about you and Vanessa Park—"

I cut him off with a forced laugh. "Oh, God, that. Trust me, there is zero truth to those rumors! To *any* of them," I add firmly, because no chance I'm letting Shannah's famewhoredom cockblock me. "I'm single, ladies! Come at me!"

Gavin's fake laugh in response is far more practiced than mine; I'm not sure he's ever used a real one. "I don't know that I'm buying this," he says in what I think is an attempt to be playful but makes me want to punch him in the nuts. "There were a whole lot of pictures of the two of you together, and I did hear she emerged from your house this morning after some serious partying last night..."

I take a deep, exasperated breath and think about K-drama, how distraught she seemed that morning and how paranoid she is that this'll be the end of her. It's bad enough she has to bone Zander Wilson of all people; I can't make it worse, even if I think it's funny as hell.

"Vanessa Park is a good friend of mine, and she's welcome to stay in my *guest house*—alone—as often as she wants, just like my other friends do. There is not, nor has there ever been, anything romantic between the two of us. *Off* set, that is," I add with a smile. At least Mickey Davis will appreciate the bit of promo there, even if he hates me for sullying the good name of one of his stars.

"Then why was she staying at your place at all, and not with her boyfriend, Zander Wilson?" Gavin asks, all bullshit-casual.

"You'd have to ask her that," I say with a shrug. "I'm just here to talk about my favorite subject: Me."

More fake laughter. "Fair enough. So, with all these rumors about you and his ex, is there tension between you and Liam?"

Seriously? I should've known coming here was a bad idea. I don't know how Holly envisions this doing anything good for me, but all it's really doing is pissing me off. "Dude," I say flatly, "this is getting boring. We all know nothing happened, so no, no one gives a shit—not Liam, not Zander, and hopefully none of our fans. Do you have any actual questions, or can I get back to something that matters?"

"Like what?" he asks sweetly.

I've never been a guy with much self-control, but whatever of it I possess goes into stopping myself from punching Gavin in the face. The worst part is, he's right. I don't know where I'm going from here, what I'm doing next. Without this bullshit drama, I don't even know why people would care to keep watching me on this stupid reality show. Because I'm rich? Because I'm hot? Because I party?

When I'm not the bad boy, I'm nothing.

And thanks to the fact that I'm in danger of losing both my money and my house, and given I've been far too occupied with a lone girl recently, I'm pretty damn close to becoming irrelevant.

"Nothing I can talk about yet." Being able to convincingly look and sound like a smug asshole at any moment is a God-given talent I'm extremely grateful for right now.

He perks up in his seat, obviously having bought it. "Not even a little hint for our loyal viewers?"

"Sorry, Gav." My shit-eating grin is so wide I swear even I almost believe I'm not talking out of my ass. "But thanks for having me. It's been fun."

He blinks in disbelief as I start taking off my mic, and a technician runs to my side. I was supposed to give him a full fifteen minutes, but there's no way in hell. He recovers quickly and we shake hands and whatever, and then I gotta get outta here. Preferably to get shit-faced and hook up with someone who's not Vanessa Park.

Except I don't really feel like doing either of those things. What I really wanna do, so help me God, is curl up on my couch with her for the rest of the day and watch more movies.

Oh, shit. I'm turning into Liam.

No. I will not let this happen. I'm not becoming that guy. And I'm not fading into obscurity either.

I whip out my phone, summon Ronen, and make some calls. If I'm goin' down, I'm doing it in a blaze of glory.

I don't know what the fuck time it is, but I am *drunk*. And a little high. And a *lot* horny. Thankfully, there's a redhead sitting at my feet who seems very happy to help with that last one, and as soon as I take this next shot with that guy whose name I can't remember from that movie that was s'posed to be a big deal, I'm gonna get on that.

"Enjoying yourself, cuz?" Wyatt asks smugly, taking a puff off the one-hitter in his hand. "You're welcome."

"You did indeed come through for me, my flesh and blood." I clap him on the back, then nab the one-hitter and take my own puff. "Looks like the Chester last-minute-party-throwing genes have extended your way." Never mind that everything from the alcohol to the weed to the girls were supplied by me and my guys; Wyatt's supplied something I can't these days—his little house in Burbank where Chuck and his fucking asshole staff of stalkers won't and can't follow.

I take one more puff—just enough that Wyatt's proud face will stop pissing me off—and pass it back. I pull up the redhead and breathe the smoke into her mouth.

She giggles and stumbles into me, and it's all so fucking predictable I could kill myself. But she isn't K-drama, which is sixty-nine points in her favor.

"You wanna go somewhere?" she asks breathily in my ear.

Ugh, the thought of getting up right now is not appealing. "Not really, but it's cool. We can just stay here. No one's watching." I have no idea if that's true or not, but I don't really give a shit. It's a town of fucking voyeurs anyway. They wanna watch my life? Let 'em watch. I cup her hip and pull her closer—the universal sign for "straddle me now"—and admire her tits while she gets herself into position.

"You sure about that?" she asks.

"Yeah. Sure." I nod toward my junk, impatient for her to get started.

She looks around, all shifty-eyed. "Um, I think people are—"

"Oh, for fuck's sake, forget it." I jerk my hips to the side to throw her off me, my hard-on already disappearing. "Wyatt!" I yell out, searching for wherever the hell my degenerate cousin disappeared to. "Bring me back that piece!"

"Ratcheting up the charm to a thousand, Chester, huh?"

My head whips back and I drop my jaw. "Liam Holloway, back to grace us with his presence. No fucking way." I slap him five, right into our bro handshake, and he laughs.

"Gracing the peons with my presence," he jokes. "I'm off 'til *noon* tomorrow. This is the most I've been able to breathe in months. Decided there was no better way to spend it. At least until Ally wakes up."

Just like that, my buzz goes south. Liam's my best friend, but hearing about how he has fucking *everything* right now—dream roles he's actually excited about, a girlfriend he's obsessed with, and so much money he could wipe his ass with it for the rest of his life and still buy my house—is the last thing I need. The reminder from earlier that he's already *had* K-drama, even if it was in bullshit capacity, is just the icing on the shit cake.

"Yeah, well, thanks for slumming it, bro." I peel myself off the couch and walk off in search of Wyatt or anyone else who might have weed or a shot handy.

"Hey! Chester!" Liam yells out, but I don't bother turning around. I don't need to hang out with Golden Boy right now. I need to hang out with someone who can get me obliterated. Liam's always been crappy at taking a hint, though, and he runs up behind me. "Dude, I was kidding."

"Yeah," I snap, spotting a stray bottle of vodka with blurry Russian letters on the label. I grab it and keep walking, hoping Liam will back off, but knowing he won't. "Except you're not. Boo-fucking-hoo that you have too much work and a girlfriend to get back to. Don't let the rest of us stand in the way of all your important shit."

"What the hell?" He spins me around, and I'm so dizzy I almost fall on my ass. I grab on to the nearest thing for balance, which turns out to be some chick's boob, and quickly grab my hand back with a muttered apology, because even I'm not that big a dick. "You're pissed at me now? For getting jobs you don't want and a relationship you shit on constantly, even though you happen to love my girlfriend?"

"Yes." I screw off the cap on the vodka and take a long drink. "You gotta problem with that?"

"No, that's just fuckin' dandy." He sounds disgusted, which is even more annoying. Because he has every right to be. But it's not gonna stop me from being pissed off.

This time, when I walk away, vodka pleasantly burning its way down my throat, he doesn't stop me.

Half the bottle and a bathroom blowjob from some groupie later, I teeter back into the party, looking for whoever's got Wyatt's bong, TamTam. I find it surrounded by a bunch of dudes, and I think one's Paz, so I walk over, then realize it's not him at all. The guy who isn't Paz is looking at me funny, and I can't figure out why I think I know him. But apparently he knows me, because he hisses "Josh Chesssster" in a way that makes me wanna punch him in the face.

I'm about to ask who the hell he is when he follows up with, "Heard you're fucking my main man's girl. Not cool, bro."

For Christ's sake, that's who this loser is—Jase Taylor, another one of the Wonder Boys, which probably means he and Zander are screwing on the DL. I'm getting pretty tired of this shit with K-drama. If I'm gonna take this much crap for fooling around with a girl, I'd like to actually get some ass out of it. This is just the worst of all worlds.

"What're you gonna do about it?" I ask, getting up in his face.

He flinches like the wimp he is. "I'm not doing anything," he mutters. "Just saying, it's not cool."

"You know what's not cool? Showing up at my cousin's party and accusing a guy you don't even know of shit."

"Wyatt invited me."

"Wyatt's an idiot, then, because you're a fucking tool and you should get outta here."

"Chill out, man." He shakes his head at his friends, but even through my vodka-blurred eyes, I can tell he's afraid of me. It feels good.

"No, asswipe, I don't think I *will* chill out. And if your little buddy is so into his girl, then why's she always with me, anyway?"

The other guys ooh and laugh, but frankly, I think it's a pretty damn good question. She's obviously not into Zander. She spends way more time with me than she does with him. Just because I'm not hooking up with her doesn't mean I won't. And Zander's a fucking idiot for taking her for granted.

"Dude, Wilson's gonna kick your ass," Jase warns me.

Now that cracks me up. I nearly collapse with laughter at the image of a single one of the Wonder Tools taking me on. "I'd like to see him try. Or you. Or anyone here, really." I push up the sleeves of my black button-down. "Anyone?"

"Chester, just take a hit and relax," says the guy closest to TamTam. He reaches for the bong and holds it out to me, but I just push it away. Now that the promise of a fight has been thrown out, it's all I want. I can feel the adrenaline pulsing through my veins, begging me to let it out in a solidly placed punch.

"Fuck that. Man up, Taylor. You wanna fight on your douchebag friend's behalf? Fight on your douchebag friend's behalf."

"You're the one in the wrong here," Jase says, standing up slowly. "Just stop plowing his girl and we won't have any problems."

"You're already my fucking problem," I snap, letting my fist fly. I couldn't stop it if I wanted to. The feeling of solid bone against my knuckles is exactly what I need, and as I watch him stumble backward and hear the scream of some random chick watching, I realize there's still plenty of fight in me. "Get back up, asshole. I'm not done with you."

"Yeah, you are, cuz." I hadn't even noticed Wyatt approaching, but I hear his voice right before he starts dragging me away. I don't even look at him, my eyes fixed on Jase Taylor grabbing his stupid glass jaw, but I let Wyatt pull me, because everything's gotten really hazy and I don't think I could walk in a straight line if I tried.

"What the fuck, man?" My tongue feels thick now that the fight is draining out of me, and I kinda wanna hit Wyatt, too, but I don't even have the energy.

"You can't punch people here, Josh. What the hell is wrong with you? You'll be lucky if he doesn't sue you. His face is, like, half his job."

"Yeah, well, maybe he should get some fucking singing talent, and then he doesn't have to rely on being pretty."

Wyatt sighs. "Just...go home and sleep it off, man. You've had enough to put down an elephant."

"You're seriously tossing your own cousin out of your house right now?"

"I'm seriously telling you to call Ronen and have him get your ass home. You need to take a breather."

"'Take a breather'?" I snort. "Christ, Wyatt. Who the hell are you?"

"Hey, you asked me to throw a party so you could chill, and I did. But if you beat the shit out of my guests, it's gonna be the last one I ever get to throw, so, yeah, I'm telling you to go home."

I yank my arm out of his grasp, pissed as all hell. "Fine. I'll go home. Gimme your keys."

He snorts. "Please. You're blitzed out of your skull, and you don't even know how to drive. Call Ronen."

"And what? Sit out here on your stoop while I wait for him to come? No thanks." I walk out into the street and hold out my thumb, hitchhiker style.

"Josh—"

"You're a fucking pain in my ass, you know that, Wyatt?"

He shakes his head. "Go inside the house and wait for Ronen."

But I don't wanna go back in that house. I don't wanna be near Wyatt, or Jase, or Liam. I don't wanna be near anyone talking about their jobs, or random chicks who just wanna blow me to have a story to tell their friends.

And for some reason, I decide the brilliant thing to do is just to run.

So I do.

Chapter Twenty

Vanessa

$\mathcal{I}$ have no idea what time I actually fell asleep last night. I do know, however, that I did it while staring at my phone, wishing I could call Bri, or that she'd call me. Not that there was anything for either of us to say. Regardless, my cell is definitely still next to my head when it blasts in my ear the next morning, startling me awake.

Groaning, I lift my head from the pool of drool on my blanket and squint at the screen. I don't recognize the number, which is usually an auto-ignore sign to me, but I'm so wrapped up in the hope that it might be Bri that against all my better judgment, I answer it anyway. "Hello?"

"Oh, thank fuck you answered, K-drama. I need you to come get me."

I rub the sleep out of my eyes and pull the phone away to check the number again. What the hell is happening right now? "Josh?"

"I'm at the Burbank PD. They made me sleep in the fucking drunk tank. Can you get me?"

"The drunk tank? Are you kidding me?"

He sighs exasperatedly, like I'm the one who stuck an IV of tequila into his veins. "I don't get a lot of time here, K-drama. One call, and Ronen's got the day off for his sister's wedding, so I made you it. Will you come or not?"

As if I'm not in hot enough water with everyone imaginable, I don't even know what would happen if I showed up at a freaking *police station* to gather Josh. It's only by the grace of my parents visiting my aunt this week that I've managed to avoid their wrath after all that publicity. "I can't, Josh. I'm screwed enough as it is. But I'll call Liam—"

"Do *not* call Liam. Trust me—he's not up for doing me any favors right now."

"And you think I am?"

"Hey, I think I did pretty good by you in that stupid fucking interview, didn't I?" I hear someone yelling in the background, and then Josh says, "I gotta go. Stop making excuses and come get me." He hangs up.

I stare at the phone for a full minute, trying to decide how much I care that Josh needs me. Of *course* he'd put this on me without a second thought, and of course he just assumes I'll do whatever he wants. I'm sort of dying to teach him a lesson by ignoring him and going back to sleep. Plus, I'm just dying for more sleep, period.

But I know I won't screw him over like that, no matter how badly I want to. If I really was his one call... It's not like I want to call his parents—even if I knew how to reach them—and he made it pretty clear Liam wasn't an option. I don't know how to contact Holly on a weekend, and *ugh*, Ally, *how* could you leave me alone with this idiot?

Groaning, I pull myself out of bed and drag my butt into the shower, but even washing off the grime of last night doesn't make me feel better about this whole thing. I can't just roll up to a freaking police station, and definitely not to pick up the guy who's already the center of a billion rumors about me now.

I throw on an incognito outfit of jeans, a plaid shirt, and sunglasses, but I still can't make myself move out the door. I can't do this alone, and I can only think of one person who might help me. Much as she might hate me right now, there's no one else I can call. I take a deep breath and dial Bri.

The phone rings three times, and I'm sure she's screening my call. But just as I'm about to hang up, I hear the tail end of a weary sigh and then, "Hey."

"I need to ask you a favor," I blurt, hating myself for even saying the words.

"Vanessa—"

"As my publicist," I add quickly, even though what I really need is hand-holding more than anything else. I quickly fill her in on my current predicament. "You know the shit will hit the fan even worse if I go myself. Plus, I just...I can't."

"This is really messed up, you know that?"

"I do know that. I promise, if I had anyone else to ask, I would."

She sighs again. "Lemme shower and get dressed, and I'll come pick you up."

"Thank you, Bri. Seriously. I owe you."

But she hangs up before the words are even out of my mouth.

I spend the time while I wait for her studying my lines, but I can't go more than a couple of minutes without glancing at my phone or out the front picture window. Finally, her Jeep pulls up, and I go out to meet her with all the anticipation I usually reserve for a full leg wax.

The ride to the police department is almost completely silent, minus the music blasting from the speakers, which her iPod identifies as Rage Against the Machine. I don't know any of the songs, and she doesn't so much as absently tap her fingers along to any.

By the time we pull up to the Burbank PD, I'm actually excited to walk into jail, if it means getting out of the cold prison cell that is Bri's car.

Inside, the process of waiting for Josh to deal with his paperwork and hand over the fine he *swears* he'll pay back seems to take for-freaking-ever, especially with Bri ignoring me the entire time. She doesn't even stand with me as I deal with everything, opting instead to sit in the waiting area with a dog-eared copy of a creepy-looking book that says *The Secret History* on it in black block letters.

When Josh finally emerges, he looks like complete and total crap, and I'm curious just how much he partied the night before. After years of living like this, he's got sky-high tolerance, so it must've been pretty epic. But judging by the scowl on his face, along with his muttered "Thanks, K-drama," I'm guessing he doesn't wanna talk about it. And he only gets more sour-looking when he spots Bri, who looks up from her book and sighs as she folds back her page and slowly stands to join us.

"What's Mini-Jade doing here?"

"I didn't wanna come myself," I say defensively. "I think I'm in enough hot water without everyone seeing me showing up at a freaking prison to pick up the guy they think I'm cheating on my boyfriend with, thank you very much."

"It's a police station, not a prison." He ignores the rest, though. Then he picks up his stuff and follows us back out to the Jeep.

The ride home is even quieter than the way there. Josh is so obviously in painful-hangover mode that Bri takes pity on him and leaves the radio off, which means we're stuck listening to him moan in pain from where he's stretched out on the back seat. It's an hour ride to Malibu, and I keep glancing over at Bri's white knuckles, her hands clenching on the wheel in annoyance every time he emits a sound.

By the time we get to his house, I'm reasonably sure she wants to kill me.

I expect we'll just drop Josh off, especially when he announces he needs to go inside and pass out. But when he says, "K-drama, walk me in?" I'm so surprised I can't even say no. I shoot Bri a quick glance and hop out of the car while she rolls her eyes and turns on her music.

He waits until we're out of earshot, then says, "Listen, whatever shit is going on between the two of you, fix it."

"There's nothing going on," I lie.

"Oh, please. I haven't seen this much passive aggression since my parents' last anniversary. If this little falling-out has anything to do with me—"

"It doesn't," I say, then realize I've just admitted to the fact that there *is* a falling out. He doesn't seem triumphant, though; I've obviously only confirmed what he already knew.

"Whatever. Just fix it. She's clearly the good friend you've needed since Ally left, and you need to work out your shit." He yawns, not bothering to cover his mouth. "You can even use my guest house. I know you're a fan of it." He reaches into his pocket, twists a key off his chain, and hands it to me. "Don't leave here angry."

Then he lets himself into the main house and closes the door behind him.

When I turn back, I see Bri watching us through the windshield. I sigh and walk over, and wait for her to roll down her window. "Can we talk?" I ask.

She purses her lips. "Okay. Talk."

"Not here." I nod toward the paparazzi who've been following us since Burbank. "Guest house?" I hold up the key.

Sighing, she lets herself out of the car and follows me back to the same place we shamelessly flirted what feels like a million years ago. It's a long time before either one of us talks, even after I close the doors.

But she stays, which means she wants to talk. Or at least it means she doesn't hate me. At this point, I'll happily take that.

"Thanks for coming," I say for probably the millionth time. It sounds just as inadequate as it did the first.

"No sweat." She adjusts the messenger bag on her shoulder uncomfortably, her eyes on the toes of the maroon Pumas she often wears to yoga. "I'll see you—"

"Bri, wait. Please."

She sighs, sounding utterly exhausted, and forces her eyes up to meet mine. They look so pained it makes my heart ache. "Why, Vanessa?"

The sound of my full name coming out in her voice just feels...wrong. We're not acquaintances. The mouth enunciating those three syllables has been on mine. This isn't how people who've had the talks we've had and done what we've done should be communicating.

And yet, I don't have an answer for her. No good reason why she should wait. Only the selfish truth. "Because I miss you. And I hate this."

"You made this choice," she reminds me, as if I don't know. As if I haven't beat myself up over it every second since. "You're not ready to come out, and I respect that. But I don't wanna be your secret girlfriend while you parade around on Zander's arm. I'm not Ally, okay? And I don't wanna be."

The mention of my best friend throws me, and I'm about to retort that Ally has nothing to do with this, when I realize that I am a complete and total moron. Because that *is* basically who I'd be asking Bri to be if I tried to get her to stay while I'm still unwilling to break up with Zander. Last year, pretending to date Liam for the tabloids while he and Ally were falling for each other nearly ruined both them and us. And maybe I didn't see the similarity here because Zander's a guy and Bri isn't, but that doesn't make it okay. I know that. And I'm not being fair to anyone here.

"I don't want you to be Ally," I say quietly. "I just need time. I'm still trying to figure *myself* out, and I need to do that before I can even consider letting the rest of the world into my head. Things are different when you're in the public eye. That might sound obnoxious or self-important, but it's the truth."

"It doesn't sound obnoxious or self-important." She sighs. "I know you're right about that part. It's not like I pay *no* attention at my job."

"So you see how important it is that I get it right," I press. "I *just* kissed my first girl. And yeah, I think I might be..."

"Gay?" she supplies.

"Maybe. Or maybe I'm bisexual. What if I am?"

"What *if* you are?" she challenges. "Like boys all you want, Park. It still won't fix this. I'm bi and I promise you, it's not a fucking light switch. You can't just set it on 'boy' because it's inconvenient that you like a girl right now. Widening your options doesn't change the feelings you have. Trust me—if I could lie awake at night thinking about *anybody* else, I would."

The truth in her words squeezes my heart so tightly I can barely breathe. I know my life would be so much easier if I liked Zander the way I'm supposed to. But I've tried for years to want the guys everyone else wants me to be with—guys hand-picked by my parents or Ally or Jade. And none of it mattered. Whatever label I give myself, or the media gives me, it won't change the fact that I've never felt about anyone the way I do for the tattooed redheaded girl in front of me.

Bri's face softens. "Look, I get the predicament you're in. I may have been a few years younger than you when I realized I was bi, and obviously I'm not a celebrity, but it had its moments of suck. But I'm out. I've been through the 'mess around with confused straight girls' phase, and I can't do it again. Not with someone capable of breaking my heart."

I don't respond. I can't. If I open my mouth, I *will* cry.

I can tell that she knows it. She sighs again, gently this time, and kisses me on the forehead. "You're gonna be okay, Park."

A single tear leaks out of one eye, and I swipe it away quickly. So freaking embarrassing to lose my shit here while Bri is walking out for the last time, all confident and noble and sure in what she wants. Another tear spills from the other eye, but Bri reaches out to wipe it away before I can.

I don't even know I'm going to kiss her until I do. But her hand is on my face, and her touch is so gentle, and she's so close, and I just do it. Just for a moment. And then I pull back like I've been burned, because I *know* I'm being unfair, and wrong, and she *just* said she didn't want this. But her fingers tangle in my hair as she pulls me back and it's not just me, it's her, and it's us, and obviously, neither of us is ready to say goodbye just yet.

Chapter Twenty-One

Josh

*T*he sunshine feels awful in my eyes as I let myself out of the house, but there's no sign of K-drama anywhere. Bri's car's still in the driveway, which makes me think she's in the guest house, and I wonder if she's fallen asleep. Can't really blame her, given that I woke her up at the ass-crack of dawn. I probably have to let her yell at me now, but I'm hoping she'll take pity on my hangover and let it go this time.

As if that's likely.

When I approach the guest house, I catch a glimpse of her through the glass doors. She's definitely not in bed. And then I see a pair of pale legs and I realize she's not alone, either. Bri must still be here, which means whatever their fight was, it was probably pretty bad. Not such a shock, considering Bri's the spawn of Satan. She seems okay as far as I can tell, but no one who sprang from Jade Harris's loins can be certifiably sane.

I'm still out of visibility for both girls, and out of curiosity, I stay that way. It looks like Bri's leaving, but I can't read the look on her face. What the hell is up with—

My brain short-circuits completely as K-drama suddenly...kisses her. Full on the mouth. Exactly the kind of thing fantasies are made of, except when it's the girl you want laying it on someone who's not you.

They part, but only for a second, and I don't even know how long they go on for, but I can't tear my eyes off of them. But as suddenly as it started, Bri yanks herself away and bolts for the door. It hits me a second too late that she's about to spot me, and though I jump out of the way, I'm not fast enough. Her face pales when she sees me, and her mouth drops open. For a second, I think she's gonna run, but all she does is join me out of Vanessa's eyeline.

"That...that wasn't what you think," she says. "I mean, I don't know what you saw. If you even saw anything." She buries her face in her hands. "Christ."

"Yeah, definitely sounds like there was nothing going on," I say. My voice sounds even dryer than usual, and I'm glad she doesn't know me well enough to tell something's wrong. "Why don't you explain, then?"

"It wasn't anything. It just happened, and it doesn't mean anything. We're friends, okay?"

I hold up my hands. "Sure, if that's your story. I wouldn't say that seemed particularly friendly, though."

"Josh." She bites her lip, and it looks borderline painful. "You can't tell her—or anyone else—that you saw that. Please tell me you won't say a word to her. Just forget it, okay? I'm begging you."

My eyebrows shoot up, and I realize there is far more going on here than I thought. But it's clear I'm not going to get any answers from Bri, and honestly, all I really want is to talk to K-drama, so I just nod curtly. "I won't," I say, meaning it.

"Thank you." There's so much relief in the way her shoulders slump that I can't help wondering what the hell I've missed. "I gotta run. Thanks for, uh..." I guess she remembers then that I haven't done shit but drag her out of her house to come pick me up from the cops. "I'll see ya." And then she's off, and I glance back toward the guest house.

Vanessa's sitting on the bed now, her mouth drawn into a frown. She rubs her lower lip with her thumb, like she's trying to seal in that kiss, and my stomach roils again as I approach the house and open the door. I'm dying to ask what the hell I just saw, but one close-up look at her face and I already know—Bri's the person she's into. Not Zander. Certainly not me.

A chick.

What. The. Hell.

She looks up in surprise at the sound of the doors opening, and I watch her quickly arrange her face into a bland expression she totally doesn't pull off.

"How'd everything go with Mini-Jade?" I force myself to ask.

"Okay, I guess. Thanks for that." She smiles weakly, and it's kind of heartbreaking. Christ. She is seriously into that girl. "Guessing you didn't get any sleep."

"Nah, too hungry. I figured I'd check and see if you wanted to grab some food." At least, that'd been my original plan when I came to the house. Now I don't have much of an appetite, but I'm dying to get out of this place.

She laughs, and it's the saddest fucking sound in the world. "Can you even imagine the shitshow if we were spotted out together now? God, I can't. Between the paparazzi at the police station and the whole mess with Zander...I need to go home, Josh. If I even still have a home, because I'm pretty sure the second I see my mother, she's going to kill me. All the gossip about me right now..."

She has a point that it sucks to be her. I can do whatever the fuck I want, and no one will care by the next week, but kids actually look up to her. She has parents she cares about pleasing. She has fans who aren't utterly depraved.

And apparently, she isn't who any of them think she is.

I sit down next to her on the bed as she drops her head into her hands. "The thing is, K-drama, sometimes you just have to accept that no one else's opinion means shit, you know? Sometimes you just have to do what makes you happy and say fuck everyone else."

Somehow, that only seems to make her sadder. "Yeah, well. Maybe someday I'll be able to do that, but that day isn't today." She braces her hands on her thighs and stands. "It's been quite the adventure, but I really do have to get home. Think you could get me a cab? My ride kinda checked outta here."

She doesn't offer why Bri left, and I don't ask. I whip out my phone. "I should probably go see Liam, anyway," I mutter as I dial. "I don't remember a lot from last night, but I'm pretty sure I was a raging asshole to him."

"You? Never."

"Funny, K-drama. Come on. Let's go."

We fix ourselves up and meet the cab out front. It's been a really shitty day for both of us, and it's pretty clear it's only gonna go downhill from here.

It takes a shit-ton of time to find Liam that afternoon. For one thing, the set's in the middle of fucking *nowhere*, which is exactly what they're going for, given that it's an army movie. For another, it's a sea of actors in camouflage—even guys I've known forever are looking alike to me right now.

He's sitting in a chair, looking over the script with— shock of all shocks—his abs on prominent display. He's sweaty and dirty and staring at the pages with a kind of focus I don't possess on my best day. He doesn't even notice me until I'm practically on top of him, casting a shadow on the sides. Then he finally looks up, blinks, and says, "Chester?"

"Hey." I glare at the actor next to him until he rolls his eyes and vacates his seat, and then I slide in next to Liam. "Thought I should probably track you down and apologize for being a dick yesterday. It wasn't my finest hour."

He raises an eyebrow. "It definitely wasn't, but you apologizing might be. Did you seriously come all the way down here just to say that? A text would've been fine."

"Yeah, it would've," I admit, feeling like an ass. "I don't know. I just needed to get out of my house, I guess."

"Heard you went to the drunk tank last night. And that Vanessa came and got your ass this morning."

"Also not my finest hour."

He sighs. "Are you hooking up with her?"

No, but someone is, and it's not her boyfriend. I think back to this morning, the fierce way she laid her lips on Mini-Jade, and feel a little shittier than I did a minute ago. "Trust me, I'm not. She's otherwise occupied."

"Oh, come on. I've fake-dated Van. I recognize her 'I'm so not into this' eyes. You can't tell me she's actually into Wilson. At all."

I'm not telling you that, I wish I could say, but I know that I can't. I'm dying to tell Liam what I saw, but... it'd be a douche thing to do. I know that. I don't really know what happened this morning, and even if I think I do, she's been a good friend—something I haven't had many of in life. In fact, I'm kinda standing in front of my only other one right now. So, if that means keeping my mouth shut, even on a secret this good—and hot—for once? I think she's probably earned it.

To Liam, I just shrug. "I don't get it either, man."

"So, are you planning on telling me exactly what happened last night to urge you to blow up at me and then get so piss-ass blitzed you got arrested?"

"Nothing *happened*, exactly. I just needed to blow off some steam."

He waits for more, and I don't really even know what else to give him.

"Things are sort of shitty right now," I say after a minute of silence. "I don't have any work coming up, this reality show is constantly in my face, my parents still haven't signed over the house, and—"

I stop myself before I can possibly say another word about K-drama; Lord knows I've said enough. I don't even know why I give a shit, except that...I'm bored.

I never, ever thought I would get bored of living like this. But now I get why George Clooney used to switch it up with a new constant every year or two. Hooking up may stay fun, but picking girls up? That gets tiresome as hell. The giggling, the "I shouldn't do this, it's so bad!" and now the hoping to be caught on camera as my arm candy...I don't want any of that. I don't want to start over every night; I wanna know who I'm going home with. I like that K-drama's someone I can tell shit to and then have as company in my car or while I eat breakfast. I like staring at her legs in my kitchen. I'm not in love with her or anything—I know that—but I've gotten used to her in a way I don't entirely hate.

"Do you *want* to have anything coming up?" Liam asks, brows furrowed.

"What do you mean?"

He shrugs. "I dunno. I just feel like you don't really care. Like, take this movie—you might've been able to get an audition, but you didn't even try. And this should be your thing, shouldn't it? It's a down-'n-dirty, hangin'-with-the-boys kinda thing, not to mention that it would've gotten you tons of ass." He rolls his eyes, because #LiamProblems. "But...do you even wanna act? In anything?"

I know I should be able to say "sure" easily—I mean, it's easy enough, and *Daylight Falls* was okay. But the truth is, he's right. I don't. I can't imagine a single part in the world right now that would get me excited or focused enough to stare at my script the way he does. It's not like I came to Hollywood to act; I act because I'm already in Hollywood.

And just as I realize that simple fact, my entire world comes crashing down.

"What the fuck am I *doing*?" I blurt out, because it comes to me so suddenly, so harshly, that I can't even keep the words in.

"Josh—"

"No, seriously, Holloway. What the fuck? I'm in my mom's reality show, so I can stay in a house my parents own. I do this acting and modeling shit not because I like it but because *I'm here*—which, again, *my parents*. How did I not realize that my parents—two people I barely have anything to do with—are somehow still dictating my entire fucking life?"

Liam cracks a smile. "I wouldn't say they've got all that much control over you, Chester. You *did* just come from the drunk tank. But for what it's worth, I gotta say, now that I'm doing movies I care about, I'm actually learning to love this stuff. And I have my own place, and I've got Ally. And still, I find life hard as hell. If it's this tough now that I finally have everything I want, how do you get through it having none of that?"

The question stings a lot more than he meant it to, I'm sure, because Liam's not an asshole. He's genuinely perplexed. And I guess I am, too. I don't know what the hell I'm doing. But he's right that it's not making me happy. I don't want the spotlight, I don't want to do what I'm doing, and I'm not having fun with life as I'm living it anymore.

But what *do* I want?

So far, unfortunately, there's only one answer to that question. And this morning gave me a pretty decent idea that that feeling isn't mutual.

Then again, Mini-Jade *did* insist it wasn't what it looked like. Maybe it was and maybe it wasn't, but it seems stupid now not to at least know for sure. Back when I used to enjoy shit a lot more, at least half the fun was in taking chances.

Now I just have to take one more.

Chapter Twenty-Two

Vanessa

 $\mathcal{G}$ let myself into the house as quietly as I can, praying that I'll get lucky for one more night with my parents' absence. Having a lot of family in the area means they're out a decent amount, but I realize as soon as I close the door behind me that I won't have any such luck tonight.

My parents are both waiting for me on the couch.

I don't think my parents have ever both waited for me on the couch.

"Hi," I greet them quietly, knowing I won't get any points for acting like nothing's wrong.

"Sit down, Vanessa." My father is a soft-spoken man—always has been—but it usually comes off as gentle. Right now, though, it's a fearsome kind of quiet. It's the most sure I've been that Something Bad is coming since my grandfather died. I immediately comply.

When I do sit and finally look at my mother, I can see that her eyes are rimmed in red. My stomach clenches at the knowledge I've made my mother cry, that I'm doing a bang-up job in general of hurting people I care about lately. Really not the kind of thing I've ever aspired to.

They're both silent, like they're waiting for me to kick off the conversation I'd rather die than have. I don't know what they know yet. Lord knows they've never been very interested in my career. They don't support it so much as they just don't get in the way of it, which, while hurtful, has always been the best I've known I could ask for.

Today, though, I suspect that's about to change.

Finally, I can't take the angst anymore, and I venture out with, "I'm not sure what you think you know, but I can explain all of it."

It's the wrong thing to say; the flash of anger in my father's dark eyes makes that patently clear. "Explanations no longer matter, Vanessa. We have allowed you to live this lifestyle for long enough. We said when you first auditioned that we would allow this as long as you behaved well and kept up your education."

"And I have," I burst out. "I have been so good. I've gone to family events, even when it's meant bailing on award shows. I had Ally tutor me for the SATs last year, and I did well enough–the second time, at least–to get into UCLA. And–"

"And that's good, because it's where you'll be going next semester," my mother says flatly. "The time has come for this hobby to end. You're eighteen now, and you cannot keep pushing off the future."

"I'm not pushing off anything! This *is* my future!" My mother's frown lines tighten at my outburst, and I force a deep breath to help me rein in my rage. Yelling has never gotten anywhere with my parents, and I know it won't now either. "Mom. Dad. I have a job, and it pays well, and I'm good at it. If I were a doctor–"

My mother snorts, and I wince. God, it's amazing how much disappointment I can see on both their faces right now. And even more amazing how quickly it drains the fight out of me.

"You can't even imagine how many people dream of being me," I tell them, quieter now. "Why can't you understand that? Why can't you understand that what I'm doing is important? Even if you don't think my show is, the fact that I'm doing it is amazing. The fact that a Korean-American actress has a starring role on a primetime network show is amazing. How can that not mean anything to you? It means *everything* to me."

Tears stream down my face, but they're not moved at all; they never have been. Even when they allowed me to audition, it wasn't with any hope or pride; at best, they saw it as a potential résumé-builder, maybe something to improve my confidence and public speaking. My mother didn't even watch me try out; she brought a crossword puzzle.

"It's a television show," my father says, still quiet, still stony. "Do not make it more than it is."

I *couldn't possibly*, I think, but I already know he doesn't understand. Neither of them do. And it breaks my heart. Because I do love it more than anything. I love it enough that I chose it over the first person I've ever had real, strong feelings for. If the fact that I passed on being with Bri for this life doesn't convey how much it matters to me, nothing will.

But of course, I can't tell them that. Because as disappointed as they are in me right now, I can't even imagine how much it would compound it to tell them their only daughter is not going to marry a nice Korean boy. Is probably not going to marry a boy at all.

"You can't make me stop," I say, forcing my voice above the whisper it desperately wants to be. "You can't. I have a contract."

"Your uncle is looking into that," my mother says proudly, as if her brother, a real estate lawyer, knows anything about entertainment contracts. I bite my tongue, though, because the only thing my parents hate more than yelling is sarcasm.

"It doesn't matter." I try to keep my voice respectful, but I *know* there's no way I'm caving on this. Especially not after what I've just given up. "I'm not going to quit. This is my life now. I wish you would respect it, and I understand that you don't. But I'm not quitting. And I'm not going to UCLA next semester."

"Then you are not living in this house." My father's voice is firm. "If you insist on keeping this job and this lifestyle, you're not doing it under our roof. You think you're an adult, earning your own money? Use that money to buy yourself a respectable apartment."

I should've known that was coming. In a sense, I think I did. And looking back on my conversations with Ally, I think she knew it, too. So there's nothing to do but nod and stand. "I will."

I think the steadiness in my voice surprises all of us, but for the first time in forever, I have no shred of doubt about the decision I'm making. They're the only two words I can manage to get out, though; if I try any others, I'll crack. So instead, I turn, walk up the stairs, and pull up the e-mail Ally sent me months ago with listings for brokers.

I've been ignoring it forever because it's so freaking overwhelming, but all it takes is closing my eyes and imagining the anger in my father's eyes to force me to push through. For I don't even know how long, I make myself look at listings and e-mail to set up appointments. Eventually, my exhaustion—physical and emotional—catches up with me, and I pass out right on my keyboard.

When I wake up, it's to the sound of a familiar, grating voice coming from my doorway and saying, "Rise and shine, K-drama."

I pick my head up slowly and wipe the sleep from my eyes and the drool from my keyboard. Seeing Josh Chester in my bedroom at my house—my *parents'* house—does not compute. "What are you doing here? My parents are gonna kill you. After they kill me."

"Oh, I've already been through the Park family wringer. They told me to make sure you're packing. After yelling at me for ten minutes."

Oof, well that's embarrassing. And yet I'm sort of sorry I missed it. "And you stood through that? Why?"

"Because I needed to talk to you, and it couldn't wait. But what the hell is going on here?"

"Oh, nothing big. Just my parents trying to get me to quit acting and then kicking me out because I won't." The words sound so crazy coming out of my mouth, I'd laugh if I didn't feel so much like crying. "And what's up with you?"

He scratches the back of his neck, looking sort of...nervous? If that's a thing Josh Chester ever gets, anyway. He closes my bedroom door and takes a seat on my princess bed, shoving one of the canopy ties out of his face. "This is weird, and I don't know how to say this kinda shit, so I'm just gonna say it, okay?"

Suddenly, I'm wide awake. I have no idea what he's about to say, but he's nervously picking at a nail and refusing to meet my eyes and I feel like I have no idea who I'm looking at right now.

And it's strangely comforting to see someone who looks just as screwed up inside as I feel.

"Go for it."

He takes a deep breath...and then mutters something I can't even hear. So much for a grand announcement. But for a second, the tiniest part of me wonders if—maybe even hopes—he's having the same kind of internal struggle that I am. I mean, Josh is one of the most notorious ladies' men in Hollywood, but hey, most people think I was with Liam, and Zander, and am now hooking up with Josh, so.

I don't even realize he thinks I *did* hear until he looks up at me with red cheeks, obviously awaiting a response, and I have to admit that I didn't.

He rolls his eyes. "You're just doing this to torture me, aren't you."

"For once, no. I really didn't hear you."

This seems to chill out his anxiety, and this time, he just says it. "I said I think I might be...into you. Which is weird, I know. And trust me, I wish I wasn't. But I'm feeling weird about a whole lot of shit right now, and I just needed to know if you felt the same. At all. Or something."

I'm so floored by his admission, I have no words. Zero. Which is awful, because he's just sitting there, waiting, and nothing's coming.

And then, I do the worst thing humanly possible.

I laugh.

It's terrible, and I clap my hand over my mouth the second it comes out, but all I can think is that of all times for a guy to actually like me—*like*; not date me because of a publicity plan, or to get a purity pledge ring on my finger, or fantasize about dating me just because I'm famous and they have some absurd image of what that'll be like—it has to be when my head and heart have finally realized I don't want a guy at all.

When I pull my hand away to apologize, though, the laughter just comes out again, and I have to clap it back.

"Wow," says Josh, a dark-red flush creeping up his neck, "tell me how you really feel."

That finally gets me to stop. "I'm sorry," I say, hoping it's clear I mean it. "It's just...your timing..." I shake my head. "There's just some weird stuff going on now, and I didn't expect that. I'm sorry."

To my surprise, the corners of his lips tug up in a know-it-all little smirk. "You really do like her, don't you?"

My entire body goes cold. "What are you talking about?"

"Don't freak out, okay? But I saw you, uh, with Mini-Ja—um, with Brianna. I wasn't sure if that was a one-time kiss thing or—"

"Shh!" Before I know it, I'm jumping out of my desk chair and clapping my hand over his mouth. "Josh, *please*. You can't tell anyone about that *ever*, okay? If my parents heard you say that—"

He pries my fingers off his face. "Okay, okay, I'm sorry," he says, keeping his voice low. "It was more than a one-time thing, huh?"

I swallow hard and nod.

"You like her?"

I nod again, feeling the lump in my throat grow.

"And it's pretty clear that's mutual."

I nod again.

"But..." He spreads out his hands, as if the fact that that hasn't translated into us being together right now is incomprehensible.

"But she's a girl," I whisper. "And so am I."

"So you're a lesbian, K-drama, not an axe murderer. Why do you say that like it's the most horrible confession on earth?"

"Because it may as well be, and you know it!" My voice heightens a little as I blurt that out, and I drop it back down to a whisper. "I have enough stacked against me as an actress, and enough stacked against me with my parents, too. I can't add this on top of everything else. I'd never work again—"

"Come on, that's not true. We've seen plenty of actors come out and continue to get work."

"Oh, please—they almost never get as much as they did before. And when they do, it's always some white guy or girl who already has so many acting credits that no one gives a shit. I mean, I don't think they'll kick me off *Daylight* or anything, but what if they do? What if fans are so pissed that they revolt and I get tossed off?"

"Then they're assholes, K-drama! What do you want me to say? Anyone who doesn't want you to be happy with who you are is an asshole. Fuck pleasing everyone else. You only live once. Who are you gonna do it for?"

"It's not that easy, Josh. I *want* to keep acting. I want my career. I want to make it here. Maybe I can say screw it and get Bri back—which at this point is a *big* maybe—but if I lose what I wanna do with my life, then I'll just be unhappy in a different way. And how long would Bri even wanna be around that?"

He sighs heavily. "So, basically, no one gets what they want—not me, not you, not her, not your parents. We're all just fucked."

"Well, that's not entirely true. Liam seems to be doing A-OK."

We both laugh. "Fucking Holloway," Josh says, but there isn't any anger behind it; I take that to mean that at least things between them are better now. "Well, I really hope you figure things out." He flicks one of the ribbons tying my canopy to a post. "She seems like a cool girl, especially considering what a train wreck she could've been, with those genes. And it's nice to see you happy."

I lean over and peck him on the cheek. "Thanks, Josh. That's really sweet. Especially considering..." I gesture between us.

He laughs. "Yeah, well, I had a feeling what your answer was gonna be, but I'm making some changes and I just didn't want to leave any loose ends." He braces his palms on his thighs and stands. "And on that note, I should head out and let you finish dealing with this crap." He glances at my computer screen. "Hell, I should probably go do the same thing. But until then..." He pulls a keyring from his pocket, jiggles a single key from it, and presses it into my hand. "The guest house. Don't know how much longer I'll have it, but it's yours while I do. Not like anyone else really uses it, anyway."

"Josh—"

"It's a temporary solution, but it's something," he says with a shrug. "I'll see you around, K-drama."

"Thank you."

He nods and walks out, leaving me staring down at the imprint of the jagged metal in my hand and wondering when Josh Chester became the on-site best friend substitute I'd been looking for.

I don't end up using the key. It just feels wrong, now that I know Josh's feelings and he knows mine. I do, however, find a place that week—a temporary thing, while I look for something that feels a little more like home—and move in the next. It's exhausting, doing it all around filming the show, and obviously my parents don't help, but it's got some basic furniture and Carly and Jamal help me bring over some clothing and pictures and stuff.

At least it's something to focus on while the press analyzes my life. I've made as many statements as possible that Josh and I are just friends and that Zander and I are on very different schedules with all that's going on in our careers and blah blah blah, but I have no idea if it's helping.

The one thing I *have* done is break things off with Zander behind the scenes. It's glaringly obvious that "relationship" was never going anywhere, and while there's plenty I'm confused about right now, my feelings for him aren't in that category. Nor are my feelings on that purity pledge. I wish I could say I did it the mature way I'd originally planned to, with an in-depth conversation to discuss our feelings and goals and whatever, but the truth is, I sent a lame-ass I *can't date you anymore* text and then deleted every one of his responses. The only reason Jade hasn't ripped me a new one yet is because I haven't told her, and I'm guessing Zander hasn't either. Like, he thinks I'm just on my period and will come to my senses eventually or something.

No, seriously. He actually said that. In a text.

Meanwhile, I haven't spoken to Bri since that day at Josh's house. I'd desperately hoped some time apart would help me forget about her, but if anything, it's only made getting my own place even lonelier.

By Thursday of that week, I'm feeling lower than low. I'm off, but the thought of leaving the house, even for a spa day or something, fills me with anxiety. Plus, I'm feeling a little gross and sluglike, especially after non-stop takeout. Finally, the idea of going to yoga pops into my head. I haven't been in weeks, and I could definitely use a night of losing myself to meditation.

I check the time on my phone. If I change and head out right now, I should be able to make the five o'clock session. I usually prefer to go at night, when it's cooler outside and traffic is less crazy, but if I don't get out of my house soon, I'll go nuts. Plus, at this hour, at least I'm guaranteed Bri won't be there.

The simple act of changing into my yoga clothes makes me feel better already, and when I get to the studio, I know I've made the right choice. This is exactly what I need right now, for both my mind and body. This is perfect. This is—

A huge mistake. Because the first person I see when I walk inside is none other than Bri. And she's talking to a tall, athletic-looking blonde I know is her ex-girlfriend within two seconds of seeing them interact. The blonde flicks Bri's ponytail in a way that makes it clear she's done it a million times before, and Bri laughs. God, I've missed the sound of that laugh.

I so badly want to run, but too many people have already spotted me, and they're already whispering. I can only imagine how much worse it would be if I left. Then Raoul calls everyone to attention, and everyone, including Bri and her Amazonian ex, get into place; I have no choice but to do the same.

He gives me a little smile and nod of recognition, and that's when Bri looks up into the mirror and spots me. The smile on her face drops, but she doesn't look away—not immediately, at least. I try to smile at her, but my lips won't curve, and eventually we both give up the half-ass effort and begin our deep breathing.

It's too late, though. Now that I've seen her, I can't clear my head. I can't think of anything else. All I can do is move into position after position while sneaking looks at her in the mirror. She never catches my eye, though; unlike me, she's focused. Peaceful.

Her ex, though...she seems to be doing the same thing I am. I can't help wondering why they broke up and just how permanent it is. It hadn't occurred to me that Bri might be here to reunite with her, that she could be over everything that happened with us so quickly, but really, what reason did I give her to do otherwise? Why *shouldn't* she find happiness with someone who can give it to her?

And if I won't, why does the idea of seeing her with someone else make me feel like there's a tornado swirling around my insides?

God, watching her hurts. I try to stop, and I can't. I can't pull my eyes from the drop of sweat rolling over her tattoo and down the back of her blue Radiohead tee. I can't not follow her graceful limbs shifting from pose to pose. Even when I close my eyes, I see her behind my lids.

Like I said to Josh, I know choosing her is just choosing one happiness over another. But when I'm with her—laughing, talking, kissing, dancing, even just swirling our hands in the sand on the beach—I never feel like I need anything else in the world. If acting's just as fulfilling, why is there such a huge hole in my heart at the sight of her?

Class is over before I know it, and as I chug my water, I watch the blonde turn to Bri. She says something to her and gives her a hug, and I hold my breath as I think, *Please don't leave together. Please don't leave together.* The blonde walks out herself, thankfully, and I release a sigh as soon as she's gone.

But my relief is short-lived when I see that Bri's just about ready to leave, too. And I know then that watching her walk out the door without a word will kill me. Even though I shouldn't, I say, "Bri, wait. Please."

She does, but she looks pretty pissed about it. We're both silent as everyone else files out, and only when we're alone does she speak.

"What are you even doing here?" she asks, her voice taking on an edge she's never used with me.

"I didn't think you'd be here," I admit. "I needed to do some yoga to clear my head, and I'm off today, and I know you don't usually come to the five o'clock because..." I flip a hand toward the door. "So, um, does that mean you and she are, um..." I can't even say it, but I know she knows what I mean.

"Vanessa, we really shouldn't be talking about this."

It feels like being punched in the gut, hearing her say that, all but confirming my suspicions. "I know," I say. "I'm sorry. I don't mean to make things weird. It's just that I feel like I'm disappointing everyone on earth lately, and it sucks, but you...it's the one that really kills me. I hate that I hurt you. I hate that I ruined any chance of anything happening with us. I mean, I still don't have everything figured out yet, but I guess I was holding on to the thought that it was still a possibility. If you're back with her—"

"I'm not." She sighs, fiddling with the sleeve of her T-shirt. "I mean, I guess she's still interested or whatever, but it isn't mutual. I didn't come to this class to see Amanda. I came because I didn't care about seeing her anymore." She laughs bitterly. "I started going to the late class to avoid her, and now I'm back here to avoid you. Maybe I just need to take up a new hobby."

My relief at the knowledge I haven't lost her completely is so strong that I almost lean over and kiss her right then and there. I know I can't do that, but I need to acknowledge the fact that there's still something between us. That I still feel it, too.

And so, without even thinking about it, I place my hand on that tiny little curve of belly.

She winces. "God, I hate when you do that. Do you just enjoy pointing out the squishiness?"

"I love your body," I rasp, admitting what I couldn't the first time I did this. "I think it's so sexy. I wish you saw it the way I do."

"You don't think that," she mumbles, casting her eyes downward.

"Of course I do." Now it's my turn for a humorless laugh. "I think that way, way more often than I should. Trust me." I drop my voice, and I don't realize just how honest I'm going to be until the words push themselves out of my mouth. "I wonder what it would be like to be with that body—with you—every freaking day."

She just shakes her head, but I can see tears forming in her eyes, and I feel them forming in mine, too. Because it doesn't matter that I feel this way. It doesn't matter if she feels the same. These are just words; I've already given up any opportunity I had to put anything behind them.

"You can't say things like that to me," she says, her voice faltering as a tear falls onto her shirt, and I know she's right.

"I'm sorry. God, I'm sorry." I take my hand back, wishing I had a pocket to stuff it in or something. "I just moved in to a new place, and I think I'm a little stir-crazy, and being dumb, and...I should go. I'm sorry."

I don't give her a chance to respond before I rush out of the studio and to my car. But I can't drive away just yet. Not until I give my breathing a chance to calm down and my tears a chance to dry up. Which is gross, because I'm just sitting in my own sweat, but I don't even care. I don't care about anything right now except—

"Hey!" I look out the window and see Bri jogging up to the window, which I immediately roll down. "You're still here."

"I'm still here."

"I was thinking..." She nibbles on her lip for a few seconds, and I can't help watching her do it. Which I'm pretty sure she notices. "I mean, you had me all curious about your new place." She squeezes the back of her neck. "I'd love to see it. And maybe we can talk. There are some things I probably...we should talk."

There is so much I don't know about what's happening with everything right now, but if there's one thing about which I'm absolutely, positively certain, it's that I want to be alone in my apartment with Bri. "I'd love that," I say softly.

"Just let me shower and change, and I'll be there soon. Text me where to go?"

"I will."

I watch in the rearview mirror as she gets behind the wheel of her Jeep and pulls out of the lot, and then I text her the address with shaking fingers. As I start off toward my new home—imagining her in it—butterflies take flight in my stomach.

I might be leading the way, but I have no clue where we're about to end up.

Chapter Twenty-Three

Josh

The only place I hate being more than my parents' house is at one of my mother's stupid friends' houses. But that's exactly where I am tonight, wasting an Yves Saint Laurent tux on a bunch of walking Botox injections, with cameras at my back. Unsurprisingly, Marsha's old costars are every bit as vapid and fame-whore-y as she is, and Lisa Torres had no problem inviting Chuck and the dick-replacements he calls cameras into her home for her bullshit "Save the Children" charity ball thing.

"I saw your interview with Gavin Lawrence the other day," Lisa's daughter Clarabel says, cornering me by the hideous modern sculpture in the living room I'm hiding behind to browse porn on my phone. "You were funny."

"I wasn't joking about anything," I reply without looking up.

She giggles. "There you go again."

Christ. The only reason I'm here at all is because it's the first time my parents have been together in the same room since my little epiphany that I want out of Hollywood—Marsha's been off at some spa for two days, which I'm sure made for scintillating reality TV, and my dad's been practically sleeping at the office, which is nothing new. Even now, he's on a conference call in the Torres' study, and I'm running out of patience with waiting.

"Clarabel, honey, can you scooch two steps to the left?"

Running out of patience with the camera guys dictating every move, too.

Apparently Clarabel's A-OK with it, because she "scooches" two steps, then resumes blathering while I scan the room for either my mother or a passing tray of drinks—they probably have about the same alcohol content by now.

"Josh, could you focus a little more on Clarabel? You're coming off distracted."

"That's so weird, because I'm not—oh, look, a bird. Gotta run." I step around both Clarabel and the camera guy and start looking for my mother in earnest, pausing only to grab a baby lamb chop from a waiter walking by. Finally, I spot the red sequin dress she's about a decade too late for in every way.

My father's not with her, but I don't care anymore—I've had enough. "Mother," I say with a smile, taking her elbow and nodding at Richard and Cara Anselm, both of whom are rumored to be banging their pool boy.

"Hi, sweetheart! Richard, Cara—you remember Joshua."

We exchange inane pleasantries for the camera, and I wonder how they're possibly going to make this interesting for viewers. And then I realize it's not my problem, and I don't care. "Can I talk to you?" I ask her.

Her eyes flicker over to the cameras, and it's clear they have every intention of following us. "Is everything all right?"

Yes, because now, suddenly, all of America will buy you as a doting mother, Marsha. "Fine. Just need to talk to you. Not to *you*," I add pointedly to the camera guy.

He shrugs, but he doesn't move the camera off us, and there isn't really anywhere in this place they won't follow. *Fuck it.* I pull her into the emptiest corner I can find, letting them film us the whole time. They'll edit out most of this, anyway. "I don't wanna do this anymore."

"We talked about this, Joshua—"

"Not really. I mean, I never *wanted* to do this stupid show, and you know that, but I don't wanna do *any* of this. I don't wanna be on TV. Or in movies, for that matter. It's time for me to go...do something."

"Like what?" she asks, her concerned-mother tone reminding me the cameras are still very much rolling. I feel like I'm in Shannah's awful preachy family dramedy. At least she's not here for any of this; I haven't seen her since the interview with Gavin in which I declared myself single, resulting in tabloids everywhere proclaiming she got dumped on national television.

"Like get out of Hollywood for a while. I don't know what. I just know I'm over this place."

"You're 'over' it?" She crosses her arms. "You are such a spoiled—" She stops and turns to the camera. "Can I please talk to my son in private?"

"Nah, let 'em stay," I say gleefully. "We *are* supposed to be opening our hearts to America, aren't we? You were saying?"

Her jaw clenches and it's kind of great, but she doesn't speak again, and finally, the camera guy gives up and declares he's taking five. She waits until he's gone and then turns on me. "Do you realize how incredibly ungrateful you are? I would've killed for everything you have. When I was your age—"

"You were clawing your way over here. Trust me—I know. But this was your choice, not mine."

"Are you honestly pretending you haven't enjoyed the fruits of your father's and my labor?" I could swear the woman is about to spit fire. "I know all about your extravagant parties at the beach house, Joshua. We've let you do whatever you've wanted for years now, and we've bankrolled it all without a word. Don't you feel any obligation at all?"

"I might have if you hadn't blackmailed me," I remind her, but a little part of me actually feels...guilty, which is decidedly not a Josh Chester emotion. She has a point. Sort of. But that doesn't mean I should have to put my life on display. "But you have to understand where I'm coming from. Don't you ever want a break from this? Don't you ever want to get out of here?"

"I *come* from 'out of here,' Joshua. I promise you, it's not better out there. You think you know, but you have no idea."

"Of course I have no idea!" I explode. "This is all I've ever done! I never got to think about whether it was what I want. But I *know* I don't wanna do *this* shit."

"Keep it down!" she whispers fiercely. "And stop thinking you're so above it all. For your information, this 'shit' is an incredibly rare opportunity. All you had to do was let a few cameras follow you around while you live your life. You make it sound like that's the hardest thing in the world. You have no idea what is to really work. You've never served plates of grease to truckers who try to stick their hands up your uniform, or walked miles in the mud because your family's only car broke down. You should be thanking your father and me every damn day that this is all you know."

I can't even remember the last time I heard my mother acknowledge her life before Hollywood, and I'm so stunned by it now, I don't even know what to say.

Of course, Chuck does. "That was *great*," he says, emerging from I don't even know where with a huge smile on his punchable face. Marsha turns flaming red at the realization that this entire conversation was caught on camera, and I almost can't blame her.

Almost.

Because this is what she signed on for. This is what she signed *me* on for. And it's ab-fucking-surd.

"Unfortunately, the lighting isn't great in this corner," Chuck continues, as if he hasn't just interrupted the most honest conversation I've had with my mother in years—maybe ever. "Let's try this again in a separate room. Yvette, you can be sitting on the couch and Josh can come find you?"

"Dude, are you kidding with this shit?" I demand. "We're not—"

"Fine," Marsha says flatly, all the fight draining from her face. "Let's go. There's a den I'm sure Lisa will be happy to let us use."

Of course she's on board. Of *course* she is. I open my mouth to blast them both, but Chuck cuts me off. "Hey, Josh, can I talk to you for a sec?"

I glance at Marsha, who's already smoothing down her hair for the reshoot, and roll my eyes. "Whatever." I'm bolting straight out of here to get blitzed, anyway, so may as well hit rock bottom first.

He waits until the camera guy has Marsha out of earshot, then says, "So, you're thinking of hitting the road, huh?"

"Do people seriously still say that?"

Chuck laughs. That bastard always laughs. It's maddening. "Where is it you're planning on going?"

"What's it to you?"

"What if I said I thought we could work something out?"

"I'd say I highly doubt it."

"Look, Josh, let's be real for a minute. I know you can't afford to send yourself on some world tour right now, and Mommy Dearest ain't gonna help you after you get this show canceled, which is obviously gonna happen without you in it."

"What's your point, Chuckles?"

"We start with six episodes. Just Josh Chester being Josh Chester, giving a glamorous insider look at some of the most gorgeous locations in the world. You get your travel budget, and we get the stuff that's actually been working for this show."

"You're out of your fucking mind."

"Am I?" He raises his eyebrows.

"Yes. You are."

But I don't walk away.

And neither does he.

And despite myself, I grin.

And so does he.

And I wonder which of us just made a deal with the devil.

Chapter Twenty-Four

Vanessa

$\mathcal{I}$ clean up as much as I can while I wait for Bri to show up, but the truth is, there isn't much there. I hate how unsettled my apartment looks. When I walked Ally around it on FaceTime, she said it looked a little serial-killer-y, and now that's all I can think. The only décor is a couple of framed pictures on the end tables and a couple of my favorite detective novels on the lone bookshelf. I couldn't fit much into my little car, so I let clothes take top priority, but now I wish there was some semblance of personality here.

Something to make Bri wanna stay.

I don't even have any food to offer; there's nothing in my fridge but mustard. But after half an hour, I start to think I'm worrying over nothing; she's not going to show up. Somewhere in between when we left yoga and now, she changed her mind and realized my mess of a life and immature, inexperienced ass aren't worth it, and—

Buzz.

I wipe my palms on my denim mini and answer the door, my insecurity about my apartment increasing by about a billion. But when she walks in without saying anything and drops onto the ugly beige couch that came with the place, I realize even when she looks around, she isn't really seeing anything at all. I take a seat opposite her, on the overstuffed armchair that's become my only happy place in the apartment, and curl my legs up underneath me.

"Do you want a drink or anything?"

She lifts her water bottle. "I'm good, thanks." She doesn't drink from it, though. She just picks at the label, her eyes on the threadbare rug, her lips pressed together. "You never asked about when or how I came out."

"I figured you'd tell me when you wanted to. It seems like the kind of thing that should come out in its own time."

"I guess it's time," Bri says wryly, the corner of those lips that haunt my brain curling up just a little. She catches herself picking at the label and stops, lifting her eyes to meet mine. "I was a sophomore. I was dating a guy, and we were fooling around a lot, and I liked him okay. But the truth was that given the choice between hanging out with him and hanging out with my best friend, Candice, I chose Candice every time.

"At first I thought I was just being considerate, making sure not to choose a guy over my best friend or whatever. But then we'd be watching a movie, and all I could think about was how badly I wanted to slip my arm around her. When we were walking around, I'd just find myself staring at her hand, wishing I could take it, wanting us to be some sort of...unit or something. I just wanted more."

I know those feelings. God, I know them. Even now, I look at all the empty space on the couch next to Bri and wish I were filling it, lying in her lap while she tells me this. To hear her talk about having these feelings for another girl burns me with jealousy, but I also know Bri's never mentioned Candice, even casually, which suggests this story doesn't have a happy ending.

Her fingers return to the label on her water bottle, absently picking. She obviously doesn't like reliving this, but it seems important, so I try to help it along. "So you tried something?" I ask gently. "And she rejected you?"

Her responding laugh is filled with so much pain that I want to hunt Candice down and destroy her. "Nope," she says with an edge to her voice that could shred that label into ribbons. "She did not reject me. She kissed me back that day, and the next day, and the next. And after every time, she would have some sort of crazy freakout about it—*oh my God! What are we doing? I'm not gay!*—and then it would just be more of the same. I'd promise myself that I'd stop hanging out alone with her, stop putting myself in these positions, but I couldn't help it. She'd get drunk and leave me these voicemails begging me to come over, and I would. Every damn time."

"All while you were dating that guy?"

"I broke up with him when I realized he was no longer the one I was constantly thinking about kissing. But as far as Candice goes, that was somehow the worst thing I could've done. She thought that was psycho-extreme, and that it meant I was a lesbian and obsessed with her. For some reason, everything was okay as long as I liked guys and she was my one random exception, but when she thought I didn't like them at all anymore, somehow that changed everything."

"But aren't you bi? I mean, *don't* you like guys?"

"I am, and I do, and the fact that she fucking erased that—that she acted like I'd been living some lie with exes I'd genuinely liked—didn't exactly endear her to me, either. But she flat-out hated that I liked girls, and I didn't *want* the fact that I also like guys to make it better. I wanted her to understand that I wanted *her*, but she was so hung up on what it all *meant* instead of how it all *felt* and..." She exhales deeply. "Anyway. We had a big blow-up and stopped talking. She told our friends that I was gay and had come on to her and..." She waves her hand. "I mean, you can imagine."

"And you didn't tell them the truth?"

She shrugs. "I guess I could have, but the shit that went down between me and her seemed so secondary to what I'd figured out about myself. And I do like girls. I didn't want to take that back. I didn't wanna be all confused and freaked out like she was. I wasn't gonna pretend about anything like she did. And I haven't." She takes a deep breath.

"But I can't be with pretenders, either. I can't be with girls who are confused and freaked out. I get that you are and why you are, and I swear I'm not judging you. But I can't step backward into that life. Not even for you."

"I understand," I say softly, and I really, really do. I don't want to be that confused girl. I don't wanna be freaked out. Hearing this only makes me crazier about Bri, for being out and proud about who she is. I want to be that girl, too, and I hate that this is a thing about me no one except Josh knows. "I haven't told Ally," I admit. "But I will. Whether I come out publicly or not, I'm going to tell her."

Bri puts down the bottle and wraps her arms around herself, looking more fragile than I've ever seen her. "The thing is, Van, if you do, you'll never be able to pretend this never happened. She'll always know you're faking it whenever you're out with Zander or whoever. You can't go back with an 'oops, never mind.' That's how it is."

"I know. That's sort of the point." I run my finger over the bumpy seam of the armchair, following the path with my gaze. There's no way I can look Bri in the eye for this. "But Ally and I have a thing about our, um... our firsts. We weren't even speaking last year when she lost her virginity to Liam, and she still told me immediately. And I know I'm screwing everything up, and that I have no idea where to go from here, but the fact that I've found someone I'd *want* to be my first... that's the kind of thing we tell each other." I snort a little as I dig a nail under a loose stitch. "Guess I really don't believe in the whole 'purity before marriage' concept. For me, I mean."

There's no response from the couch, and my heart sinks as I wonder just how badly I've freaked her out with that. But it's out there, and what's more is that it's true. I want to be with Bri with every fiber of my being, and though I know it's not in our future, the fact that I feel that way at all just seems so incredibly... significant.

Finally, the silence becomes too loud for me to bear, and I look up to see her staring back at me. She doesn't look horrified, or repulsed, or even scared.

She looks awed.

"That's really how you feel about me?" she asks, so quietly I can barely hear, but just loud enough to raise goose bumps all up and down my body.

"I'm not trying to push you into anything by saying that," I add quickly. "I know why you don't want to be together, and I get it and respect it, I promise. But I am so, so tired of pretending. I know it's selfish, but just this once, I need to be honest about how I feel. Even if this is the only time I get to say it. I need you to know how I wish things were and how much I care about you and—" *Want you.* I can't say the words, but I hope they're coming out loud and clear. Judging by the way her cheeks flush and those light-green eyes smolder, I'm thinking they do.

"Thanks for that." Her voice is still so soft, so quiet, I have no idea what she's thinking. And then the look in her eyes shifts, like she's made up her mind about something, and she stands.

I know I'm watching her leave for what's probably the last time, and there's a distinct dagger-in-the-heart feeling as I walk her to the door. "I'm sorry," I can't help saying for the millionth time as I follow behind.

Her hand reaches for the knob, but she doesn't turn the handle; she turns the lock. "Don't be," she says, taking my hand and twining her fingers with mine. "Please, please don't be." And then she wraps her other arm around my neck and kisses me so deeply that everything else on my shoulders—on earth—falls away. And then I'm walking backward toward my bedroom, pulling her as our lips meet over and over, taking care to make sure I'm using only enough force to guide and none to pressure.

We slip onto my bed easily, like it'd been waiting for us, like this had always been the plan.

"Is this okay?" she asks softly, and I'm so drugged from kissing her that it takes me a few seconds to realize she's talking about her fingers, trailing down my body, gently stroking every curve on their way down.

"Uh huh," I manage as the tip of her nose brushes my earlobe, her breath warm on my neck. Her mouth covers mine again, and God, when did making out get so dizzying? I swear, I've done this a million times, but it's never felt like this—not with Zander, not with anyone.

Now that she's drawn my attention to her fingers, I can't help noticing everywhere they travel–up my shirt, over my bra...every touch is so slow, so gentle, so careful. It feels like she's afraid I'll bolt any second, change my mind, and declare that I don't like girls after all.

I shift on the bed, trapping her hand in my shirt but freeing my mouth to speak. "Bri, I want this. I *mean* this. You know that, right?"

She bites her lip, smiling sheepishly. It's adorable. But I want to be the one biting her lip. "I guess it still feels a little surreal. And scary."

My eyebrows shoot up. "You're scared? Hi, you're the one who's done this before."

"Yeah, and you haven't, which is kind of a big deal," she says softly. "I just wanna make sure you're okay."

"I'm okay."

"Okay, then." She smiles against my lips, and then we're kissing again, and her hand slides back down my shirt to tug at the hem. We break for her to pull it over my head and toss it on the floor, and I do the same with hers, taking the time to graze her skin, her curves, that tiny little tummy that's such a turn-on I can barely breathe. All I can think is how soft this all feels, how different, how perfect. So perfect I forget to be nervous when she unhooks my bra and slides it down my arms. So perfect I don't even have a moment to be self-conscious when she looks at me–really looks at me–and murmurs, "God, you're beautiful," before kissing me again. And again. And again.

And then her fingertips are traveling down, down, down.

"Is this okay?" she murmurs.

I open my mouth to say yes, but I'm not sure it is. I think it is. And when her fingers brush the right spot over the fly of my jean skirt, it's obvious my body thinks it's plenty okay.

But there's no going back after that, is there? If we keep going, if we take this further, I feel like that makes it official. Not just me and Bri, but everything. That I like girls. That I'm—

"Guess not," she says, but she's smiling as she slides her hand back up to my waist, settling it in the curve there. "See? Only what you're okay with, Park. Always. I promise."

When she kisses me this time, it's gentler, a step back. And I know it's not what I want. This girl—this fun and crazy and thoughtful girl, this careful girl, this girl who's making my entire body tingle with nothing but kisses and fingertips on my skin—does things to my head and my heart I didn't even know were possible. I don't want to push her back because of a label, because I'm scared. I want the fact that I've finally figured out what I want to *matter*. I've spent so much of my life playing someone else, and tonight, with her, I'm just me.

"It's okay," I whisper, though I'm trembling, and I know she can feel it. "It is. Please."

"You're shaking."

"I know. I'm a little terrified," I admit. "But I swear, I want to."

"Then we will, at some point." She kisses my collarbone, and it's nice, but it feels like she's comforting me or something.

I don't want to be comforted.

I want to know what I've been missing.

And just like that, the shaking stops. "Bri. Please." My voice sounds ragged, breathy, just short of begging. Embarrassingly desperate. Which is exactly how I feel.

"Jesus, Park." She'd been bracing herself over me on an elbow, but now she collapses on my side, laughing into the crook of my neck. "I'm trying to be noble here, but you're killing me."

"Good."

She rolls up and places her palms on the mattress, one on either side of my head. Those light-green eyes that used to be so unsettling are blazing as they meet mine. "Really?" she says flatly.

"Really."

"Really."

"Real—"

Her mouth crashes down on mine, and I know even before her hand finds my thigh and starts a slow slide up the inside that there is definitely no going back.

I focus on the soft warmth of her mouth, the way her tongue is sweeping mine, while her fingers forge a path of fire up to the lace edge of my boyshorts. *Don't stop*, I think as she slides just the tips of her fingers beneath them. *Don't—*

My entire body arches off the bed as she brushes against me, and my moan is pathetic against the lips that are still pinning me down. They curve into that smile I know so well, and she nips at my lower lip. Her voice is huskier than I've ever heard it when she says, "Huh. Guess you weren't kidding about wanting to."

I want to come back with a smartass reply, but the truth is my brain is a fog. For all her teasing, when her eyes flit down my body and then back up, I can see the wonder in them. She may like to tease, but I know this means as much to her as it does to me. So I give up and let my eyes flutter closed again, letting the rhythmic stroking of her fingertips soothe me until I can gather myself.

And then she asks, "Still okay?" sounding genuinely worried I might say it's not. But it's so, so much better than okay. Especially when she asks.

Words are still failing me, but I reach down and tug up my skirt, giving her better access—the only response I can manage right now. She sucks in a sharp breath through her teeth, and then I feel her fingers slide free.

My eyelids flutter open. "I wasn't—" The rest of the words die on my tongue when I feel her fingers curling against my waistband. She wasn't stopping; she was undressing me. Completely.

It shouldn't be a big deal; I wear bikinis on set all the time, get photographed in next to nothing, have to change in front of people constantly. Even getting bikini waxed every two weeks on the dot is a standard occupational hazard.

But this is so not that.

And still...

I lift my hips off the bed, and her eyes never leave mine as she slides the skirt and boyshorts free—not even when they get stuck on my ankle on the way off, and we both laugh, just a little, breathless.

And then she's kissing me again, and her hand is there again, soft and cool and teasing as it strokes and circles until I'm so dizzy I swear I might just pass out. Finally, I turn away so I can reclaim my mouth. "Just do it already."

She laughs. "Well, that's romantic."

"You know what I mean." I sound ridiculously helpless, and it makes her smile widen, just enough to show that dimple. "Bri, just..."

"Yeah," she says, the hand that's stroking me stilling while the other one sweeps damp black strands of my hair off my face. "I know what you mean."

This time, when her mouth takes mine, her finger slowly enters me too, as gentle as anything she's ever done. But my body's had enough gentle, as much as I appreciate the gesture. I arch into her hand, and my first thought is, *More*. Or maybe I actually say it aloud, because the next thing I know, a second finger has joined the first, and oh *God* this is what I've been missing, what everyone has been talking about while I haven't had a fucking clue, while I've been worrying that I'm some sort of defect of nature around Ally and Liam, or Josh and...whoever that day's prize is.

This. This. This.

I slip a hand into the wave of hair cascading over her face and hold tight, both to press her mouth closer to mine and to steady myself as she quickens her pace and my body rocks to match it. The build-up inside me is so strange and intense that I almost wonder if something's wrong, and then, just as quickly, it becomes clear this is all going somewhere very, very right.

And then I can no longer share my breath, and I pull back and cry out as waves of bliss radiate out from every limb, my body near-vibrating as they crawl out of my fingertips, my toes.

It takes me an hour or maybe a minute to open my eyes again, and when I do, I see her looking down at me, biting her lip as she tries to keep from smiling. And just like that, insecurity slowly creeps in to replace the euphoria of only seconds before.

"Oh God, what?"

She shakes her head, kisses me hard, then collapses next to me. "That," she says, dropping another kiss onto my bare shoulder, "was the hottest fucking thing I've ever seen."

"Oh."

"Yeah." She brings my hand to her mouth and bites a knuckle. "Oh."

I can't stop smiling like an idiot as I watch her intertwine our fingers. "That was... Good Lord. Is it always like that?"

She laughs. "Not always." Her lips press against my shoulder, and my eyelids flutter shut. When she speaks again, her voice is low and breath is warm against my ear. "Sometimes I use my mouth."

Dying. I am dying right now. And it's the most perfect death. "You know, you're gonna have to teach me some things," I warn her, my face flushing with heat. "How to do them, I mean."

Her lips curve into a smile against my neck. "Cannot fucking wait, Park." She kisses me again and adds, "I'm gonna go wash up. I'll be right back."

I wait until I feel her slip out of bed and then watch her disappear into the bathroom through my haze as I pull the sheet up and over my body. *This*, I think, watching her retreating back, *is what happiness feels like*. The door closes behind her, and I look around the room, surprised to register that it seems a little more like home now that something monumental has happened in it. *This is what being excited to grow up feels like.*

And as much as I love acting and my parents, I don't think I want a life that doesn't allow for the potential to feel the way I do now. And I don't know how long I could love a career that wouldn't support me being... me.

Besides, what I want—what I've always wanted— is to be a role model, to show kids that not fitting into the industry standard doesn't mean there isn't a place for you. That doesn't have to stop with race. It *shouldn't*. God, it seemed so important when Zander and I were talking about setting good examples, but I don't want to be the kind of example that tells kids how to conduct their sex lives. I wanna be the kind that conveys that who they are is okay. Great, even. That where you come from and who you love should never be the kinds of things that hold you back.

I wonder what the hell kind of ceremonial ring they make for that.

I'm shaking a little with the force of all this by the time Bri emerges from the bathroom, but when she tips her head and asks what's wrong, I tell her I'm just a little chilly. Lord knows I've already started enough promises to her I haven't kept.

But I know what I have to do. And as she slips off her jeans, climbs into bed, and curls around me, holding me close to warm me up, I let go of the fear, embrace the only certainty I have, and let myself fall completely.

Chapter Twenty-Five

Josh

I toss back my second bottle of beer as I watch out the front window of the house, waiting for headlights to glare against the glass. When I finally see Liam's Range Rover pull up, I chug the rest of it, put it down on the sill, and head outside.

"You made it," I declare, greeting my guests with open arms.

Liam and K-drama slam their doors behind them and walk up. "We were pretty officially summoned," Liam says wryly. "What's the big occasion?"

I don't answer, ushering them inside instead, knowing it'll drive them both nuts.

"Ooookay," Vanessa says slowly, gesturing toward the dining table. "Is that champagne? What's going on here, Josh?"

"Are we celebrating something?" Liam asks, bracing himself on one of the dining chairs. "Are those In-N-Out burgers and fries?"

"Indeed they are. Sit," I urge them, pulling out a chair for K-drama. She gives me a funny look, then drops into it. "I have some news."

"Champagne news?" K-drama arches an eyebrow. "Please tell me you're not getting engaged to Shannah Barrett."

"Funny." *Especially since I came on to you like an idiot just two weeks ago.* "No, definitely not. I'm done with Shannah Barrett. I'm done with my parents' stupid shit. And I'm definitely done with Chuck and that reality show."

"I see you took our conversation to heart," says Liam, grabbing a burger and sliding into a chair. "Does this mean you found a new passion to pursue?"

"Actually, no." I pop open the champagne, and K-drama squeals and laughs as the cork goes flying and I spill all over the table before moving my mouth underneath to capture the escaping suds. After a couple of swallows, I hand it over to her and grin as she chugs a little straight from the bottle. "But I *am* gonna go looking for it. I'm leaving," I tell them, wishing I had a mic to drop for maximum dramatic effect.

"You got your own place?" Liam asks.

"Clearly, I was a positive influence," K-drama says smugly, putting the bottle down. She plucks a fry from the pile in the center of the table and pops it in her mouth.

"Nope, not that either." I take a huge bite of burger and swipe my tongue over the sauce on my lip. She doesn't even watch, so I guess she's totally gay now. "I mean, I'm leaving. Leaving LA. Leaving the US, actually."

K-drama's fingers freeze mid-air on the way to nab another fry. "To go where? For how long?"

I shrug. "Everywhere. I don't know. I just know there isn't really anything for me here. But there's gotta be something more fun out there, right? So, I got a one-way ticket around the world. Heading to Hawaii first. Figured I'd get in a week of surfing with Wyatt, and Aspen's gonna come do a shoot there for a couple of days. Then Japan and then...we'll see, I guess."

"Wow." Liam pulls off the top bun and takes a bite of his burger. I should've guessed he's cutting carbs. Man, I'm so glad to be getting out of here. "So you're just...wandering."

"Just wandering," I confirm. "I mean, there's always plenty to do and lots of people around. But yeah, I wanna see new stuff. Do new stuff. Have experiences and shit. Maybe even do some volunteer stuff so I can see what it's like not to be an asshole for five minutes."

"Deep," Liam says with a nod.

K-drama rolls her eyes. "So, basically, we're here to help you set up for another massive party to send you off?"

"Nope." I sweep my arm over the table. "This is it. Welcome to my goodbye party."

"This?" Her eyebrows shoot up. "No one's eating swords or doing body shots off a Victoria's Secret model."

I shrug. "New plan, new Josh."

Suddenly, the skepticism falls off her face, and her eyes widen a little. "Wait. When are you leaving?"

"The new owners of the house take over on December 1 to redo it. I sure as hell don't wanna be here for that, so, as soon as possible, basically."

She knots her fingers in her lap, a weirdly nervous gesture, and I can't help smiling. She is so gonna miss me. I take another swig of champagne as she says, "Can you stay until then, though?"

"Suddenly realizing you're gonna be sad and bored without me, K-drama?"

"Actually..." Her eyes dart to Liam, then back to me. "There's something I need to do. And I need to do it next week, while Ally's home for Thanksgiving. And I'd really, really like for you to be here, too. It'd mean a lot to me."

It's obvious from Liam's face that he's completely confused, but I'm not. Not for a second. I reach over and cover her nervously twisting hands, squeezing. "Yeah," I say quietly. "I'll stick around for that."

"What am I missing?" asks Liam, looking between the two of us, then dropping his eyes to our clasped fingers.

"I'll fill you in as soon as I fill your girlfriend in first," she promises. "I just want to talk to her in person."

He nods, already over it. "Cool." Then he puts his burger down. "It's weird, you know? I feel like you guys are figuring all this shit out lately. I'm kinda jealous."

"You?" I snort. "Dude, you've, like, set up your whole life already in the past few months."

He shrugs. "Not really. I mean, yeah, I've figured out that I wanna do movies, and that I'm not so into being a teen heartthrob or whatever. And obviously I know I wanna be with Ally. But...I dunno. It's tough to do it all, ya know?"

Vanessa smiles as she squeezes my hand one more time before pulling it back to nab another fry, and at the same time, we say, "Hashtag LiamProblems."

There isn't a lot I'll miss about being here, I know, but this little party is to say goodbye to the few things I will. And it's not exactly the most kickass shindig I've ever thrown, but I feel pretty sure it's the right way to go.

★ ★ ★ ★ ★

The next week, as I open yet another bottle of champagne with Liam and K-drama—this one in a limo, en route to LAX—I'm glad I stuck around for just a little longer.

"Shouldn't we wait until we actually *get* Ally before opening the champagne?" asks Liam, frowning as he looks down at his phone like he can make it light up with a sext from sheer force of will.

"I have another one," I assure him as I pass the bottle directly to K-drama, knowing she could use the liquid courage. "This one's just to get us into the celebratory spirit."

"I still can't believe you got her parents to let us pick her up," Liam says to her. "I barely got them to agree to relinquish her to me for Saturday night."

"I'm practically Pam's third daughter," she tells him, taking a swig from the bottle. I happen to know she told Ally's mom exactly why we need to pick her up from the airport, but she's still trying to keep that information quiet until she gets to tell Ally in person.

"Yeah, yeah." Liam grins and grabs the champagne, then takes a long drink. He looks the happiest I've seen him in months. "You excited for your trip?"

"You know it. Had to sell some shit in order to finance some of the finer things, but when I think about the fact that this time next week, I'll be on the North Shore...yeah, it's worth it." I take the bottle from Liam, but I only sip. These are the last couple of days I'll have with my friends for a while, and for once, I wanna have a clear head. "You sure you don't wanna come with?"

"I'm sure I'll end up meeting you somewhere," he says, glancing at his phone again. "Once I've got these movies behind me, I'm definitely gonna chill for a bit. But..."

"But you're gonna be chillin' in NYC," I finish for him, and it's gratifying to see him blush a little in the dim interior of the limo.

"I think so, yeah." He scratches the back of his neck. "I'm hoping to talk to Ally about it this weekend. She seems to like doing the whole dorm thing, so I don't know if she'll want to get a place together or anything, but I think me having one there will be good. Somewhere I can go when I'm not filming *Daylight*, maybe do some stuff shooting there instead. Anyway, it's not like you'll be in LA, so…"

"Truth." I take a longer swig of the champagne this time. "It's weird how other people have real roots here, isn't it?"

"Well, you seem to have an unexpected one these days," he says, keeping his voice low as he nods at where K-drama is spacing out, staring at the lights of LA through the tinted windows. "Are you *sure* you're not hooking up?"

"Dude, no. Definitely not. Never have, never will." *And in about an hour, you'll know exactly why.*

"You try?"

It's on the tip of my tongue to admit that I did once, that day in her bedroom after I saw her with Mini-Jade in my guest house, but it hits me that…no, I didn't. I told her I was into her, but I didn't kiss her. I didn't touch her. I didn't even attempt a move. If anything, I sent her straight back to Brianna. And I'm not sorry about it.

Somewhere along the way, the thought of kissing her became sort of…gross.

"Oh God."

Liam leans toward me anxiously. "What?"

I lean in to meet him and keep my voice low. "I think I might…love K-drama. Like, as a friend. Is that a thing? Like, with girls? Can you do that? Without wanting to fuck them and stuff?"

Liam's loud laughter fills the limo.

"What's so funny?" K-drama asks, sounding a little dazed.

"I think our little Joshie's growing up." Liam grabs the champagne from me and lifts it in the air. "Something we can all drink to."

Chapter Twenty-Six

Vanessa

The knit cap on my head itches as I make my way through the crowd at LAX to the reception area for Ally's flight, but it's worth it—nobody's stopped me yet. Of course, that might be because people care more about reuniting with their families for Thanksgiving than one of a billion C-list actresses being in their midst, but I prefer to think it's the knit cap.

It's probably my very last day of being able to fly under the radar, and I'm determined to make the most of it.

I hold up the sign I brought with me—"Duncan" in big block letters—and try to stop my hands from shaking. Liam and Josh agreed to wait in the limo while I got her so we could have a little time alone to talk, but now I'm wishing I had some company to keep my mind off our impending conversation.

Just then, my phone buzzes with a text, and I look down and smile at Bri's message.

Stop being so nervous. Ally's your best friend, and she loves you. No matter what.

Another text follows a few seconds later.

I'm the one who should be nervous. I have to pass the best friend test. Which means you need to save me some of whatever alcohol Josh Chester has poured down your throat in preparation.

I laugh as I type back, *Do you have a camera on me or something?*

Yes, she responds immediately. *And your legs look great in that dress.*

Nice try—jeans.

I tried. Willing to bet your legs still look great.

A cloud of butterflies takes flight in my stomach, and I think, *Ally will love you. She has to. Because I'm pretty sure I do.*

All I actually write back is, *Cute.*

This time her response takes a minute, and I crane my neck to look for my best friend's familiar auburn waves to no avail. Then my phone buzzes again.

I am, aren't I?

The text is accompanied by a picture of Bri perched on her bed, wearing a little Nirvana T-shirt and even littler shorts, her black-framed glasses, and a pair of headphones. She's not wearing any makeup, and she's childishly sticking out her tongue, and she looks so beautiful I have to curl my toes in my sneakers to keep myself from running to the limo and demanding it take me straight to her.

God, yes, you really are.

"Van?" I look up, and there's Ally, looking ten shades paler and somehow five years more sophisticated than when she left. I slip my phone in my back pocket, drop the sign, and accept a hug that nearly tackles me to the ground while both of us crack up. "What are you doing here? I thought my parents were getting me."

"I asked if I could," I say, readjusting my cap and drawing her away from the crowd. "I needed to talk to you about something, and I really couldn't wait."

"Is everything okay?"

"That...is a really, really good question." I can't help breaking into a laugh, which makes her cock her head like I might be crazy. "Yes, it's more than okay. I'm hoping it'll stay that way."

"You're kind of freaking me out. Whatever it is, just say it."

I still haven't said the actual words aloud to another person; I think I've been waiting for Ally to be the first to hear them. But now that the time has come, I can't even get them out. Instead, a single word emerges from my lips. "Ukelele."

The bag she'd been carrying hits the floor. "Vanessa Hyun-Jung Park," she whispers fiercely, yanking me even closer. "You had sex? With Zander?"

I shake my head.

"Please, please do not tell me you had sex with Josh Chester."

And just like that, any fear I have of telling Ally about Bri lifts from my shoulders. Because after that, there's really nowhere to go but up. "I did not, nor will I ever, have sex with Josh Chester," I assure her.

"Then—"

"Bri, Ally." My eyes dart around to make sure no one's listening, but no one cares about two teenage girls standing in the corner of crazed LAX the night before Thanksgiving. "I had sex with Bri. I'm *with* Bri. That's what I had to tell you." I swallow hard. "So... yeah. I'm gay. In case you didn't catch that."

For a moment, there is dead silence. Just...nothing. And my stomach drops into my toes as I wonder what the hell is going through her mind right now. What—

Ally flings her arms around my neck and squeezes so tightly I can barely breathe. "I have about a bajillion questions for you, but I thought a hug seemed like the right place to start. Is that okay?"

"It's the okay-est thing in the world," I assure her, squeezing my eyes to blink away the tears gathering there. I feel so light right now, I could actually float out to the curb.

"How about you? Are *you* okay? God, no wonder you sounded so freaked out on the phone. This must have been so terrifying and confusing and...I don't even know what."

"It was all that, and still is," I admit. "Trust me when I say I didn't see it coming either. But it just feels *right*, finally."

"I wish you could see the smile on your face right now. Is that what I looked like when I started dating Liam? You're gonna blind half of LAX." She squeezes my hand. "Seriously, I'm so happy to see you this happy, Vanny."

"I'd be happier if you never called me Vanny again."

"I know, but that's unlikely, so you should just keep enjoying this whole relationship thing."

"Remind me why you're my best friend again?"

"Because I'm always the one to order the fries so the calories don't count for you. Duh."

"Oh, right." My phone buzzes in my pocket, and I realize we've been lingering in the airport for a while now. "We should get going—Liam and Josh are waiting for us in the limo, and I wouldn't tell Liam anything until I told you."

"Josh knows?"

"Josh...may have seen us kissing," I confide, heat rushing to my cheeks.

Ally just shakes her head as she hauls her bag back up on her shoulder and we start for the doors. "And he didn't alert the media? I don't even know who this non-asshole version of Josh Chester *is*."

"It's weird, I know. But we're kinda friends now."

"After all the crap you gave me—"

"I *know*. Trust me, I know."

"So when do I get to meet the girlfriend? Please tell me she's in the limo too. I'm dying of curiosity."

"Not until tomorrow," I tell her with a smile, "but trust me, she's antsy to meet you, too."

"Fine. I suppose I can wait one day," she grumbles. "*If* you provide me with details until then. Like...*how*? *When*? I know you decided not to do the purity pledge thing, but what happened with Zander? And did you tell your parents? And—"

"One thing at a time, A." I push open the doors into the balmy LA air. "I broke up with Zander, but I haven't told him about Bri, nor have I told my parents. I'm hoping to do that as soon as we drop you off. And I'm pretty sure neither one is going to go very well."

She squeezes my hand. "I'm here if you need me, you know. I'm sorry I haven't been so present this semester. College and a long-distance relationship are way harder adjustments than I thought they'd be. I'm glad you've had Bri to make up for my being a crappy best friend."

"You could never be a crappy best friend, A. This is the stuff that matters." I squeeze her hand back. "Plus, you're around for the most important part—like, a kind-of-crazy thing I'm planning on doing tomorrow."

"I'm in. Whatever it is."

"I know you are," I say, squeezing her hand one last time as Liam jumps out of the limo. It looks like it's requiring every ounce of restraint he has not to pounce on her, and I laugh and let go of her hand. "She's all yours, Holloway," I declare, relieving her of her bag so we can stash it in the trunk. His name isn't even fully out of my mouth before he practically attacks hers.

I roll my eyes and get back in the limo.

"I take it that went well?" Josh asks as I slip my phone back out of my pocket.

"Not as well as *that's* going." I jerk my thumb toward the window. "But, yes, all good."

"You ready for the rest of it?"

"Not even a little." Checking my texts, I see I'd gotten a response from Bri to my last one, followed by, *I'm guessing you're with Ally now—lemme know how it goes.* And then, sent fifteen minutes after that, *I promise I will always do my best to be worth all this, Park. I hope you know that.*

My heart squeezes inside my chest, and I write back, *She can't wait to meet you,* as Ally and Liam finally join us inside the limo. *And you already are.*

But by the next morning, I'm not so sure anything is worth this. The Duncans were as easy as I knew they would be; the Parks...not so much. I managed one hour of their reaction of alternating silence with suggestions of therapy before begging Ally to pick me up and bring me to Zander's so I could get this night over with. My conversation with him lasted less than five minutes and ended with him telling me that I really should see someone about being Saved.

Then I spent the entire night tossing and turning, wanting to call Bri to make me feel better and resisting because I didn't want her to know how badly everything was going.

And now, as I pull on jeans and my favorite comfy Union Jack sweater in preparation of introducing my two favorite people, I really just want to puke.

"You can do this," I pep-talk myself in the mirror as I slather lotion on my face and concealer under my eyes. It comes out more like a grumble, though, and I'm silent as I draw on eyeliner. I can't make myself bother with anything else but mascara, and it's just as well, since the doorbell rings as soon as I toss the tube back on the bathroom counter.

I know it's Bri at the door, coming to pick me up, and that I should be excited about that, but right now, all I want is to be left alone. I don't want her to see how lousy I look. And I really don't want the tiny bit of regret that's beginning to seep in to show on my face.

But when I open the door, my mind goes completely blank.

"Too much?" she asks.

I shake my head, my throat suddenly feeling dryer than the Valley in August. I have just learned three things about Brianna Harris: 1) she owns leather pants; 2) she possesses no shame in wearing an "I Heart My Girlfriend" T-shirt in public; and 3) she looks otherworldly hot in both.

Worth. Everything.

"Excellent—then let's go. I have an important good first impression to make." She tries to tug me out the door, her silver bangles jangling, but I laugh and point out that I'm not wearing shoes yet. Sighing, she follows me inside, closing the door behind us as I hunt down my shoes and a bag.

It takes me a couple of minutes, but I finally reemerge. "Now I'm ready."

She looks up from where she'd been examining the framed picture of the two of us on my end table. "Are you?" she asks, putting the frame down and walking over. "You know, you haven't said how things went last night."

I shrug. "They went."

"They went badly." She indicates the table. "The picture of you with your parents isn't there anymore." It's true. When I got home last night, I shoved the frame in a drawer. "I wish you would've told me."

"I didn't want to upset you. And anyway, we didn't think it would go well," I remind her, although I think a part of me kind of believed it would, or at least hoped enough to believe. My heart pings, thinking about the conversation and about how many more will be ahead for the next few days, weeks, months.

"That doesn't make it easier." She tucks a strand of hair behind my ear, her fingertips lingering on my neck. "My mom's entire response when I came out was, 'Good—stick with girls and don't get pregnant.' Candice and a few of our mutual friends, though...they sucked. That whole thing sucked. I hate that you're going through this now. But promise me you'll stop trying to go through it alone, okay? I'm here. That's sort of the point."

I take a deep breath and inhale the now-familiar scent of her apple shampoo. "Okay," I promise softly, sliding a hand just under the hem of the "I Heart My Girlfriend" T-shirt. I love how smooth her skin is underneath, inked with what I now know to be a hibiscus flower. "Thank you."

"Thank *you* for being sure enough about me—about us—to go through all this," she says, brushing a strand of hair behind my ear and touching her lips gently to mine. "You're pretty fucking great, Vanessa Park."

"You're not too bad either." I pinch her tiny tummy, and she laughs and swats me away.

"I take it back—you suck," she says, but she's grinning, and then she kisses me again. "Are you ready?"

"As I'll ever be. Let's do this." I tap her on the butt with my bag and lead the way out of my apartment, off to the LGBT Youth Center where Ally, Josh, and Liam are meeting us to serve early Thanksgiving dinner— and to put me in front of the cameras and into our future.

Chapter Twenty-Seven

I break out one last bottle of champagne—this one for the Duncans, to serve with Thanksgiving dinner. They invited all of us to come back after we spent the afternoon at the LGBT Youth Center, slinging turkey and mashed sweet potatoes while "journalists" went all vulture on us. Of course, that was kinda the point—bringing attention to the center—but it didn't exactly make me sorry to leave this shit behind.

"I'm so glad you could all make it," says Ally's mom, wrapping one arm around Ally's shoulders, the other around Vanessa's. "And I'm honored you're spending such an important day with us, sweetie," she adds, kissing the top of Vanessa's head. "We're so proud of you. And happy for you."

"Thanks, Pam." She's blushing, but the truth is, she was fucking awesome today. When a reporter asked what we were doing there, she took the mic and handed it right off to the director of the center to let him talk about the city's displaced LGBT youth. Then she took the mic back, declared "Oh, and I'm gay" like a fucking boss, handed it back, and scooped up some green beans.

It makes me a little glad I'm leaving, because somehow, seeing her own herself today kinda made me want her again, just a little. Apparently my dick and my brain are slow to get on the same page.

"And it's great to have you, too, Brianna." Ally's mom smiles at her warmly and gives her a hug before releasing her to let her clasp hands with Van. "All of you." She gives me a hug, too, and I try not to squirm; for all that I like touching the ladies, hugging someone else's mom when I've never hugged my own off-camera is just too weird.

"Hi, Josh," Ally's little sister, Lucy, says shyly. She's got a monster little-kid crush on me, and I love it. Though when she's legal in six or seven years, she's gonna be trouble. "Is it true you're traveling around the world? That's so cool."

"It is! Do you wanna come with me? I'm sure your mom will be down with you hiding in my backpack."

She giggles. "I'll ask her."

"No, honey," Pam calls back. "I'd say when you're eighteen, but even then, not a chance."

I grin. "Wise choice, Pam."

She scowls at me, but it's playful. I think.

"So, how are you feeling?" Ally asks Van, holding her by the shoulders.

"I...don't even know." She shakes her head. "God, this is crazy, isn't it? I'm sorry about all the paparazzi out front."

"Eh, that's what blinds and curtains are for," says Ally's dad with a dismissive wave. "As long as they don't think they're getting any turkey."

"I didn't even ask, Bri," Pam says apologetically. "Are you a vegetarian?"

"Not even a little bit. I—" She's cut off by the sound of the doorbell, and we all freeze. The front lawn is packed with vultures, but ringing the bell, especially on Thanksgiving, seems like a whole other level.

Even I've only had that happen to me once, and I'm pretty sure that photographer's still weeping over his priceless shattered lens.

Ally walks up and looks through the glass. "Ha. Well, if it isn't." She opens the door and steps back, letting in...Jade.

"Fucking creeps," Jade mutters as soon as she's inside, patting her spiky platinum hair like the crowd's been running their fingers through it. Then she stalks over to Vanessa. "I could kill you, Park." Her creepy green devil's eyes are filled with irritation as she glances at her daughter. "If you weren't making my only child very, very happy, I probably would."

Lucy gasps, and I hear Ally whisper, "She's being hyperbolic, Luce. She wouldn't actually kill Van, I promise."

"No, I would," Jade says coolly without so much as a glance at the Duncan sisters. "I'm up to my ears in shit thanks to this impromptu announcement, and Zander's not remotely ready to deal with this."

"I warned Zander in advance," Vanessa says firmly. "Considering his response was to tell me that I was a sinner and he's glad he avoided making the terrible mistake of committing to me and burning in hellfire, you'll understand that I don't really care what happens to him."

"Mom—" Bri starts, but Jade winces at the name. Bri sighs. "Jade. It's done. If you're going to blame anyone, blame me. Or better yet, don't blame anyone—just sit down and eat with us. If that's okay with the Duncans," she adds quickly.

"Of course it is," says Pam. "Ally, honey, go grab another setting."

"I shouldn't."

"Well, your daughter will be eating with us, and it's Thanksgiving," says Ally's dad, "so, we'd love if you would, too."

"We have enough Hollywood orphans at the table," Liam adds wryly. "Given that you're the only parent of one here who actually supports your child's identity, maybe you should stick around."

Surprisingly bold words coming from Liam, but they work. We all take seats around the table, and I even see Jade give Brianna a quick hug. Very, very quick.

But even with the tension between Jade and K-drama, and the paparazzi roaming around outside, it's impossible not to feel like everyone around me has their shit together. Which I'll take as a good sign, because it means I have to be next. I don't know what the fuck I really wanna do or what I think I'm gonna find, but there's a way better shot it's in actual China than the Chinese Theater.

Some space will be good. A little scarier than I'll ever admit, even to these people, but good. And worst comes to worst, I'll bang a lot of foreign chicks, smoke and drink some good shit you can't get in the States, and...I don't know what. I don't wanna plan. I just wanna go.

Ally's parents are both good cooks, which I already knew from occasional dinners here while Ally was my assistant. It occurs to me as I shovel turkey and stuffing into my mouth that this is probably the last place I had home-cooked food. It's no In-N-Out Burger, but it's pretty damn tasty.

On my right, Ally's grilling Bri on every single detail of her life while K-drama laughs; on my left, Lucy's staring at me adoringly while Pam watches with disapproval. It's everything the way it should be, but it isn't my life. I'm just a guest here, which is all I've really ever been anywhere—in my house, on the set of *Daylight Falls*, and now at A Duncan Family Thanksgiving.

If I'm gonna be a guest, it might as well be somewhere fucking awesome.

I get a whole lot of questions about my trip that I have no answers to, but mostly, this is a Welcome Home Ally party meshed with a Happy Coming Out for K-drama, so I don't feel too bad when I tell everyone I have to leave early, and I don't think anyone cares all that much when I go. Then I hear K-drama excuse herself, too, and I wait for her to join me and walk me to the door; going outside together at this point is basically suicide by paparazzi flash.

"Thank you," she says once we're out of earshot of everyone else. "For staying. I couldn't have done it without you today."

I roll my eyes. "Oh, come on, K-drama. You're the new rebellious rock star of the Teen Hollywood set. You don't need shit from me."

"Trust me," she says dryly. "You're the last person on earth whose ass I'd kiss if you didn't actually deserve it." Her expression grows unsettlingly sincere. "Thank you for being the friend I've needed the past few months, Josh. I'm guessing I won't be hearing from you much while you're gone, but I don't even know where or who the hell I'd be right now if it weren't for you, so...thank you. Really."

I open my mouth to give another sarcastic response, but she narrows her eyes. "Just say 'you're welcome,' Josh. Instead of whatever asshole thing you're about to say, just say 'you're welcome.'"

I nod. "You're welcome. And you might even hear from me once or twice."

She leans over and pecks me on the cheek, tells me to call her before I go and to travel safe. Then she heads back to her girlfriend, her best friend, her life.

And I head out to mine.

I don't go straight back to Malibu, though. Instead I have Ronen steer me to the house I usually avoid like the plague. But when we pull up in front of my parents' Bel-Air monstrosity and I roll down my tinted window, it's obvious nobody's home. The entire place is dark, and both cars are gone. Fuck Thanksgiving, I guess; they're certainly not thankful for me. Or each other.

"Are you going to ring the bell?" Ronen asks.

"Nah. Let's just go back to Malibu." I roll my window up and drop my head back as we pull away. If I ever had any doubts that leaving was the right move, they're gone now.

And in a matter of hours, I will be, too.

Chapter Twenty-Eight

Vanessa

*D*ear Vanessa, I love you on *Daylight Falls*—you are the perfect Bailey! But I don't understand why'—that's the letter Y, by the way," Bri clarifies, shifting onto her other elbow amid the piles of letters surrounding her prone body on my bed, "'you have to be gay. You obviously like boys on the show.'" She looks up. "Do you want to know all the horrible spelling mistakes, or should we just go ahead and drink?"

I turn in my desk chair and curl my legs up underneath my butt. "Hmm, I'd say drink, but does that one get a full shot for 'Why do gay people have to tell us they're gay when I don't have to tell people I'm straight'? Or just a sip for 'Obviously you're not gay if you kiss boys all the time'?"

"Hmm, tough call. Maybe two sips."

I pick up the Thermos we've been sharing—a combo of raspberry Bacardi and Fresca—take two sips, and pass it over before turning back to my e-mail. "There are a whole lot of wonderfully sweet teen girls praying for my eternally damned soul. Aren't concerned fans the best?"

She puts the Thermos down on the floor instead of drinking from it and rolls up into a sitting position. "Don't forget about all the letters and tweets thanking you," she says softly, gesturing for me to join her on the bed. I do, letting her wrap me up in her arms from behind. "The people hating on you don't matter, Park. The ones who need to see a queer girl actually making it in Hollywood—a queer girl of color, no less? They really, really do. And you matter to them, so much. And to me, by the way."

"Oh, whatever," I tease, but a little shudder goes through my body as she presses her lips to the back of my neck.

"Not 'whatever,'" she grumbles into my ear, resting her chin on my shoulder. "You wanted to be a good role model with that stupid purity ring crap, and now you are, with something you actually believe in." She keeps one arm wrapped around my waist and reaches out for an open letter with her free hand.

"Look at this one. 'Dear Ms. Park, I've been trying to figure out how to come out to my best friend for two years. When I saw you rip off the Band-Aid on TV, I realized I should, too. Thank you for making me feel like it's okay to be who I am.'" She holds it up in front of my face so I can see the purple scrawl. "How can you even for a second give a damn about people quoting the Bible at you when you get something like that?"

I can't help smiling at that, and at the knowledge that her best friend was every bit as cool about it as mine was. I just hoped her parents were cooler. I'd only spoken to mine once since my coming out hit the airwaves, and it was to listen to them declare it all "yet more Hollywood nonsense." I haven't spoken to them since. They've never even seen my apartment, and I've been here almost a month, filling it piece by piece.

And Bri's stayed here almost every night.

"It's hard not to care about people who seem to think I'm a different person somehow," I admit, feeling my throat grow thick with tears I'm tired of shedding. "Even–"

My cell phone rings, cutting me off, and I instantly grow cold. I just spoke to Ally an hour ago, and obviously Bri's right here, which means the odds are high it's yet another reporter who somehow got my phone number. I reach behind Bri–I know it's somewhere in these sheets–and snatch it to shut it up.

It's my mother.

Bri looks at me questioningly, and I mouth "my mom" to her.

"Pick it up!" she urges, so I do.

"Hi, Mom," I say cautiously, eyeing Bri to make sure she doesn't go too far, just in case I'm in for another evisceration.

"Vanessa." Her voice is stiff, but not icy. "Your father's here as well. I'm putting you on speakerphone."

Oh, good, a double whammy. No way this can possibly be horrible.

I wait until the static settles on the other end, and then my father says, "Hello, Vanessa. How are you?"

How am I? Seriously? *Now* they wanna know? Weeks after they kicked me out of their house, turned me away when I came out to them–came out to the world? I look helplessly at Bri, but she just gives me an encouraging smile, then slips out of the room to give me privacy I don't even want.

"I'm fine," I reply. "I have an audition tomorrow for a summer movie, and the apartment's coming together, too. Bri's been helping me decorate." I say this last bit a little more deliberately, just in case they've managed to convince themselves it–or she–is a passing phase.

"That's...I'm glad to hear it, Vanessa." It's hard to say whether I believe her or not by her voice alone, but she's trying, and that's more than she's done in a long time. I grip the phone tighter.

"And how are things over there?"

"Also fine," she says.

I'm just wondering the purpose for this call, since it doesn't seem to be to have a real conversation with me, when my father says, "Uncle Robert and Aunt Jeanine are hosting Christmas dinner this year, and they would like to know if you will be joining us."

"I..." *Didn't know I was invited*, I almost say, but I know that won't go over well and they'll just play dumb. "I didn't realize they were hosting it."

"Yes, they are, and they asked about you," says my mother. "I told them I assumed you would be, but that I would check."

I assumed you would be. So, I'm still part of this family, then. Even though my parents know. And Uncle Robert and Aunt Jeanine—they must know, too. Not that they watch much TV, but considering pretty much everyone in America knew within ten minutes, even on Thanksgiving Day...

"You can tell them I'll be there. Please," I add quickly. "And what about...can I bring a guest?"

There's a long silence, then a sigh on the other end, though I'm not sure which parent it comes from. Then my father says stiffly, "We would like to meet this guest first, for dinner at our home."

Dinner. With Bri. And my parents. I can't imagine anything more awkward, or anything I want to do more. "Just tell me when, and we'll be there," I say quickly, afraid the slightest hesitation in response will make them rescind the offer. I know I should ask Bri first, but given I came out on a national scale for her, I'm thinking she'll probably give me this.

"Sunday night," my mother says. "Six thirty. Do not be late."

"We won't," I promise. "We'll see you then."

She makes some sort of grumbly noise of agreement, and then they hang up.

I jump off my bed and soar out into the living room, knocking Bri over onto the fluffy purple shag rug as I fling my arms around her and squeeze her tightly enough to cut off her breathing.

Surprised laughter bubbles up from her throat as she turns in my grasp to face me. "Please tell me this is joy."

"It's a start," I say, but I can't stop smiling. "Sorry about knocking you over. Oh, and about the fact that we have the world's worst dinner plans on Sunday night."

Her eyebrows shoot up. "We're having dinner with your parents? Holy crap. That is terrifying."

Okay, yeah, I definitely should've asked her first. "I'm sorry," I say. "I was just so relieved for the invitation, I—"

She clasps my head in her hands and cuts me off with a long, slow kiss. "It's a 'worth it' kind of terrifying," she assures me when we part, then rolls us over so she's on top. "Just, you know, tell me how to dress and act and behave and all that."

I laugh, reaching up to toy with a strand of her fiery hair. "As long as you eat kimchi, they'll love you just as you are," I assure her. "Or at least tolerate you as much as they'll tolerate anyone."

"Best I can hope for, I guess."

"Best any of us can hope for with the Parents Park. I should probably also warn you that this came up in the context of going to my aunt and uncle's for Christmas dinner. Not that you have to come," I add quickly. "I just wanted it to be an option, especially if Jade is as...Jade-like about Christmas as she is about everything else."

Bri grins. "She's actually been a little...different since we got together, but something tells me it won't be quite as dramatic as suddenly learning how to cook. Maybe let's see how this dinner goes first."

"Deal."

She lowers herself for another kiss, which quickly escalates until the rug is littered with discarded clothing and we're both panting for air. "Have I mentioned how happy I am that you got your own place, by the way?"

"Only about a hundred thousand times." I slide my hand through hers, admiring the way the different shades of our skin look intertwined. "May not be exactly how I planned for it to go down, but that seems to be the theme of the past six months, doesn't it? Can't really complain about how things have turned out...yet."

"Good." She brings our hands to her mouth and nips my index finger's middle knuckle. "See? Going off script isn't always a bad thing."

"Was that seriously a Hollywood pun, Brianna Harris?"

She laughs. "Yes. God, sue me. I'm the worst."

"Nah," I say with a grin, kissing her again. "You're not so bad."

Besides, I can't really blame her when I can't stop thinking that I got my Hollywood ending.

Epilogue - Three Months Later

Josh

The view from my villa in Santorini is predictably beautiful—it'll make a great background for Pensive Josh, or maybe Playful Josh, or whatever the hell Chuck decides he wants from me today. I don't even care anymore. There's a traditional Greek breakfast spread out in front of me—including baklava with extra pistachios because the owner's daughter, Zoe, thinks it's the way to my heart—and the Aegean's sparkling like it's been outfitted by Jacob the Jeweler. After running out of my own cash about a week into Tokyo, I'll take what I can get.

It isn't so bad now that we're thousands of miles from Hollywood and things are on my terms—or, at least, the terms Holly set out after learning the more me-centric episodes of our stupid reality show actually tested pretty well. I'm pretty sure she's gonna drop me soon, but for now, I do shit on their dime and Holly makes some cash. Everybody wins.

"What are you thinking about?"

I blink away from the sea and glance over at my breakfast companion—a gorgeous Turkish girl named Pelin I picked up inside the Hagia Sofia a couple of weeks ago—but I'm so thrown by a different face staring back at me that I have to think back to how much ouzo I had the night before. But nope, it's definitely her, smirking at me from the cover of an imported American *Cosmo* in Pelin's dainty brown hands.

"Nice going, K-drama," I murmur, lifting a glass of fresh-squeezed orange juice to my lips. She looks good, even in a weird jumpsuit thing unzipped to show a barely necessary bikini top, *Vanessa Park is Out, Proud, and Loud!* blazing in pink lettering at her shoulder.

"Ne?" Pelin takes a sip of her rancid-smelling Greek coffee, which might as well be mud.

"Nothing." I take a sip of juice, put down my glass, and get up. "I gotta make a call."

Pelin just shrugs and returns to her coffee and magazine, and I allow myself a few seconds to appreciate the way her satin robe slides off her bronze shoulder while I pull out my phone. It only occurs to me on the third ring that I have no idea what time it is in California. Hell, after three months of traveling around, I have no idea what time it is in Santorini, either.

I'm about to hang up when she answers. "Hello?"

"Hey, K-drama."

"Josh." I'm not sure if I'm imagining the smile in her voice because I want it to be there, but I'll take it. "Checking to make sure I'm taking good care of your loan? Ronen has been a fabulous security guard, thank you."

"Damn straight. I hope you two let him watch every once in a while as a reward."

"I'm gonna ignore that. Where are you?"

"Santorini. It's fucking gorgeous. Where are you?"

"Bed. It's pretty glorious too."

"Alone?"

"Tonight, yes. I'm supposed to be getting my beauty sleep for new headshots tomorrow," she adds pointedly, though I can tell she's not mad I called.

"There aren't enough hours in the night."

She laughs. "Every time I wonder if maybe I miss you, you remind me how much better off I am with you halfway around the world."

"Hey, do I not send good souvenirs?"

"Yeah, thanks for that ridiculous pornographic postcard from Bangkok, by the way. I wanted to burn it, and of course Bri hung it on my fridge. I completely forgot about it when my parents came over, so that was a fun hour I spent explaining the unexplainable."

"Isn't it nice that I'm facilitating conversation between you and your parents?"

"So nice."

The sun is beating down, and I duck into the shade. "Well, I just saw you on the cover of *Cosmo*, so I guess things aren't going too bad over there."

"Not too bad," she agrees. "Not too great, either. Shockingly, no one's banging down my door to star in their hetero rom-coms. But things are going well with *Daylight*. They're even thinking of writing Bailey as bi and giving me a female love interest next season. Which is *massively* on the DL, obviously, and still totally up in the air."

"So what are you doing this summer?"

"College, if you can believe it," she says with a snort. "My parents said if I didn't line up a movie, I had to sign up for summer session."

"And you agreed?"

"Let's just say I'm doing all the parent-pleasing I can these days. The whole girlfriend thing's been kind of a huge shock, and they're really trying to be cool with it. So I'm meeting them as halfway as I can.

Besides," she adds, "Bri's gonna take some classes, too, so hopefully that'll make it suck a whole lot less."

"Ah, Bri. So how's lesbian sex? As good as I've imagined?"

"It's pretty damn good. How's anonymous sex with foreign strangers?"

"'Bout the same as it was five years ago." I glance over at Pelin, who's put her feet up in my chair. I hadn't really planned to hook up with the same person for this long, but Chuck seems to like the idea that I've "found love on the quest to find myself" or whatever. Truth is, it's been kinda nice, but I won't be sharing that bit of info with K-drama.

"Where are you off to next?"

"Ally didn't tell you?" I tap my fingers on the white railing next to me and look out at the glittering sea. "I'm meeting up with her and Liam in Rome for a couple of days during her spring break."

"Ohhhh right. I forgot that was coming up next week. I still can't believe they're letting you tag along with them. And I can't believe you *want* to."

The truth is, I miss Liam. And I miss Ally. And I even miss K-drama a little bit. But again, I have no plans to share any of that. "I'm surprised you're *not* coming," I say instead. "I thought you got off on third-wheeling with those two."

"Thanks, but I'm good with my own wheel," she says. "Although, now that you mention it, a couple of days in Rome *would* be nice..."

She's so predictable. "You're going to book tickets the second you get off the phone with me, aren't you?"

"Of course not," she says huffily. "I wouldn't tag along without asking Ally first."

As if Ally would ever turn down a chance to spend a couple of days with Van. "Guess I'll be seeing you and Bri next week."

"You might be," she concedes, and I can hear the smile in her voice. "I still can't believe you ended up on a reality show after all that. You're such a tool."

"You're just jealous because you wish you were this close to the Isle of Lesbos right now."

"God, you really are the worst." She's quiet for a beat, then says, "Do you think all this stuff is worth it? Just, like...everything?"

"Thinking of ditching it all to become the brain your parents so desperately wish you were?"

"Ha ha. And no. I'm just curious, I guess."

"I think—" I hear someone call my name and see that the camera guy is trying to get my attention to come back for filming. "I think it doesn't really matter," I tell her. "I think once you start, you just have to learn how to keep going."

"That sounds about right. Or, at least, for as long as they'll let you keep going, anyway."

"Well, yeah, there's that."

"Have fun in Greece and try not to spread too many diseases to the natives, will you?"

"I'll see you next week, you BFF-co-dependent drama queen."

She laughs and says goodbye, and then she's gone.

I head back to where Pelin's sitting with our breakfast, the sun shining on her perfect, camera-ready skin. "Let's get this party started. I need to get into that baklava already." I offer myself to be mic'd up, then take my seat back at the table. "Lights, camera"—Pelin smiles at me before taking a tiny bite, then licking the honey off her lips—"and my personal favorite: action."

Acknowledgments

Sometimes it's hard to remember when and how a book began. In this case, there's no forgetting the text message from Patricia Riley that said, "What if that imaginary Josh sequel wasn't so imaginary?" Thank you, Patricia—my editor and friend—for setting this story free and loving every turn it took along the way. (Except Liam. I'm sorry about Liam. I swear, that never happened.)

Huge thanks to Lauren Meinhardt for setting the course of this book by asking for Vanessa's story. I had no idea then who she was or that she'd completely own this book once I figured her out, but it's been my favorite writing journey thus far, and I'm endlessly grateful for that challenge and all your editorial guidance and support.

To Maggie Hall—I don't even know how to begin. I don't think I ever would have finished this book with my sanity intact if you had not been with me every step of the way. And then, after everything you did for both the story and for me, you went ahead and made the most perfect, beautiful cover I could ever have imagined. Thank you, for everything.

Endless gratitude to my critique partners, Gina Ciocca, Marieke Nijkamp, and the aforementioned Maggie Hall, for figuring out all the ways this story was broken and helping me glue the right parts together. I'm forever awed by your skills at saving what I think is hopeless, and so in love with how far we've all come together. Best year ever? Best year ever.

Huge thanks to Lyla N. Lee and Audrey Coulthurst for incredibly helpful, insightful, and encouraging early reads, and to Christina Franke, for brainstorming me out of a tough spot and being generally fabulous. Thank you to my wonderful line and copy editors—Asja K. Parrish, Sarah Henning, and Becca Weston—for helping make my twisted little book as coherent as possible; Jenny Perinovic, for the lovely internal design; and to my kind, patient, wonderful publicist, Patrice Caldwell, for all her hard work.

Much love and gratitude to all my wonderful author friends who are there for the millions of non-writing parts of the process. Lindsay Smith, my amazing accountabilibuddy—I don't know what I'd do without you (drink less?) and I never want to find out. Thank you for always pushing me to my limits and beyond. Sara Taylor Woods, Katie Locke, Emily Henry, Paula Garner, Ami Allen-Vath, and Candice Montgomery—handsy hugs to you all for ensuring I always had both the proper subtext-y inspiration and people to crack me up or hold my hand when I needed it most. Love to my wonderful pub-sisters, especially Kelsey Macke, Megan Whitmer, and Michelle Smith, for kindness, companionship, and inspiration. Thank you, Leah Raeder, for much-needed pep talks and instilling in me the determination to nail the whole shebang, and the YA Misfits, OneFour KidLit, and the Binders (especially my amazing, beloved co-mods) for guidance and commiseration. Finally, heaps of appreciation to the incredible bloggers who supported both this book and *Behind the Scenes*.

To my family—whether Adler, Fisch, or Croog—thank you for unflagging love and support. Very special thanks to Eyal, for helping me out with some tough LA research questions, and to Julia, for being my biggest fan even though your mom won't let you read my books until you're sixteen.

Yoni—you are above and beyond the love interests of stories, even the ones whose abs have their own fan clubs. You are more than I knew a partner could be. Thank you for being by my side through everything, always.

This book is for those who love fearlessly, and those still trying to. Thank you for being exactly who you are.

About the Author

*D*ahlia Adler is an Associate Editor of Mathematics by day, a Copy Editor by night, and a YA author and blogger at every spare moment in between. She lives in New York City with her husband and their overstuffed bookshelves.

CPSIA information can be obtained at www.ICGtesting.com
Printed in the USA
LVOW04s1010250615

443821LV00004B/5/P